I0543838

Loose Enas

S.R.Claridge

GLOBAL PUBLISHING GROUP

Global Publishing Group

Printed in the United States of America

First trade edition: June 2013

10 9 8 7 6 5 4 3 2 1

ISBN 978-0-9898467-4-5

The author would like to offer special thanks to her brilliant team of editors, whose expertise is invaluable: Cash, Jerrye, Gary, Matt and Beth

She would also like to thank her family and friends for their love and encouragement, her children for their ongoing patience and humor, her husband for his strength and constant support, and God for every blessing.

~

Loose Ends is the fifth book in the Just Call Me Angel series. A complete list of series books and other books by S.R.Claridge is located at the back of this book.

For previews of upcoming novels, reviews and information about the author, visit AuthorSRClaridge.com or find her on Facebook.

CHAPTER 1

Two steel canisters, placed in a welded metal container were delivered to a Chicago warehouse on the south side and placed under the watchful eye of Richie and Hank Sabona. The Sabona brothers were well-known security contractors, often hired to guard or transport items that were not of a legal nature. This particular evening, their job was to guard the container until it was picked up for appropriate disposal. Pacing in front of the container, Richie took a drag from a cigarette, exhaled and then flicked the butt to the ground. "What are we guarding anyways?"

"Dunno," Hank shrugged. "Some type of military grade nerve gas."

"This shit must be deadly if they got us guarding it," Richie said, leaning in closer to the container.

"What are you doing?" Hank asked.

"I thought maybe there'd be a label or something to indicate what's inside."

"Moron," Hank chuckled. "They ain't gonna label something they don't want no one to know about."

Richie set down his gun, reached into his shirt pocket, retrieved a pack of cigarettes and lit up another smoke. "You want one?" He asked, extending the pack toward Hank.

"Nah," Hank moaned. "That shit will kill you. I'm gonna take a leak."

Hank sauntered across the warehouse and exited through the side door into the night air. Although there were indoor restrooms, they were two buildings away, so he opted to go outside because it was quicker and he could stay close. Just as he zipped up his fly and leaned down to retrieve his gun, he heard footsteps from behind. Hank whirled around but it was too late. Two bullets from a silenced .45 soared through the air and exploded into his chest.

Richie took a long drag from his cigarette, and upon hearing the door open, turned to face it. He was obviously expecting to see his brother, because his weapon sat propped against the container, out of reach. One shot to the chest threw his body backwards onto the warehouse floor, where Richie gasped desperately for air. The assailant, dressed head to toe in black, approached rapidly and fired another shot directly between his eyes.

"All clear," the assailant spoke into a headset microphone that looped around his left ear. Within moments, two men carrying welding torches entered and began opening the container.

"Careful," the assailant warned as they lifted out the steel canisters. "It's deadly."

CHAPTER 2

Angel washed her hands, reapplied her lip gloss and then checked her reflection in the restroom mirror. Dressed in a black, Versace cocktail gown and black stiletto heels, she could barely contain her excitement. Tonight was not only the grand opening of the newly renovated Tetterbaum's Pub, but it was the first official Maratinzano family gathering since her father's murder, twenty-five years ago. After his death most of the Maratinzano family was either murdered or fled for their lives, so tonight marked a rebirth. Chase and Big Mike had just taken the Omerta oath and become Made members of her family. In addition, Sean Shepherd, also known as The Snake, had been given Giovanni's blessing to transfer from the Maratinzano family in New York to Angel's clan in Chicago. With her entire family present to celebrate the rebuilding of the Maratinzanos in Chicago, she felt giddy. Not only that, but even she had to admit that she looked damn good in her dress. Turning toward the full-length mirror, she drank herself in from every angle and couldn't deny that being the granddaughter of both the Capo di Tutti Capi and the Head of the Costa Nostra afforded her luxuries she wouldn't have normally had; luxuries like Versace gowns.

The pub had been closed for several weeks, and after the mass shooting that took the lives of several wait staff and patrons, followed by the bomb set off by the Cobra gang, Angel wasn't sure if it would ever re-open. She considered taking Olga's advice and selling it. She even entertained lucrative offers from potential buyers, but couldn't bring herself to let it go; and tonight she

7

understood why.   For her, Tetterbaum's pub held a very personal history. It was here that she met Grayson Galante and the secrecy of her family's Mafia roots unraveled. It was here that she and Andrew discovered Tetterbaum's tapes which revealed incriminating evidence against the five Chicago families, and proved that Venito Barone had been masquerading as her father's Compare and amassing wealth that rightfully belonged to her. It was here, at Tetterbaum's Pub, that she was reunited with Tony and realized he had never stopped loving her; and it was here that she first met Andrew.

Angel moved closer to the mirror, allowing her eyes to scan the length of her body. It was obvious she didn't look like the other Mafia Bosses, and not just because they were all men. There was a softness in her that they lacked; a softness, not to be misinterpreted as weakness, and she had every intention of holding onto it for as long as possible.

Now, taking a deep breath and exhaling slowly, Angel smiled at her reflection. For the first time in a long time she felt comfortable in her own skin, or maybe that was just the glowing effects of Versace. As she exited the restroom, she decided to make one more pass through the dining area and then return to her own party. The bar was bustling with people and the restaurant was booked with dinner reservations through the entire evening. Angel understood people wanting to see the newly renovated Tetterbaum's, but she also knew part of the draw was her recent hiring of two of the finest Italian chefs in Chicago. Chef Randolfo Alortini and Chef Inigo Conaletti. Both had come highly recommended by Joseph Venturini, Andrew's father and Boss of the Venturini family.

As she strode between tables, greeting patrons, she couldn't help noticing the large number of bogata brothers in the pub, particularly from the Galante and Cullato families. She mentioned it to her bartender, Johnny, and asked him to keep a watchful eye on them.

"Notify me immediately if you see trouble brewing," she told him. "I'll be in the back."

"I'll handle it, Boss," Johnny said with a crocked grin, flipping his blonde hair to the side in a Bieber-esque manner. "Go enjoy your party and don't worry 'bout nothin'. Johnny's on it."

Johnny was a little rough around the edges, but Angel saw goodness in him. He was new to the city, had no crime family affiliation and desperately needed money. He showed up sober, on time and was always smiling. Aside from the annoying habit of referring to himself in the third person, Angel found him refreshing.

After checking in on the kitchen staff and commending Chef Conaletti and Chef Alortini on the extravagant menu they designed for her opening, Angel returned to the back room where her family sat.

The men rose from their seats as she entered and remained standing until she returned to her chair. It was a sign of respect but Angel wondered if she'd ever get used to it. It was an old-fashioned gesture, sort of like opening doors and removing hats; but she appreciated it nonetheless. *Wouldn't it be nice if these gestures of respect became fashionable again,* she mused. The dinner plates were removed and an assortment of desserts were placed in the center of the table. The dessert platter had no sooner touched the table when Olga leapt upward and snagged two Cannoli, one for Salvatore and the other for herself. Angel's eyes widened in surprise at how quickly Olga had snatched the dessert.

"If you snooze, you lose," Olga said, plunking her rounded hips back into her seat. Angel shook her head and smiled. Good 'ol Olga. She was always good for a laugh.

The evening felt surreal. Angel sipped her wine, letting her thoughts drift as her eyes traversed the table. A twinge of sadness threatened her joy as she recalled the many sacrifices that had been made along the way. She owed her life to the people in this room and to the efforts of several good men who had lost their lives protecting her. It was something she didn't take lightly, and even now in the midst of celebrating, it brought a melancholy feeling.

She had come a long way from the naïve MU Journalism graduate, who spent her evenings gossiping with her great aunt, Olga, and snuggling with her cats, Midnight and Mo. She had been blown off of a dock, thrown out of a plane, fired on by a grenade launcher, tear gassed, shot at and Tasered. She imagined not many women could say that. She had learned to handle a gun, exposed traitors within her own family, killed to protect her mother, and been intimately involved with a couple of the hottest Italian men in the city. Some might say she was living the dream; but there were moments when it felt more like a nightmare. The unspoken truth about mafia life was that the dream only ended one way, in death.

Faces of lost friends and loved ones filled her mind. Stefano Carlachi. Grayson Galante. Miquel Cusanelli. Scotrovi. Giovanni's bodyguard, Freddie. The Nelson couple. Big Mike's family. Her father. The list went on and on. Countless innocent lives taken, and families devastated by loss. This was not something Angel could easily dismiss, and she wondered if, over time, she would become hardened to it like Giovanni and the other

Bosses. She wondered if one day she would look in the mirror and the softness would be gone.

Her thoughts were interrupted as Giovanni rose from his seat and raised his wine glass into the air. "To my granddaughter, Michelangela May Maratinzano, my pride and joy, the image of her father's strength and the beauty of her mother's soul."

Her name rolled from his tongue with a flare of grandfatherly pride. He gave a slight nod and then the others raised their glasses, said "Salud" in unison and drank.

Angel lifted her glass. "Grazie, Nonno," she said and Giovanni's face lit up. It was no secret he wanted her to learn Italian and was outwardly delighted anytime she spoke it. Even one word uttered in his native tongue brought a sparkle to his eye.

Sipping her wine, Angel let her eyes take in the entire new room, which she had added to the back of the pub specifically for family gatherings. The table was a gift from Giovanni and it was round, made of mahogany and large enough to comfortably seat twelve. The room held the new table, a small bar area and a private restroom. For added privacy, a set of wooden, double doors closed it off from the rest of the dining area. There was also a door to the left which led directly to the kitchen and a door to the right which exited into the alley on the side of the building. The additional doors were added per Giovanni's specific directions. "A wise man never enters a room with only one way out," he instructed. In addition, an emergency activated, bullet-proof divider was inset into the walls surrounding each doorway. In less than one second the room could be entirely sealed off and secured. Not even a grenade launcher could blast through the emergency dividers.

Angel would have liked to have installed large windows to make the room feel bigger, but Giovanni warned against it. "Windows invite spies," he told her. This was just one small example of what Angel considered Giovanni's over-the-top paranoia, but she obliged his wishes. To compensate, she had a special ventilation system installed, consisting of eight floor and ceiling vents designed for rapid air circulation. This would keep the room from ever feeling stuffy. It also allowed for heavy cigar smoke to be easily dissipated.

Angel sat closest to the double doors that led to the rest of the dining area. To her immediate left was her mother, Sophia, and to her right sat feisty, Aunt Olga. Next to Sophia was Joseph Venturini and next to Olga was Salvatore Buscetta, who was Sophia's father, Angel's grandfather and head of the Costa Nostra in Sicily. Angel had thoughtfully ordered these seating arrangements, knowing that Olga had the hots for Salvatore and that Sophia and Joseph were romantically involved. In fact, if Olga's meddling premonition was correct, Joseph was expected to propose to Sophia tonight. A part of Angel envied her mother's freedom to marry. Since she was not technically a Maratinzano, she could marry whomever she chose, regardless of familial affiliation. Angel had no such liberty.

At this very table sat two of the men she adored most, either of which would make a fine husband and neither of which she could have. Tony Andriachini, rugged, passionate and fierce; and Andrew Venturini, logical, romantic and steady. Not only couldn't she choose between them, but by birth name she was forbidden to have them. Unfortunately, family custom held no regard for love. With the knowledge of her true identity came a most painful realization. Loving someone

12

she could never have was far worse than never loving at all.

Next to Joseph sat Andrew and then Tony. Tony's father, Charlie Andriachini, who was Boss of the Andriachini Crime Family was next and then Giovanni. Next to Giovanni sat the Snake, Chase, and Michael Maletta, better known as Big Mike. The Galante and Cullato families were not invited to the celebration because Giovanni was still uncertain of their loyalty.

Chef Alortini entered the room and greeted both Giovanni and Salvatore with a bow of his head and kiss on their right hand. This was the highest sign of respect and Angel could see in Giovanni's expression that he approved of her Chef selection. He gave her a wink across the table and Angel smiled. She couldn't escape the feeling that she was probably the only person with whom Giovanni felt comfortable enough to wink. A man of his stature and power was not known for playful affection.

Chase was fidgeting in his seat, chatting with Big Mike. The Snake spoke mainly to Giovanni, but occasionally turned whenever Chase irritatingly tapped him on the forearm. Olga was talking poor Salvatore's head off and Sophia and Joseph were holding hands under the table, whispering quietly to one another. Tony was leaning forward, listening intently to whatever his father was saying and Andrew was leaning against the back of his chair, with his arms folded over his chest, appearing to be lost in thought.

Angel's eyes locked with Andrew's and she tried to determine what he was thinking. His expression was somber and though he forced a smile when their eyes met, she could see an uneasiness. Placing her napkin atop the table, Angel pushed her chair out and stood, as did all of the men. "Andrew, will you join me in the kitchen?" She asked, and everyone at the table quieted, making her feel awkward by the sudden attention. "I want to show you some of the other renovations," she stuttered, "since you know the place better than anyone."

Angel saw Tony's jaw tense as Andrew rose from his seat and held open the kitchen door. Moving quickly through the door, Angel led Andrew through the kitchen and into the hallway where Mr. Tetterbaum's wooden roll-top desk sat.

"You kept the desk?" Andrew asked, surprise in his tone. "I thought that would be one of the first things to go."

"I like it," Angel shrugged. "It has a history."

She made an immediate left and turned to face the brick wall just before the entrance to the bar area. Reaching downward, she pulled open a small panel in the wall, located three feet off the floor. It was over-laid in brick to match the rest of the wall so if a person wasn't aware of its existence, it would be almost impossible to find. Angel punched in a four-digit code and then closed the panel. A door, overlaid in brick to match the wall, slid sideways, revealing an opening. It was just wide enough for Andrew to turn and slip through. Angel followed him inside and then closed the door by pushing a control button on the left side of the interior wall.

"This is the new entrance to Tetterbaum's secret hiding place," she said, moving her hand up from the control button to the light switch and flipping it upward. Three tiny hanging lights illumed the area with a yellowish glow.

"No more lifting the steel table and climbing under the floorboards?" Andrew smirked.

Angel shook her head. "I left that entrance as a viable second option, but thought we needed easier access."

"You've gone high-tech on me," he teased.

The room was a small, narrow space that ran the length of the bar and sat between the wall at the back of the bar and the wall at the front of the kitchen. Andrew and Angel had discovered it together when they were searching for Tetterbaum's tapes.

Andrew ran his hand along the shelves that lined the entire wall to the left and held the new surveillance equipment that Chase had installed. "New equipment, too?" He asked and headed for the back of the space.

"Yep." Angel joined him. "Chase upgraded the video and audio surveillance so he can now monitor everything from his laptop."

"Everything?" Andrew turned to face her and Angel felt her stomach flutter at his close proximity. His brown eyes sparkled with a hint of seduction that pierced right through her. She slowly licked her lips.

"Well, not, everything," she sighed. "This room, for example, is not monitored."

The words had barely escaped her when Andrew lunged toward her, pressing his lips on hers in a burst of passion. Her defenses were nonexistent as he entangled his fingers in her hair, pulling her in deeper, caressing her soul as well as her body. It felt like an eternity since she had been in his arms.

"I missed you, Sweetheart," he uttered breathlessly between kisses. She hoped her kiss was saying *I missed you too* because she couldn't bring herself to pull her lips away to respond. Despite the chaos of mafia life and her complicated relationship with both he and Tony, she couldn't deny how much she loved Andrew.

Andrew pressed her against the shelving, letting his hands caress the outline of her breasts as his lips and tongue explored her neck. She gripped his muscular arms and ran her fingers up the back of his neck and through his hair. The musky scent of his skin, his touch, his body and his kiss ignited a burning passion inside that could only be quenched one way, and she was willing.

Angel was ready for complete surrender when Andrew abruptly pulled away. "We should head back before Giovanni sends someone to find you," he said.

She moaned. This wasn't the first time Andrew's logic had stifled a moment of passion. In fact, it was hard to believe, but they had only made-love once and Angel was aching to do it again. Wrapping her arms around his neck she pulled him into another kiss. "Let them search for a while."

"Sweetheart, as tempting as this is, we need to head back." Andrew took her hands from his neck and held them for a moment, gazing down at her fingertips. Angel had the instinctive feeling that he wanted to say something but was holding back.

"What?" She asked, redirecting his gaze from their hands to her face. "What are you thinking?"

He paused and then grinned. "Nothing." Despite the forced smile, Angel knew there was something he wasn't telling her. She had sensed it earlier in the evening. He pulled her close and planted a lingering kiss on her forehead, then tugged on her hands, beckoning her toward the door.

"No," Angel said flatly and withdrew her hands from his. "I'm not going back until you tell me what's on your mind." Crossing her arms, she glared at him.

"There's that Maratinzano stubbornness I know and love," he teased. Wrapping his arms around her waist, he pulled her close. "Sweetheart, you look...."

His words were cut short by the sound of two shots just outside the door. Angel instinctively ducked and then reached under her dress and grabbed the 9mm from a holster that was fastened tightly around her left thigh. Andrew drew his .45 and pressed his ear against the door.

"What do you hear?" Angel whispered.

"Nothing." Andrew pulled his cell from his pocket. "Put your phone on vibrate," he said. "Someone from the family will be calling to find out our whereabouts and we don't want the sound to give away our position." Angel reached back under her dress and retrieved her cell phone from a small strap around her right thigh.

This made Andrew smirk. "You got anything else under that dress you want to show me?"

"In the words of Olga, you snooze, you lose," she sneered, still a little miffed that he had pulled away from their kiss. Andrew gave her a glare that said her comment wasn't fair and Angel rolled her eyes. This conversation would have to wait. "Do you think there's more than one shooter?" Angel asked.

"I don't know," Andrew answered, his eyes blazing with intensity. "But I need to get out there and see if I can subdue him before more shots are fired."

"You can't just open the door. What if he's standing right there? He could shoot you dead before you even know what hits you." Angel studied his face. She could tell Andrew was in cop mode, assessing their odds of making it out without being seen. "There's another way out," Angel whispered.

"I thought of that, but for all we know the shooter could be in the kitchen and it'll take us longer to get through the floor. We'll be sitting ducks. Besides, we don't know how many assailants are out there."

"No, I had another exit put in." She pointed to the back of the room. "It's a stairway that leads to the underground cellar where Mr. Tetterbaum kept his old surveillance monitors."

"Where Antonio was killed?"

Angel nodded. That was a memory she didn't want to re-live.

"Who else knows this exit exists?" Andrew asked.

"Just me and Chase, and now you." Angel could see the wheels spinning in Andrew's brain.

"Let's sit tight and give it a few more seconds." Andrew glanced down at his phone. "It's been forty-five seconds since we heard the shots, which means our shooter might already be gone."

"Or dead," Angel remarked.

He shook his head. "I only heard two shots and it sounded like they were fired from the same gun. Unless the last shot was to kill himself, I don't think anyone else took him out," Andrew explained.

"Then maybe he came in to kill someone in particular, someone in the restaurant, hit his mark and then left," Angel posed, shuddering at how nonchalant and cold it sounded. After all, hitting a mark meant taking a life. It wasn't target practice, it was murder. She felt compelled to keep the distinction fresh in her mind. That distinction was the only thing that made her different from the old school mobster minds like Giovanni, Salvatore and Carl Cusanelli. "I noticed there were a lot of bogata boys in the restaurant tonight."

Andrew shook his head and glanced back down at his phone. "Something's not right," he mumbled.

"Well, we know that," Angel snipped and Andrew gave her a scolding stare. Her sarcasm was obviously not appreciated.

"No, I mean, someone should have called one of us by now."

Angel stared momentarily into Andrew's eyes, thoughts bouncing in her mind. What was he implying? Was her family all dead? Was that why no one had contacted her? It made more sense to think that they didn't hear the shots, but that seemed ludicrous as well. Angel rushed to the surveillance equipment and flipped the audio switch for the main dining room. She heard nothing. No talking. No laughing. No clinking of glasses or scraping of forks against plates. It was complete silence. She frantically flipped the switch for the private room but heard nothing there either.

"What's happening?" Panic rose in her voice. "I can't hear anything."

"Are you sure the equipment works?" Andrew asked.

"Positive. Chase and I tested it out earlier today and it was working perfectly." Andrew didn't comment but instead started rapidly punching keys on his phone. "What are you doing?" She asked.

"Notifying the police," he clenched.

"But..."

"I know," he cut her off.

"If they see Giovanni and Salvatore and your father and Don Andriachini together, they'll..."

"I know," Andrew gritted and then quickly ran his hand through his hair.

Angel leaned her back against the wall. Whatever Andrew thought was happening was bad enough that it warranted the risk of handing the Capo di Tutti Capi, head of the Cosa Nostra and two Crime family Bosses, one of which was his father, over for police interrogation. Even if the police found no grounds to hold them permanently, there was enough accusation and speculation of their crimes to make life a living hell for a while; not to mention that the media would have a hay day. Giovanni would be livid.

There was an unspoken mafia rule and it was a simple one: the families didn't call the police. They policed themselves. Civilians called the police, but bogata brothers lived by the code. They didn't rat each other out to the cops and the ones who did, didn't live long. Even more potent was the fact that Bosses met in private and those meetings were never disrupted by the police. If the cops were able to find out about a Bosses meeting, it meant traitors were in the families and it historically resulted in a house cleaning blood bath. If there was one thing you didn't do, it was call the police on a Boss, especially not the Boss of all Bosses.

Angel knew that the fact that Andrew notified the police meant something was terribly wrong, more wrong than a single shooter after his mark.

"What's going on?" She asked, searching his face.

"Is this room completely sealed from outside ventilation?" Andrew blurted in a hushed tone, while briskly moving about the room, peering between shelves and up at the ceiling. He had completely ignored her question. Angel watched him intently. "Sweetheart, is this room air tight?" Andrew stood directly in front of her, peering down.

"I don't...I don't know," she uttered and he seemed irritated by her ignorance. "Why?" The concern on his face stirred fear inside of her. *What's going on?!* She screamed on the inside, but kept her outward composure.

"There were too few shots fired to render the restaurant quiet. We've got four armed guards stationed, but the shots we heard were rapid and in one location." Andrew shook his head. "Even if they somehow made their way into the back room and shot the two guards inside of the room, our men would have fired to take the shooter out."

That made sense. At the first sound of gunfire, the Snake, Tony and Big Mike would have drawn their weapons and moved to intersect the shooter; not to mention that the other guards would have fired when the shooter took out the first man. "Maybe there were more shots but they used a silencer?"

Andrew shook his head. "We'd be hearing other sounds, like people crying and praying and footsteps. Our shooter is gone."

"Then why is everything quiet?" Angel threw her arms in the air in a frustrated gesture and almost hit Andrew in the head with the barrel of her 9mm.

He gave her an irritated glance and then turned his attention back to the surveillance equipment. "Is there a viewing monitor so we can get a visual of the back room?"

Angel shook her head. "We can retrieve the data from Chase's laptop or on the monitors at the Towers."

"Then there has to be an uplink we can use…"

Before Angel could respond, Andrew was on his phone, dialing his FBI friend, Sal, for help. While he waited for Sal to answer, he instructed Angel to dial Sophia's and Tony's phones and the number of anyone else who was in the back room. Angel made the calls while Andrew spoke to Sal; but all of her calls went to voicemail.

"Damnit!" Andrew blurted as he disconnected the call. Before she could ask, he holstered his .45, turned to her and took her by the shoulders. "Sweetheart, I think we've got a big problem. Sal can't tap into the surveillance inside the building because Chase has security codes in place that will take too long to decipher. That means we can't get a visual on what's going on out there."

Angel nodded. "What do you think is going on out there?" She studied his face for answers.

He took a deep breath. "Three days ago, a biological, military-grade nerve gas was shipped from an underground weapon's facility in Washington DC. The FBI notified local precincts here in Chicago because they had Intel that suggested that it was headed here." Andrew moved his hands from her shoulders and placed her face between his palms. "I think whoever stole it may have used it here, tonight."

Her mind instantly recalled the time when Frank Vilachi's men flooded the Towers with tear gas and kidnapped Aunt Olga. "That can't be right," she said, pushing his hands from her face and beginning to pace. "Tear gas burned my eyes and my chest and I was coughing and spitting. If that were the case we would hear everyone in the restaurant choking, moaning and even vomiting."

The look in Andrew's eyes told her the outcome was worse. "Sweetheart..."

"Tear gas doesn't kill people," she blurted, anger rising in her throat, making her voice quiver.

"Tear gas doesn't but nerve gas can. This is a chemical weapon called CoBroGas. It is still in the testing phase and because it can be combined with other ingredients, no one knows its capability yet." He ran his fingers through his hair. "It's complicated to explain."

"Try," Angel said flatly, sliding her gun back into the holster around her thigh and crossing her arms over her chest.

22

"Basically, it combines the chemical compound Bromoacetone, which was outlawed for riot use years ago, with carbon monoxide." Andrew stared at Angel as if he were waiting to see the information register in her brain. It had, but she wasn't sure how to process it. She knew nothing about Bromoacetone and very little about carbon monoxide, except that it was silent and lethal.

Angel swallowed, trying to hold back panic. "What if it's seeping into this room right now?" She began nervously chewing on her index fingernail. "We've got to get out there and open windows and doors and flood the place with fresh air before..."

Andrew grabbed her shoulders, cutting her sentence short. "We don't know how potent this is. This room must be somewhat air tight and if we open that door we could be dead in a matter of seconds."

"Then we'll go out the other exit, the one that leads to the cellars."

They stared at each other for several seconds before Andrew spoke. She could tell his brain was analyzing every possibility. "Sweetheart, I don't know the capability or the longevity of this gas. If we open any of the exits..." his voice trailed off.

"But if we just sit here everyone else might die," Angel gritted.

"For all we know they're already dead."

The words stung her heart and just as quickly as sadness enveloped her, anger pushed it aside. "I am not sitting in here when there's a chance I can do something to save my family."

"You are one stubborn woman," Andrew mumbled, shaking his head and pulling off his sport coat. She watched intently as he unbuttoned his black collared shirt, pulled it off and proceeded to tear off the sleeves. She stared at his muscular chest and the bulges of his biceps. Had they not been worried about dying, Angel would have been tempted to wrap herself in his naked manliness; but that thought would have to wait.

"You're not wearing a vest?" She said with surprise. This was unusual because Andrew was almost always adorned in Kevlar beneath his shirt.

"I wasn't anticipating any trouble tonight," he uttered. "A mistake I won't make again." Angel could tell Andrew was rattled. In every situation Andrew was always the stable, calm influence; so to see him shaken scared her. "I'm not sure it will even help, but tie this around your nose and mouth," he said, handing her one of the sleeves, "like a bandit." She tied it around her face and then waited while he put on his now sleeveless shirt and tied the other sleeve around his face.

Angel showed him the exit and gave him the code to open the door, which, similar to the entrance from the hallway, was designed to blend in with the brick wall. "The first step down is lower than a normal step, so be careful," Angel explained.

"Got it," he said and then turned to face her. "Listen, Sweetheart," he spoke calmly, taking a piece of her hair and moving it away from her face. "As soon as the door opens, we're going to stay low and move as quickly as possible. The faster we get outside the better." Angel nodded in agreement and Andrew lifted the sleeve from his face and kissed her forehead. "If we live through this, I want to see what else you have beneath that dress."

"I just might let you," she smiled from behind the sleeve.

With her gun held firmly in her right hand, Angel slid her left hand into Andrew's and gave it a squeeze. As soon as she stepped down onto the first step, she knew she had a problem. The heel of her black stiletto lodged into a crack in the wooden staircase. Angel tugged on Andrew's arm, causing him to whirl around.

"My shoe is stuck," she moaned, pointing downward.

Without hesitation, Andrew reached down and removed her foot from the straps. "Take off your other shoe and leave them here," he said.

"But they're Gucci," she objected and then realized, in the grand scheme of what was happening, how foolish she sounded. Leaving her shoes behind, she again slid her left hand into his and they hurried downward. It was twenty-two steps straight into darkness and Angel instinctively held her breath until her feet hit the cold, concrete floor of the cellar below.

"Go left," she whispered. "There should be an open archway straight ahead."

Andrew released her hand so he could feel his way through the darkness, and Angel held the back of his pants. They located the first archway and she instructed him to turn left again. "We should now be in the room that used to hold Tetterbaum's surveillance monitors, so from here we'll need to find the narrow hallway that leads to the right."

She didn't like being down there. Memories of stumbling over Antonio's body raced through her mind and made her nerves stand on end.

As they moved through the tunnel, Angel tightened her grip on Andrew's pants. As scared as she felt, she reminded herself that at least the air down there seemed to be uncontaminated; though if they were dealing with carbon monoxide they could conceivably fall over at any moment. She pushed the thought away. All they had to do was navigate through the hallway, find the steps that led to the street level and they would be out into the fresh night air.

The steps were concrete and uneven so moving quickly was impossible in the dark, not to mention she was barefoot and kept ramming her toes into jagged pieces of rock. They had to hold onto the stone wall to their right to navigate carefully upward. Half way up, Angel saw a light coming from the room at the top. It was dim and it was moving. Andrew pushed her against the wall and touched his finger to her lips, signaling her to be quiet. She slowly reached under her dress, retrieved her 9mm and held it tightly.

It was pitch black except for the tiny, moving light that sporadically cast a glow on the first two concrete steps. Angel suddenly felt Andrew's lips against her ear lobe and heard the intensity behind his whisper. He had removed his sleeve, at least long enough to talk to her. "Don't move. I'm going up. You stay here."

She froze. The prospect of being left alone in the dark was unacceptable. She wanted to object but before she could even turn her head toward Andrew, he was gone. Instinctively, she crouched down, held her gun in front of her and leaned her back against the damp, cool, stone wall. The darkness engulfed her and she fought to keep herself from imagining the worst. Angel focused all of her energy on listening and breathing. She heard a random shuffle of footsteps but no one spoke so it was impossible to imagine how many people might be in the room at the top of the stairs. She listened for Andrew's movements, but heard nothing. The silence was deafening.

All of a sudden, there were elevated male voices and then a gunshot. Every muscle in her body tensed as if she had been hit with a jolt of electricity. The second shot didn't prompt a muscular response, but her nerves maintained heightened awareness. She quickly turned and aimed her gun upward. Since Andrew knew she was armed, she surmised that he would announce himself before coming toward her in the dark; thus, she prepared to fire at anyone that came quietly onto the steps.

There was a loud scuffling sound from above and then the light that had been moving became still. Angel heard grunting, a scraping sound and what sounded like fists meeting flesh, but the shuffling of shoes against the concrete floor made it difficult to ascertain exactly what was happening. Was Andrew engaged in a fist fight? Had he lost his gun? Had he been shot? What if he needed help? Should she creep upward and try to peek inside the room? He told her to stay, but how could he expect her to stay when he might be fighting for his life?

Against Andrew's instructions, Angel crept step by step until she was no longer in pitch darkness. Inching her neck around the side of the wall, she peered into the room. A man lay dead to the left of the steps. There was a bullet hole in his head and a cell phone clutched in his right hand. The cell phone light was what they had seen moving around. Next to him was another man. He had been shot in the chest and Angel presumed he was also dead. She peered in further, to see Andrew and third man rolling around on the floor to the right. They were entangled to the point that there was no way Angel could fire a shot without the risk of hitting Andrew. *Where is Andrew's gun?* She wondered, scanning the floor to see if it had been knocked out of his hand. Was the scraping she had heard earlier the sound of Andrew's gun being strewn across the concrete floor?

All of a sudden, the door to the left of the steps flew open and a large man filled the doorway. Without hesitation Angel fired three rapid shots into the man's chest, sending him hurling backwards into the alley. "No!" Andrew yelled, drawing Angel's attention back to the fight. Upon seeing the man he had been fighting rise up, Angel fired again, the bullet soaring past Andrew and imploding into the man's neck. Andrew leapt to his feet, his eyes wide with horror. Dashing to the doorway, he looked down at the body in the alley. "We've got to go now, Angel. Now!" He hollered.

Angel ran toward Andrew, leaping over the two bodies inside the door and halting dead in her tracks when she saw the man lying on the ground in the alley. She threw her hand over her mouth and gasped.

"Keep moving!" Andrew barked.

"But...I...He's..." she stuttered.

"We've got to go!" He seethed. Grabbing her arm, Andrew pulled her down the street in the opposite direction of Tetterbaum's Pub, into a side alley and maneuvered her behind a dumpster. He pressed her back against a brick building and removed the sleeve from her mouth. "I told you to stay!" He scolded.

Angel opened her mouth to speak but no sound came out.

"Damnit, Angel!" Andrew slammed his hands against the brick wall on either side of her. "When are you going to learn to follow instructions?"

Tears filled her eyes as the sound of sirens filled the cool night air. "What about my family?" She sniveled.

"We can't get to them now," he shook his head. "We can't go back. It's out of our hands now."

CHAPTER 3

Angel climbed into Andrew's black, Chevy Equinox, and watched Tetterbaum's disappear in the side mirror as they drove away. Flashing lights from police cars, two fire trucks and several ambulances surrounded the pub. The weight of what she had done and not knowing if her family had survived was almost more than she could bear. She stared out of the window and waited for Andrew to finish talking to whoever was on the other end of his cell phone.

When he finally disconnected the call, Angel looked over at him. Swallowing the impermeable lump in her throat, she asked, "Was he dead?"

"I don't know," Andrew answered in monotone. "If he had a vest on, maybe not."

"So, there's hope?" Tears pooled in her eyes.

He shook his head. "If he lives then he knows who shot him. And if he's dead, then a Mafia Boss just personally assassinated the Mayor of Chicago."

"Does the Mayor normally wear a bullet proof vest?" Angel asked.

Andrew shrugged. "Sweetheart, I don't know what the Mayor was doing walking into that building. Maybe he had a vest, maybe he didn't. Maybe he was armed, maybe he wasn't. Maybe he was meeting the men in the room or maybe he was drunk and looking for a private place to take a leak." Andrew pounded his fist against the steering wheel. "I don't have the answers. Hell, I don't even know if those men had anything to do with the shooter at Tetterbaum's or if they were the Mayor's security detail for the night." Andrew's voice escalated and Angel couldn't remember seeing him so angry. "I don't know if everyone is dead or alive, gassed or not gassed… and now I've jeopardized my career and I won't be able to get that information."

"I'm sorry," she whispered, tears now streaming down her cheeks. "I thought you were in trouble and I knew you weren't wearing a vest and I just wanted to…" her voice tapered off. It didn't matter what she had thought at the time, the fact remained that she had made the situation undeniably worse.

They drove in silence for several moments and then Andrew explained that he was taking her to his father's second home on the outskirts of the city.

"Why can't I go to the Towers?" She asked.

"Because that's the first place the cops are going to come looking for you." Andrew ran his hand through his hair.

"How do you know they'll come after me? I mean, if the Mayor is dead then it's a moot point and if he survived, chances are he didn't even see who shot him."

Andrew gave her a cockeyed glance. "Don't play detective, Sweetheart."

It was infuriating when he spoke down to her. She crossed her arms over her chest and stared out of the passenger window. "Take me to the Towers," she barked.

Andrew made a sharp right turn, squealing the tires as he swerved the Equinox into an alley, and hit the brakes so hard Angel's seatbelt locked around her and her head slammed against the back of the seat. Unhooking his seatbelt, he angled his body to face her. "You listen and you listen good. We're in damage control mode right now; do you understand what that means?" Angel stared at him, her eyes wide and her mouth agape. She didn't know how to respond. She'd never seen Andrew like this. "It means unless I can gain control of this situation...and I mean fast, you're, no, we're, in a shitload of trouble." He exhaled angrily. "There are surveillance cameras all over the place; cameras that saw the Mayor take three hits to the chest."

"But they didn't see me pull the trigger," Angel argued. "And even if there was a camera inside the room I was basically wearing a mask with the sleeve over my face and it was dimly lit. There's no way anyone could identify that it was me."

"Maybe not, but surveillance cameras from the outside will reveal both of us stepping over the body and running down the alley." Angel gasped. She hadn't thought about that. "And whether he is dead or alive, they're going to pull bullets from a 9mm out of his chest, and out of the neck of the other guy." Andrew's jaw tightened. "And my .45 is somewhere in that room, registered to me, Special Investigator Andrew Venturini, with my prints all over it." He dropped his head and exhaled. "Our families and friends might all be dead. The Mayor might be dead. And my career on the police force just ended."

"Can't you tell them what happened at Tetterbaum's and that we escaped and came upon these men and they fired on you?" Angel asked. "Can't you say it was self-defense?"

"They didn't fire on me. The one guy pulled a gun, but he didn't fire on me. I took them both out just before I was jumped by the third guy," Andrew's voice grew weary. "I don't even know if the second guy was armed. I was hoping to subdue the third guy without shooting him, so we could get information from him."

31

"And then I shot him…"

"And then you shot him," Andrew repeated.

"This doesn't look good," Angel muttered.

"It isn't good," Andrew spewed.

"Maybe you could say you were following these guys because you had a hunch they were the ones who stole the CoBroGas?" She scrunched up her face.

Andrew looked more deflated than she had ever seen him. "Maybe," he sighed. "Now, I've got some guys taking steps toward damage control, but you've got to disappear for a while." He rubbed his eyes. "If everyone is dead, it won't take long to notice you're not among the bodies."

"What makes you think whoever did this was after me?"

Andrew raised his eyebrows, indicating disbelief. "History."

He strapped on his seatbelt, threw the gear shift into drive and pulled back into traffic. All of a sudden, a thought struck Angel. "Couldn't we have Chase erase the surveillance video feed that shows us leaving the building and in the alley?" The words were barely out of her mouth when reality hit. Chase might be dead. The thought made her sick to her stomach.

"I've got Sal working on it, but there are no guarantees." Andrew placed his hand on Angel's left thigh and gave her a tender squeeze. "I'm going to take you to my dad's private home. You'll be safe there and since my dad is or was one of the victims inside the pub and not a suspect, the police won't have reason to search his estates, at least not initially."

It took thirty minutes to get to Joseph Venturini's estate, and they spent most of the drive in silence. A long gravel driveway led to the white, colonial home. Andrew circled around to the back and pulled into a free-standing, five car garage which sat directly behind the house. It was white and matched the home's colonial design. Angel was startled when a man appeared in the passenger side window and tugged open her door.

"That's Rex," Andrew said, motioning for Angel to step out of the car. "As in T-Rex," he continued and Angel could see that his size had fostered the nickname. Rex was six foot, six inches tall and built like a concrete wall. He had a rigid jaw line, a long nose, slits for eyes that showed only black pupils and no hair of any kind on his face or head; not even eyebrows. Angel tried not to stare. Rex and Andrew shook hands and Andrew got right down to business. "We're going to need a few days' worth of clothing and food," he said.

"Already on it, Boss," Rex grunted in a deep tone.

Andrew stopped abruptly. "Don't call me that," he said with a hint of what Angel thought was irritation in his voice.

Rex nodded. "My apologies."

Angel had forgotten that Andrew, though the youngest of Venturini's three sons, was Joseph's chosen to become the next Boss. It was typically a position considered for the oldest son, but for some reason Joseph didn't believe either of the other two boys could handle it. Andrew and his father had argued over it for years and, sadly, Joseph's favoritism had driven a wedge between Andrew and his brothers. Part of the problem was that Andrew didn't want to give up his career on the police force so he never took Joseph's proposition seriously. Angel wondered, in lieu of all that happened tonight, if he would consider the position now.

They entered the house through the back door and into the basement level den. It was decorated in navy blue and burgundy colors and had a warmer feel than Angel would have imagined. The floors were dark red wood and in the middle of the room was a giant navy rug with the outline of a white sailboat on it. A red wood bar ran the length of the room to the immediate left and a navy sectional filled the room to the right, sitting in the center of the rug, facing a seventy inch, built in, big screen television and a black rod iron, glass top coffee table. There were no windows. She followed Andrew through the den and into a hallway that jetted off to the left. Passing two bedrooms, one on the left side of the hall and one on the right, Angel tried to peek in as they strode by, but Andrew's pace was too fast for her to see anything.

They hurried up the staircase, which wound around to the left and emptied them onto the main level and into a gigantic Great Room. It looked like a library and tavern game room combined. The ceiling was twelve feet high which made the room feel that much more open and spacious. A white brick fireplace sat in the very center of the room, with a rectangular seating ledge that went all the way around it. Circling the fireplace were navy leather couches and two burgundy leather arm chairs. The far right wall consisted of floor to ceiling bookshelves and held hundreds of books. In front of the shelves stood a competition length pool table with navy blue felt which was imprinted with a white sailboat. To the far left was a rectangular dining room table, with six chairs on each side and one on each end. Beyond it was a set of glass French doors that led to the kitchen.

Andrew stopped at the fireplace and turned to Angel. "Wait here," he said, "and this time, do it."

Angel rolled her eyes and walked over to take a gander at the bookshelves. She didn't appreciate his sarcasm, even if it was deserved. He disappeared into the kitchen and came back several moments later with a woman in tow.

"Angel, this is Mrs. Rosen," Andrew announced and Mrs. Rosen outstretched her hand. "She will attend to your needs while you're here."

"It's nice to meet you," Angel said. Mrs. Rosen shook Angel's hand, then gave Andrew a slight nod and returned to the kitchen without ever saying a word.

Angel guessed Mrs. Rosen to be in her early fifties. She had petite features and long, dark hair that had tiny streaks of gray and was pulled back into a low bun. Her eyes were bright green and she wore a solid, black dress with a white apron tied around her waist. Tiny diamond stud earrings glistened from each lobe and Angel got the feeling that she was more than just hired help. Now wasn't the time to burden Andrew with questions, but she made a mental note to ask him about Mrs. Rosen later.

Rex suddenly appeared from a doorway inset into the bookshelves, a door Angel hadn't even noticed. "Boss, we're ready for you," he said and Andrew exhaled annoyingly. "Sorry." Rex shrugged. "Old habits."

"Now you know how I feel when Chase calls me Boss Lady," Angel snipped.

"You are a Boss and you are a lady so I really don't see the similarity, Sweetheart," Andrew retorted with a snide grin. Angel slid her hand inside his and he gave it a tender squeeze. "I'm sorry. I'm on edge," he said.

"Me too," she whispered and leaned her head on his shoulder. Andrew pressed his lips against her forehead in a slow kiss and then pulled away.

"I've got a quick meeting and then I'll have Mrs. Rosen get you settled." He released her hand and headed toward the bookcase door.

"Can't I come with you?" Her question stopped Andrew in his tracts. She could tell he was uncomfortable by her asking.

"That wouldn't be a good idea," he said.

"Why not?" Angel pried, inching her way closer. After all, Andrew had been a part of almost every family meeting she had held at the Towers for the past year.

"This isn't the Towers. Women don't come to meetings here. Sorry, Sweetheart." Andrew stepped through the door and closed it behind him. Angel felt like the air had just been knocked out of her. She had never seen this chauvinistic side of Andrew. He had never once remarked that she didn't belong in a man's mafia world. He had never once made a derogatory comment about her leading or attending meetings. All this time she had thought that she had his full support; now it seemed as if he actually viewed her as inferior.

Angel sat stewing on the couch, gnawing on her index fingernail. It was hard to believe that her night of celebration had suddenly become a night of horror. So much had gone wrong that she had difficulty focusing on any one thing. Her thoughts bounced from the fear that her whole family had been poisoned by a lethal gas, to the fact that she had shot and probably killed the Mayor. The worst thing was the not knowing. She dialed her mother, Tony and Chase's cell phones again but they all went straight to voicemail. Part of her wanted to curl into a ball and cry, but experience had taught her to dig down deep and cling to even the smallest amount of strength and the slightest hope. Leaning forward, Angel placed her elbows on her knees, buried her face in her hands and quietly prayed.

When she opened her eyes, she was startled to find Mrs. Rosen standing in front of her. "I didn't want to interrupt," Mrs. Rosen said. "Can I get you anything?"

A time machine, Angel thought, *so I can go back and un-do this whole mess.* "No, thank you," Angel answered quietly.

Mrs. Rosen lowered herself onto the couch next to Angel. "You're head of the Maratinzano family, right?"

Angel nodded.

"It must be scary being the only female Boss." Mrs. Rosen folded her hands atop her lap and Angel couldn't help noticing her perfectly straight posture.

"It has its challenges," Angel uttered.

"Weren't you the one who uncovered the list of traitors in each family?" Mrs. Rosen asked, her eyes narrowing and her lips pursing together to make her face appear even more pointy. "The list with the names of the Russian infiltrators?"

Angel nodded again. "Well, it wasn't just me; I had a lot of help uncovering it…"

In the middle of Angel's sentence, Mrs. Rosen abruptly stood up, turned and strode briskly into the kitchen. Angel wasn't sure whether to follow her. She waited for a few moments but when Mrs. Rosen didn't return, Angel got up and began to make her way toward the kitchen. Before she reached the French doors, Andrew and Rex came bounding in through the bookshelf. Rex headed for the kitchen and Andrew made a beeline for Angel.

One look at Andrew's face told her that he had good news. "Sal was able to alter the surveillance video before investigators saw it," he grinned.

"So, we're in the clear?" Angel asked.

"As far as shooting the Mayor, yes, we're in the clear," he explained. "That is, unless he remembers something."

37

Angel's eyes widened. "He's alive? I didn't kill him?" Andrew laughed out loud as she excitedly threw her arms around his neck and hugged him.

"Oddly enough, he was wearing a vest," he explained and Angel slid her arms from around his neck and gave him a questioning look.

"Is it normal for the Mayor to wear a bullet proof vest?"

"I wouldn't call it normal but it isn't abnormal either. Government officials have been known to take extra security precautions, especially in some of the more urban areas." Andrew took Angel by the hand and led her to the couch. "What we need to find out is why he was entering that building and what connection he has, if any, to the men inside and to what happened at Tetterbaum's. We also need to come up with a story for your whereabouts and mine. I called the police from inside the building and then disappeared with you. They're certainly going to have questions about that."

"Can't you just tell them that we sneaked off to make-out?" Angel grinned, and a big smile filled Andrew's face.

"We'll call that plan B, Sweetheart," he said. "Not that I would mind having everyone think I was lucky enough to be making-out with the Boss."

Angel raised an eyebrow. "See, if there were no women bosses you'd never be able to have that reputation."

"True, indeed," he smiled.

"You're a good cop, you'll figure out what to tell them," she said, but despite her encouragement, it didn't take long for Andrew's playful grin to fade and a somber gaze to replace it. Angling his body so that he was facing her, Andrew took both of her hands and held them between his. She could already tell that whatever he was about to say wasn't going to be good and she braced herself for the worst.

"Sweetheart," he began and Angel couldn't control her emotions as fear within her leapt alive.

"They're all dead, aren't they?" She blurted, a lump wedging in the back of her throat. Angel pulled her hands from his and buried her face in her palms. At least they didn't suffer. At least there was no pain. At least they died happy, surrounded by people that loved them. Her thoughts drifted to her mother and how she and Joseph were holding hands and whispering like giddy teenagers.

Andrew pulled her hands from her face. "No one is dead."

"No one?" Angel gasped, relief and disbelief slowly snuffing out her fears.

"Listen," Andrew said softly and tucked a piece of hair behind her ear. "Paramedics and the police are just now removing people from the building."

"What took so long?" Angel interrupted.

"They had to wait for hazmat suits before they could enter," he explained.

"Couldn't fireman have gone in right away with their suits and masks?"

Andrew exhaled and she could tell he shared her frustration. "Evidentially, because they were dealing with an unfamiliar military-grade nerve gas, the powers that be made them wait for hazmat suits."

Angel grunted.

"The point is, no one in the pub died." Andrew's eyebrows lifted as if to highlight the good news, but there was still concern behind his eyes.

"If they're just now removing people, then how do you know no one is dead?"

"As soon as the hazmat teams gained access to the building, they flooded it with oxygen and started checking vital signs. According to the police report Sal intercepted for me, no one was pronounced dead on the scene."

Angel narrowed her brows. "What about the gunshots?"

"No one was shot." Andrew leaned against the back of the couch and closed his eyes. Angel could tell that not having details and being able to be on the scene was driving him crazy.

"Then what were the two shots we heard?" She asked but Andrew didn't answer. He just gave a shrug with his hands and let them flop onto his lap. "So where is everyone now?" She asked.

Andrew opened his eyes and sat up straighter. "The ones with the weakest vitals were removed first and taken to Northwestern Memorial Hospital. Everyone else is being treated on-site and will be transported to the hospital for evaluation as soon as possible."

Angel blinked slowly. Her family survived. *Thank you, God.* She silently prayed and then stood up. "We should get to the hospital right away."

Lacing his fingers in hers, Andrew tugged on her arm. "I need you to sit back down, Sweetheart."

She sank onto to couch and studied his face. "What is it?"

"CoBroGas is still in the testing phase. No one is one hundred percent positive about its short-term or long-term effects," he explained.

She had been bracing herself for more bad news but this seemed the least of their concerns. "All that matters is that everyone is alive. Whatever the effects are, they'll get medical treatment and get better." Angel started to stand up again but Andrew stopped her.

He inhaled deeply through his nose and Angel could now see that he was fighting to control his own emotions while he spoke. "Mild exposure to this gas can have minor affects, such as headaches, confusion, or lightheadedness. Prolonged exposure can poison the central nervous system, damage the lungs and the heart; and that's just the carbon monoxide part of it. Bromoacetone is a nerve agent that was outlawed because of its high toxicity levels and because people who were exposed to it died shortly thereafter or were left with severe neurological damage." Andrew shook his head. "This type of weapon is hardest on older people."

It was the way he emphasized the word 'older' that told her what he was struggling to say. Giovanni, Salvatore and Aunt Olga were all in their seventies. They would be the ones most affected and most damaged by the gas. If anyone was going to die, odds were it was one or all of them. Fear knotted her stomach as sorrow gripped her. She pursed her lips together and swallowed hard. "Do we know anything specifically about my grandfathers or Olga yet?"

Andrew shook his head. "Only that they are alive and were the first to be taken to the hospital."

"Can we go to the hospital now?" She rose from the couch. "I want to see them."

"Yes," Andrew rose and nodded. "I've arranged for security to meet us there and I'll have Rex follow us."

Andrew opened the French doors and called for Mrs. Rosen, who appeared immediately. "Where are Joe Jr. and Sammy?" He asked.

"Joe Jr. is in Reno and I haven't seen Sammy for two days," she answered without batting an eye. He has a new girlfriend.

"He always has a new girlfriend," Andrew quipped.

41

"Well, he seems to be smitten with this one," Mrs. Rosen added.

"Contact Joe Jr. and tell him dad's in the hospital and to get home right away," Andrew checked the clip of his .45 while he spoke, slid it back into place and then holstered the gun.

"Is Don Venturini okay?" Mrs. Rosen gasped.

"He's alive, that's all we know right now," Andrew responded, placing his hand on Mrs. Rosen's shoulder and giving it a gentle squeeze. "Tell Joe Jr. to find Sammy and to meet me tomorrow morning, 9:00am, at the house in the city."

"Yes, sir," Mrs. Rosen nodded.

Rex was already in the garage when Andrew and Angel entered. He opened the passenger door to a shiny, black Range Rover with tinted windows and tan leather interior, and motioned Angel inside. Then he loaded two semi-automatic rifles with scopes into the backseat, two Kevlar vests, a black leather bag filled with ammunition and three hand guns varying in size.

"She's all fueled up," Rex told Andrew, tossing him the keys "I'll load my gear into your car and meet you at the bottom of the driveway."

"Why aren't we taking your Equinox?" Angel asked.

"Extra precautions," Andrew mumbled as he climbed into the Range Rover and adjusted the seat. "I'll explain later."

Angel looked at the guns and then glanced at Andrew. "Are we going to war?" She said, half-jokingly. "Because I'm not really dressed for it."

Andrew smirked. "You know what they say about love and war."

"All is fair?"

"No. Come prepared." He gave her a wink and then backed the Range Rover out of the garage, turned the wheel to the left and sped up the driveway. Angel glanced at the passenger side mirror and saw Mrs. Rosen dart out of the basement door, across the driveway and into the garage.

She was about to mention it to Andrew when she felt his hand inching its way under her dress and up her thigh. "What are you doing?" She asked.

"We're alive and you said if we lived I would get to see what else you kept under that dress," he feigned innocence.

"I said you might get to see," she corrected him, "but not until you prove you can finish what you start." Angel raised one eyebrow and looked sideways at Andrew. It was a dare. She knew it and she knew that he knew it.

"Oh, I think you know I can finish what I start," he rebutted.

"Hmmm." Angel wrinkled up her nose and shrugged. "It's been a long time and a lot has happened since then." She flirtatiously taunted him and it felt good. "My memory isn't so good."

Andrew chewed on his bottom lip and shook his head. She could see by the fact that the corners of his mouth were curling into a smile that he, too, enjoyed their banter. "As soon as everything dies down, Sweetheart, I'm going to refresh your memory."

CHAPTER 4

Andrew parked the Range Rover in the Northwestern Memorial Hospital visitor's parking lot and killed the ignition. Turning to Angel, he went over the details one more time. She would wait in the lobby while he flashed his badge and gained information as to the whereabouts of the pub victims, and then he would come and get her. They were both supposed to keep a low profile, but especially Angel. Andrew was working under the assumption that whoever released the CoBroGas had every intention of taking out Angel with the rest of them. "When they find out you got away, they'll try again," he told her.

"If they were trying to kill everyone in the restaurant, and they find out no one died, won't they try again anyway?" Angel argued, but it fell on deaf ears. Andrew's jaw was set and Angel knew that, that meant there was no sense in arguing.

"There are too many unknowns not to precede with extra caution, Sweetheart," he said, patting her cheek with his palm. "Just keep your head down and don't say a word."

That wouldn't be hard considering she was embarrassed to show her face, what with the way she was now dressed. Since the Kevlar vest wouldn't fit under her Versace gown, Andrew had stopped at a gas station and purchased a pair of flip-flops and a black, tourist sweatshirt with a picture of the Chicago skyline on it. It hung down below her hips so just the bottom of the dress shown. The flip-flops were white with yellow sunflowers. She could imagine Olga wearing them with her yellow, fleece robe, but they weren't exactly designed to be worn with a Versace dress. Stepping out of the car, Angel looked down at her outfit and grimaced. "I look like an escaped mental patient," she moaned.

Andrew grinned. "It's not that bad."

"It isn't good," she rebutted and he chuckled.

"I'll tell you what," he said, draping his arm around her shoulder, "as soon as we're done here I'll get you out of those clothes."

Inwardly, her stomach fluttered with anticipation, but outwardly she rolled her eyes. As good as it sounded, now wasn't the time to think about the joys of de-clothing.

Andrew strode straight ahead to the Emergency check-in desk while Angel turned right and entered the waiting area, choosing a spot in the corner by the windows. Peering out the window, she saw Rex pull the Equinox into the parking lot and watched as two men climbed out. Both were dressed in black and judging by the bulge in their shirts, both were heavily armed. Angel's pulse quickened. She assumed they were the security Andrew had arranged, but if the past year had taught her anything it was not to assume and never to blindly trust. Reaching under her dress, she discreetly retrieved the 9mm from her thigh holster and quickly shoved it into the front pocket of her sweatshirt. Keeping her hand tightly on the gun, she watched the men enter. A moment later Andrew, Rex and the two men escorted her from the waiting room toward a private wing that had been specifically set up to address the needs of the CoBroGas victims.

"What did they tell you?" Angel asked Andrew as they passed the emergency check-in desk, preceded through two sets of double doors and headed quickly down a long hallway that emptied into another hallway with a nurse's station to the right and individual rooms on both sides.

"Only that everyone who was brought from the pub was placed in this wing," Andrew answered.

"And everyone is alive?" Angel asked.

"No documented deaths yet," Andrew said.

As soon as they turned the corner Angel noticed that the nurse's station was crawling with police. Two officers, Daniel Lisben and Harry Monahan, immediately approached Andrew and pulled him to the side of the hallway. Lisben was short and stocky with gray hair parted to one side, hiding a bald spot, and dark gray, bushy eyebrows. His skin looked leathery and his jowls hung loosely on his face, indicating to Angel that he was probably nearing the age of retirement. Monahan was six foot, three inches tall, had bright red hair, green eyes and was covered from head-to-toe in freckles. She couldn't have envisioned a more Irish looking man in his mid-twenties if she had tried. Angel wasn't able to hear what they were saying but she saw one of them slip Andrew a gun and she assumed it was the .45 he had lost at the scene. It was obvious that these cops were part of the damage control he had mentioned earlier.

Angel approached the long, half-moon shaped nurse's station and asked if she could see Giovanni, Sophia, Olga, Salvatore and Tony. "I'm sorry," the gray-haired woman said without looking up from her computer screen. "Immediate family only."

"I am family," Angel said. "Sophia is my mother. Olga is my great aunt and Giovanni and Salvatore are my grandfathers."

The nurse looked up and gave Angel a once over. "I'll need to see some ID," she said flatly.

Angel held up her hands. "I don't have my purse with me," she shrugged. "We were at a dinner party and my purse is back at the restaurant." Even if she had had it with her, she wouldn't have been able to prove that she was related to any of them, because when she discovered that her last name was really Maratinzano, Angel hadn't rushed to the DMV to change her license. It still read Angel Martin.

"I'm sorry. I can't help you," the nurse scowled, picked up a clipboard and walked away.

Angel slid her right hand into the sweatshirt pocket and angrily wrapped her fingers around her 9mm. *Who the hell does she think she's dealing with?* Her eyes narrowed and her jaw tensed. She was contemplating her next move when Rex placed his hand on her shoulder and leaned down, whispering into her ear.

"Don't pull your gun, ma'am," he said with a deep, throaty tone. "We have a way to get you in."

Rex led her back down the hall, making a quick left into what looked like a storage room and closing the door behind them. The two men whom Angel had seen getting out of the Equinox, stood guard outside of the door. The room consisted of metal shelves stacked high with white blankets and blue scrubs. "Brilliant!" Angel exclaimed, retrieving a pair of scrubs from the shelves and pulling the sweatshirt over her head. She unfastened the Kevlar vest and handed it to Rex. After struggling with the zipper on her dress for a few seconds, she turned to Rex. "Can you help me?" Turning her back toward him, Angel lifted her hair and waited. Rex set the vest on the floor and quickly unzipped her gown. When it fell around her ankles she heard him inhale sharply, and then, out of the corner of her eye, she saw him spin around and face the door.

47

"Would you like me to step outside, ma'am?" Rex asked.

"It's okay," she said, sliding on the scrub pants and retrieving the bullet proof vest from the floor. She fastened it around her and then pulled the scrubs shirt over her head. "Thank you for turning around, though." Angel slid blue surgical booties over her flip-flops and placed a blue hat resembling a shower cap over her hair. "How do I look?"

Rex hesitantly turned and gave her the once over. "Like a doctor or a nurse or somethin' medical."

Angel nodded. This was good. Now, she could go find her family without being hassled. Retrieving her 9mm from the sweatshirt pocket, she reached down into her pants and holstered it around her thigh. It would be hard to retrieve quickly, but at least she would have it if the need arose.

Exiting the supply closet, Angel handed Rex the Versace gown and sweatshirt and instructed him and his two guards to find Andrew, tell him about her wardrobe change and that she was going to search for the family. "I'll look less conspicuous without an entourage," she explained and Rex agreed. "Tell Andrew to text if he needs me," she said and then hurried down the hall.

At the end of the hall, Angel decided to start her search by heading left, away from the nurse's station. There was no sense in risking contact with medical personnel. Peering into the first two rooms, Angel didn't see anyone she recognized. She found Johnny in the third room and gasped at the sight of him. He was lying on his back, covered with a sheet that stopped just below his chest. His face was bright red, as were his hands and forearms, an oxygen mask covered his nose and mouth and he was hooked up to a heart monitor.

She walked closer and Johnny opened his eyes. The whites of his eyes looked yellow and she saw fear on his face. "Johnny," she whispered. "What happened?" He shook his head slightly and Angel assumed it meant he was too weak to speak. "Did you see who did this?" He nodded, blinking slowly. She gave his hand a tender squeeze and he yelped in pain. "I'm sorry," she gasped, releasing his hand.

Johnny moved his arm toward his face and tried to lift the oxygen mask, but he was too weak. Angel carefully removed it from his mouth and upon seeing that his mouth was filled with blood, a wave of nausea flushed her. "So...da," Johnny rasped.

"Soda?" Angel repeated. "You need a drink?" Johnny's eyes rolled back into his head and Angel returned the oxygen mask to his face. "I'll get you some water. I'll be right back." She slowly backed toward the door, unable to peel her eyes away. "You're going to be okay, Johnny," she said, but not even she believed those words. He looked like he was dying.

Suddenly, an alarm sounded and several nurses rushed up the hall to the right of the nurse's station. "Code blue, room 134," one of them hollered.

"Code blue 134," another nurse repeated. Panic gripped Angel. You didn't have to be medically trained to know what Code Blue meant. She dashed from Johnny's room, and headed toward the commotion.

"Clear," a nurse blurted and then Angel heard the sound of paddles jolting someone's body. She peered into the room to see Giovanni lying on the bed, his chest bare, his eyes staring blankly upward, an oxygen mask on his face, white circular monitors stuck to his chest and medical personnel surrounding his bed. The heart monitor remained flat-lined and Angel's knees went weak.

"Clear," the nurse blurted again and the paddles jolted Giovanni a second time, lifting his chest from the bed and slamming it back down. Angel couldn't breathe. *Not Giovanni*, she silently cried. *Not Giovanni.* It felt as if time stood still as Angel silently prayed and fought the urge to rush to his side. *Don't die,* she willed him. *Please don't die.*

"Clear" the nurse said a third time and his body lifted from the bed. Suddenly, the room was filled with the most beautiful sound. Beep. Beep. Beep. Her eyes darted from Giovanni's face upward to the machine monitoring his heart. There were blips of movement on the screen; tiny spikes of hope. His heart was beating and Angel's heart was racing. The nurses high-fived and the paramedic returned the paddles to their holder.

"That was a close one," one nurse said.

"Let's get him to ICU," another nurse ordered.

Angel stood frozen. Her mouth was dry, her eyes were teary and she couldn't look away from her grandfather. She had almost lost him and it made her realize, despite their differences, she loved him and she wasn't ready to run the family without him.

Angel stepped into the hall as the hospital personnel prepared Giovanni for transport to the ICU. She wanted to stay with him, to hold his hand and to be there the moment he woke up, but knew she needed to find her mom, Olga, Salvatore and the others. "I'll come see you soon," she whispered as they wheeled Giovanni away.

Making her way down the hall, Angel peeked into every room. She didn't recognize most of the people, but noted that their skin was as red as Johnny's. Through the last door on the left she found Tony. He was sitting up, had an oxygen tube in his nose, his muscular chest was bare and his legs were dangling over the side of the bed. His skin looked flushed but not fire red like the others.

"Tony!" Angel exclaimed and rushed into his room, throwing her arms around his neck.

"Babe," he grunted with a voice that was raspy and low. He then attempted to clear his throat and speak again but his voice still sounded unusual. "What happened?"

Angel fought back tears. She was overjoyed to see that he was in better shape than Johnny and Giovanni. She released her hug and laced her fingers in his. "Does it hurt when I touch your skin?" She asked.

His lips curled at the corners, "Only a little, Babe, but don't let that stop you from touching wherever you want."

Tony! Angel smiled. That was a typical Tony response and it reassured her that he was going to be okay. "Do you remember anything?" She asked.

He either didn't hear her question or was suddenly distracted by the way she was dressed, because he looked her over, looped his right hand around her backside, pulled her in closer and said, "I wouldn't mind playing doctor with you."

His smile broadened, revealing blood on the inside of his mouth. *Oh, no! Tony!* She removed his hand from her bottom and held in firmly between hers. "I think you should lie down," she told him, planting a tender kiss on his cheek.

"You want me to lay down here?" Tony asked. "Right here, Babe?" His words slurred and Angel became aware that something was wrong; he was disoriented and behaving oddly, even for Tony. "You want to examine me here, Doc?"

Angel lowered him backwards on the bed and lifted his legs so that he was lying flat. She then reached down and raised the bars on both sides of the bed so that he couldn't roll off. Leaning over him, Angel looked into his eyes and noticed the whites of his eyes were slightly yellowed; but not as bad as Johnny's. She planted a tiny kiss on his forehead. "Tony," she spoke softly, "do you know who I am?"

"Babe," Tony grinned, "how could I forget you?"

Always the charmer, Angel thought. "What's my name?" She asked, watching as his smile faded and his eyes glazed over. It was obvious he couldn't remember. As she stared at Tony, Andrew's words replayed in her mind. *"Mild exposure to this gas can have minor affects, such as headaches, confusion, or lightheadedness. Prolonged exposure can poison the central nervous system, damage the lungs and the heart."* Angel swallowed hard, forcing herself not to cry. She licked her lips, took a deep breath and leaned over him.

"Tony, I'm going to leave now but I'll be back in a little while." She started to straighten when he grabbed her by the arm.

"I'll be here, Babe," he rasped and something in his eyes told her that those words held deeper meaning. It was as if he was promising not to die.

She took his fingers from her sleeve and kissed them. "You better be," she smiled through tears. *You better be.*

Angel stepped into the hall and could no longer hold back her emotion. The tears came faster than she could wipe them away and a tall, dark-haired man in scrubs coming toward her, noticed. "Are you new here?" He asked, stopping in front of her.

Angel nodded.

"You can't let patients and families see you break down. You have to show strength. You have to toughen up and accept that people die." His dark brown eyes pierced through her. "We'll all die someday." As he sauntered down the hall, he added, "Why don't you step outside and get some fresh air."

Anger boiled in her toes. Who did he think he was? Probably some hotshot doctor who thought he was God's gift to medicine. She knew better than anyone that people die. She'd seen more people die than the average person, but she wasn't accustomed to watching them die slowly, especially people she loved. In the mob world, people died quickly. One pull of a trigger and they were gone. That didn't make accepting death easier, but forced the living to move on that much faster. Watching someone suffering, being unable to help them and unsure if they would ever recover was brutal.

Lost in her own thoughts, Angel glanced up to see a hospital employee at the end of the hall, pushing a gurney. Whoever lay on the gurney was fully covered with a sheet. He stopped at an elevator and as the door opened Angel rushed toward him. "Wait!" She yelled and the employee turned to face her. "Who is it?" She panted, pointing to the body.

The employee shrugged. "Someone brought in from Tetterbaum's pub. Evidentially some kind of bomb went off there tonight." He grabbed the clipboard that was sitting atop the body. "A guy named Stephen Manucci. Twenty-five years old."

"Can I see him?" Angel asked.

"Be my guest," he said, obviously thinking she was a hospital employee.

Angel lifted the sheet to reveal Stephen's face. She noticed right away that his skin didn't look bright red, like Johnny's, and there wasn't any dried blood at the corners of his mouth. She wondered if he had had some previous medical condition that rendered his body less able to fight for life against the effects of the gas. Unable to stomach the view, Angel shuddered and lowered the sheet. "Is there a list somewhere of everyone brought in from the pub?" Angel asked him.

"Yeah, in the computer." He wheeled the gurney into the elevator and Angel guessed that he was heading for the morgue. "You coming down?"

She froze. She hated hospitals and bodies and the thought of going downstairs to a place where she would be surrounded by dead people was horrifying. She stared blankly, her knees on the verge of buckling.

"I thought you wanted a list of everyone from the pub?" He said and Angel instinctively threw her arm up to block the elevator door from closing.

"Can you get me that list?" She asked.

"Yep. I can print it from my computer downstairs."

She stepped inside the elevator with a siren going off in her head. Red flags were waving. Her instincts were telling her something was wrong, but it was too late. The elevator doors closed.

CHAPTER 5

"You were supposed to stay with her!" Andrew barked, motioning Rex and the two men with him, into an unoccupied hospital room.

"My apologies, boss," Rex groaned. "But she instructed us to find you."

"Yeah," one of the other men chimed in. "She told us that she would be less conspicuous without an entourage."

"And less protected!" Andrew seethed.

"We didn't think of that," Rex uttered. "We were following orders."

"You work for me. You follow MY orders!"

"Got it, boss."

"You better be damn glad I'm not the Boss yet because if I were, you three wouldn't be standing here right now. Find her!" His jaw tightened and his nostrils flared as Rex and the two men scurried from the room. Andrew was angrier than he had been in a long time. Pulling his cell phone from his pocket, he dialed Angel again but it went straight to voicemail. She hadn't responded to his calls or texts and he couldn't escape the feeling that something was terribly wrong.

Officer Daniel Lisben stuck his head inside the room. "Is this our holding room?"

"Temporarily," Andrew sighed. "Until they need it for another patient, we're free to use it." Andrew stared out the window into the parking lot. "Any news yet?"

"We've got confirmation that the Mayor has just been moved upstairs. Room 486."

"How many on his security detail?" Andrew asked.

"Five men.   We can't get near him, not here anyway," Officer Lisben explained and Andrew gritted his teeth. This was more bad news. He had a hunch that the Mayor was somehow connected to whoever stole the CoBroGas and would be able to fill in some crucial blanks; that is, if Andrew could find a way to talk with him.

"How long are they going to keep him here?" Andrew asked.

"Probably until the media dies down. They'll want to play it up long enough to garner the sympathy of the voters and then release him when people lose interest in the story," Officer Lisben said with certain sarcasm. "You know the political game."

Officer Harry Monahan entered the room with a big grin spread across his freckly face. "It's a media zoo out front," he said, shaking his head. "I've never seen anything like it. I think I just got my mug on the news."

Andrew and Officer Lisben shot each other a glance and said in unison, "Rookie." Officer Monahan blushed at the truth. He had only been with the Chicago police force for a few weeks while Officer Lisben was getting ready to celebrate thirty years on the force and Andrew was approaching his tenth-year anniversary.

"Special Investigative Officer Venturini..." Officer Monahan began and Andrew cut him off.

"Let's drop the titles," Andrew said. "Call me Andrew and I'm gonna call you Monahan." Monahan's face lit up.

"Well, all right then!" Monahan clapped his hands together and shuffled his feet. "Andrew." He then directed his attention to Officer Lisben. "Should I call you Dan?"

Officer Lisben scowled at him like an old dog that had just been introduced to the new family pup.

"Call him Lisben," Andrew said, gripping Lisben by the shoulder and giving him a squeeze.

"Well, all right then!" Monahan said, his face glowing with excitement. "Andrew and Lisben," he repeated.

"Go get us coffee," Lisben barked.

"All right. Black? Cream and sugar?" Monahan asked. "How do you take it?"

"Quickly and quietly," Lisben scowled.

"Get the coffee from the fourth floor and, while you're up there, see if you can snoop around and find out anything about the Mayor's condition and when he will be released," Andrew instructed.

"No problem. I'm friends with one of the guys on Mayor Tompkins security team. We go way back. I can find out anything you want to know," Monahan told him and Andrew raised his eyebrows with sudden interest. This was good news.

"Any chance you can get me in to talk with the Mayor?" Andrew asked.

"I'll see what I can do," Monahan said, bounding out of the room as fast as he had entered.

"What do you know? The big oaf's got contacts," Lisben remarked.

"Cut the kid a break," Andrew scolded. "You were a rookie once too."

"Yeah, well, I don't trust his dumb act and neither should you." Lisben chided. "Nobody that stupid can make the force. You mark my words and watch your back around that one." Lisben shook a finger of warning in Andrew's face. "And if he says 'well, all right then' one more time, I just might shoot him," Lisben snarled.

Andrew chuckled. He had to admit that Monahan's constant use of that phrase was annoying but not annoying enough to shoot him.

Rex suddenly burst into the room. He was winded, panic stricken but abruptly stopped when he saw Lisben. Rex motioned with his head for Andrew to follow him into the hallway. "We got trouble," Rex panted. "We've scoured this whole wing of the hospital and we can't find Angel. We even checked the cafeteria and the gift shop."

Andrew exhaled angrily. It was doubtful that Angel had gone for food or flowers at a time like this, and evident that he wasn't working with the sharpest tools. "Giovanni has been moved to the ICU. She might have gone to find him."

"I thought of that, but I wasn't allowed in the ICU." Rex shifted his weight and lowered his voice, talking out of the side of his mouth. "I can't find our men either."

"What do you mean you can't find them? Weren't they with you?" Andrew threw his arms in the air.

"Yeah, boss, they were with me and now they ain't," Rex nodded. "I left them on this floor to go to the ICU and when I came back, they were gone."

"Did you call them?" Andrew asked.

"No answer on either phone. That ain't the usual protocol." Rex shook his head side to side. "The protocol is to always..."

"I know protocol," Andrew interrupted. He instructed Rex to walk each floor again and continue calling their cell phones; and then he called Sal and asked him to run a trace on their phones.

"Who we dealing with here?" Sal asked. "Criminals or family?"

Andrew hesitated. Technically, it was both. "Two Venturini men are missing. Start your search within the Northwestern Memorial Hospital building. I have a feeling they didn't leave the building." Andrew gave Sal the numbers.

"It will take me a few minutes," Sal said.

"Also, run Angel Maratinzano's phone through the system," Andrew said and he heard Sal's breath catch. Sal knew about Andrew's feelings for Angel.

"You want me to run her number first?" Sal asked.

"That'd be great." Andrew hung up and told Lisben he was going to go room by room and see if he could locate his father. He had been so distracted with Angel and the Mayor that he'd almost forgotten that his father was also one of the victims. Actually, he had been trying to keep his mind occupied so that worry couldn't consume him. Being the son of a mob Boss made things difficult. Any time there was a medical emergency within a crime family it had to be handled with the utmost sensitivity and secrecy; but especially when a Boss was involved. He couldn't just waltz up to the nurse's station and ask to see Joseph Venturini. The mere mention of his father's name would cause unwanted media attention, and could alert the attempted assassin to the fact that his father had not been killed in the pub. Having the head of the Costa Nostra, the Capo Di Tutti Capi and several Crime Family Bosses in the same hospital at the same time was an assassin's dream. Andrew knew he needed to stay alert and focused, which is why Angel's vanishing was even more maddening.

Poking his head into each room made Andrew realize that the effects of the CoBroGas were worse than he had feared. The yellowing of the eyes and the reddening of the skin made him question the magnitude of internal damage. When he got to Tony's room, Andrew stepped inside and closed the door.

"There you are!" Tony blurted and struggled to sit up in bed. "I've been looking all over for you." His words slurred slightly, as if he had had too much wine.

"Have you seen Angel?" Andrew asked.

"Yeah," Tony grinned. "That babe is hot."

"No, I mean have you seen her tonight?" Andrew clarified.

Tony's brows narrowed, like he was trying to retrieve a memory. "She's in a black dress. God, she looks good in that dress." His eyes glazed over. "You took her away." He stared at the wall and mumbled, "Don't go with him. Stay with me."

Andrew observed Tony and quickly realized that he was suffering from disorientation. He stepped closer and lightly tapped Tony's face with his palm. "Hey, man, tell me your name," Andrew said, forcing Tony's gaze to meet his own. Tony stared at him. "What's your name?" Andrew repeated.

Tony shook his head. "I'm drawing a blank."

Andrew leaned down into Tony's face. "Your name is Tony Andriachini, son of Charlie Andriachini. You live in Chicago. You were dining tonight at Tetterbaum's Pub when someone flooded the building with a chemical agent called CoBroGas. You're disoriented from the effects of the gas." He studied Tony's eyes to see if anything rang a bell. "Repeat what I said," he ordered and Tony mumbled it word for word. "Now, does any of that sound familiar?"

Tony shook his head. His eyes were blank.

"Has anyone else come into this room? Anyone that looked familiar to you?" Andrew asked.

"There was a sexy doctor who kissed my forehead..." his voice tapered off. "She felt familiar."

"That was Angel!" Andrew blurted. "Did she say where she was going?" Tony stared and slowly licked blood from the corners of his mouth.

"I don't remember what she said," he slurred. "I just knew I didn't want her to leave."

"I know the feeling," Andrew uttered under his breath.

Leaving Tony's room, Andrew made a beeline back to the nurse's station, flashed his badge and asked for the whereabouts of the other people who had been brought in from the pub.

"We didn't have room for everyone in this wing so we put them in available rooms on the second floor," explained a young, petite blonde whose name badge read: Emily.

"Can you get me a listing of everyone brought in from the pub?" Andrew asked.

Emily clicked on the computer keyboard in front of her. "Yes, sir," she said, with her fingers dancing across the keys almost as quickly as Chase. Her blue eyes widened and she gasped, "Wow, there sure are a lot of John Does."

This was to be expected. None of the Bosses carried identification and most of the Made members didn't either. The only ones who still carried their own personal ID's were the lower ranking bogata brothers or civilians.

"Can you print me a copy of that list?" Andrew asked.

Emily handed him two sheets of paper. The first sheet had the names of those located in the first floor rooms and the second page held the names of those located on the second floor. Andrew thanked her and started to walk away when her voice stopped him.

"Officer?" Emily called out. "I show that several persons are deceased, and one John Doe is in ICU."

He already knew Giovanni was the John Doe in ICU. "Do you have names for the deceased?"

"A couple of real names and the rest are John Doe and one Jane Doe," she shrugged and handed him a print out of the names.

Sorrow pierced Andrew's heart. Assuming most of the civilian women in the restaurant carried identification, it stood to reason that Jane Doe could only be one of two people. Olga or Sophia.

CHAPTER 6

"I've traced her phone and she's in the morgue," Sal spoke poignantly, "or at least her phone is, and so are your two Venturini buddies."

Andrew spewed obscenities. What the hell was Angel doing in the morgue? Andrew knew she had a fear of dead bodies so he couldn't imagine why she would have gone there, unless she was forcibly taken. He phoned Rex and instructed him to meet at the first-floor elevator. Then he called Lisben and Monahan for back-up. Like it or not, there was a lack of manpower, so the cops and the mob were going to have to work together on this one.

Once inside the elevator, Andrew drew his .45 and Rex, Monahan and Lisben followed suit. "We don't know what we're walking into," Andrew explained. "So be ready."

"Well, all right then!" Monahan blurted, pulling a Taser from his belt. He now held a .45 in his right hand and a Taser in his left.

"I don't think you need both, sunshine," Lisben laughed. "The gun ought a do the trick."

"The gun leaves no witnesses," Monahan retorted, "and at the academy they said to always bring in a witness from the scene of a crime."

Lisben shot Andrew a thoroughly annoyed look that screamed, "This kid's clueless."

"A witness would be great," Andrew said, "but it's most important to have the four of us go in alive and come out alive. Got it?" He stared at Monahan.

"Yes, sir. I got it."

The elevator doors opened and they stepped into a dimly lit hallway. The floor was tiled in white and black squares, the walls were painted white and fluorescent bulbs hung from the ceiling, every other one lit. Andrew led the way with Rex slightly behind and to his right, Monahan slightly behind and to his left and Lisben bringing up the rear. At the end of the hallway were gray, steel, double doors with darkened glass, rectangular windows that prevented anyone from looking inside. The doors were locked and Andrew tapped on them with his gun.

A man's voice came from inside the room. "Ca...can I help you?"

"Yes. I am Special Investigation's Officer, Andrew Venturini, and I have been sent to analyze the bodies of the deceased victims from Tetterbaum's Pub," Andrew explained.

"I didn't re...receive that order," the man stuttered.

"If you'll unlock the door, I'd be happy to show you the paperwork," Andrew lied.

"Can you come back later? I'm...I'm on my break," the man nervously answered.

"No. It's a mad house upstairs, as I'm sure you know. We need to see the bodies now," Andrew answered with a stern calm.

Lisben shook his head and whispered. "I say we shoot through the damn door."

Rex readied his gun. "I can do it, Boss."

Andrew held up his finger and motioned for them to be quiet. "Are you opening up or are we going to do this the hard way?"

"I..I'll op...open," the man stuttered, his voice shaking.

Just as the lock clicked open, Andrew exploded through the door, gripping the man around his throat and pushing him backwards against the wall. Rex, Lisben and Monahan rushed inside and spread out. Andrew dragged the man to the right, through another doorway and handcuffed him to an examination table.

"Please, pl...ease don't sh...shoot me," the man begged. "I didn't do anything. I sw...swear. I didn't touch her."

Andrew gritted his teeth and placed the barrel of his .45 against the man's forehead. "You didn't touch who?" He seethed.

"Ms. Mar...Mara...Maratinzano," he stuttered.

"Where is she?" Andrew hollered. The man's entire body trembled beneath the barrel of Andrew's .45. Andrew cocked the gun and pressed it firmly against his temple. "I'm going to ask you one more time." Andrew drew in a deep breath and spoke slowly. "Where is she?"

A puddle of urine formed between the man's shoes. "She's...she's in a drawer...drawer 58."

Andrew hollered to Rex. "Look in drawer 58." Then he turned back to the trembling man before him. "You better hope she's alive."

"She...she...is...she...is alive," he uttered. "I...I... gave her oxygen."

"We got her!" Rex yelled and Andrew left the man and rushed into the other room. Angel was lying on her back, zipped into a black body bag. A tube ran from her nose to a small oxygen tank that was next to her left thigh. Her skin was ice cold. Rex lifted her out of the drawer and Andrew maneuvered the body bag from around her. Rex gently placed her and the oxygen tank onto a gurney while Andrew checked for a pulse.

"She's alive," he sighed. "Keep the oxygen on her and stay with her," he instructed Rex. "I've got an idea."

"Uh-oh," Lisben chided. "Why do I get the feeling that your idea is going to force me into early retirement?"

"Probably because you know me so well," Andrew chided and then turned to Monahan. "You help Rex. Lisben, you're with me."

"That's what I was afraid of," Lisben muttered under his breath.

Lisben followed Andrew back to the examination room, where the man stood cuffed to the table. His eyes were widened and his lips quivered.

"Golly, Moses, Venturini," Lisben gasped, "you made him wet himself?" He looked at the man and shook his head. "That's humiliating."

"Maybe I should put him out of his misery?" Andrew sneered, raising the .45 and aiming it at him. It was good cop, bad cop and Andrew and Lisben played it well.

Lisben held up his hand, motioning Andrew to lower his weapon. "Now, just a minute, there. I think this kid will cooperate." He stepped closer to the man. "You'll cooperate, won't you?"

He nodded his head spastically up and down. "Y...y...yes, sir."

"Okay, son," Lisben said, "let's start with a basic question." Lisben slid a round stool on wheels over toward the man and sat down. "What's your name?"

"Ia...Ian, sir," he stuttered. "Ian Flanko."

"How long have you worked in the morgue, Ian Flanko?" Lisben asked.

"Almost a year, sir."

"Get to the point," Andrew barked at Lisben. "We don't have all day."

Lisben raised his eyebrows and adjusted his weight on the stool. "My friend here is a little hot-headed. He's not the most patient person so I'm gonna let him ask you some questions."

"Don't let him shoot me!" Ian blurted.

"How did Ms. Maratinzano end up in the morgue?" Andrew asked.

"I brought her down to give her a list of all of the names of the people brought in from the pub," Ian said.

"Who told you to do that?" Lisben asked.

"No...no one," Ian answered. "She stopped me at the elevator upstairs and wa...wanted to see who was on the gurney and then sh...she asked me for a list."

"You were pushing a gurney with a dead guy and she asked to look at the body?" Andrew squinted. He could hardly accept the fact that Angel would have asked to see a dead man.

"Ye...yes. He was a DOA from the pub," Ian answered.

Andrew neared Ian and cocked his gun. "There were no DOA's from the pub," he seethed. "And why didn't you print the list from the nurse's station upstairs?" Andrew barked.

"Be...because I'm not authorized to use those computers."

"So, you brought her down here and then what happened?" Lisben interrupted.

"We walked in here and a guy shoved a gun in my face. Then the dead guy from the gurney jumped up with a gun."

"The DOA came to life and had a gun?" Andrew scoffed. "This is ridiculous. I'm just going to kill him."

"N...no! I swear it's true," Ian begged.

"Let's at least let him finish his story," Lisben said. "Continue, Ian."

"Th...they said that some...someone was trying to kill her because she's a mafia boss. I knew right away that there was only one woman boss so it had to be Ms. Maratinzano. They paid me five hundred bucks to hide her in one of the drawers." Lisben shot Andrew a skeptical glance. "It's true," Ian said. "I sw…swear it's the truth."

"Would you be able to ID these men?" Andrew asked.

Ian shrugged. "Yeah. The dead guy's name is Manucci. The other guy was tall, had dark hair and a scar on his left hand."

"Where's the money?" Lisben asked.

"In my ri…right pocket."

Lisben stood up, stuck his hand in Ian's right pocket and pulled out five, one hundred-dollar bills. He tossed them to Andrew.

"Hey, that's mine!" Ian objected.

"Listen, sunshine, you're not in a position to be making demands," Lisben sneered.

"Why did you give her oxygen?" Andrew asked, studying Ian intently.

"Because they se…sedated her and sedatives slow the metabolism. I…I was worried that the sedative, coupled with long term refrigeration could kill her."

"Why would you care if they killed her?" Lisben said.

"They said if she died, I died."

"What did they use to sedate her?" Andrew asked.

"I don't know. They grabbed us the se…second we walked in."

"Did they say they were coming back to get her?" Lisben asked.

"Not exactly, but I as…assumed they were because they told me to lock the door and not let anyone in." Fear had driven all color from Ian's face and he was visibly shaking.

Andrew and Lisben exchanged glances and then Andrew motioned with his head for Lisben to join him in the other room.

"Sit tight, sunshine," Lisben said to Ian as he followed Andrew out.

They entered the room with the refrigeration units, where Angel was lying on the gurney, covered with a blanket. "Her skin is starting to warm up," Rex announced.

"What do you think?" Lisben asked Andrew. "You think he's telling the truth?"

Andrew exhaled and gnawed on his bottom lip. "Something doesn't add up." He rubbed his hand through his hair and then down around his chin. "If these men didn't tell Ian to bring Angel to the morgue, then what were they doing down here in the first place?"

"That crossed my mind too," Lisben muttered. "Doesn't add up."

Andrew took out his cell phone to dial Sal and realized there was no reception. "Damn," he blurted. "I wanted to see if Sal could pull surveillance feed from the hospital security cameras and see if we could get a visual of these men." He put his phone back into his pocket. "I'll have to wait until we're upstairs."

"Andrew, come look at this!" Monahan yelled excitedly from the far back corner of the room.

Andrew instructed Rex to stay with Angel and he and Lisben rushed to find Monahan. There were three long rows of refrigeration units with cooling drawers. Monahan was in the last row, standing over an open drawer. "He ain't dead," Monahan said and pointed at the body in the unzipped black bag.

Andrew looked down and gasped. "That's Chase!"

"You know him?" Monahan said with surprise.

"How do you know he's not dead?" Lisben grimaced.

"I used this stethoscope. I found it hanging in the examine room when we first came in."

"And you just started opening drawers and checking for heartbeats?" Lisben narrowed his brows. "There's something wrong with you." He looked at Andrew. "Who does that? There's something wrong with him."

Andrew found himself momentarily speechless. It did seem to be a randomly odd action. Nonetheless, Monahan had found Chase, so Andrew felt equally as grateful for the action as he was curious.

"Well, being as how Ms. Maratinzano was in a cooling drawer, I thought maybe others might be too. It reminded me of when I was kid and read this book called, 'Hidden Bodies.' In the book the bad guys buried people alive in body bags and cooling drawers. They'd stick them in there alive but by the time they were found by hospital personnel, they'd be dead," Monahan explained. "I don't know why I started opening drawers. I guess I just remembered the book and got curious."

Lisben shook his head. "You're sick," he said to Monahan and then glared at Andrew. "I'm telling you he's crazy and you can't fix crazy."

They lifted Chase's body bag out of the drawer and laid him on the floor. If his skin had been reddened from the CoBroGas, it wasn't evident because of the blue-ish tint it had from the cold. "We need to check all of the drawers," Andrew blurted.

"What!" Lisben exclaimed. "I'm not pulling out bodies and checking for heartbeats."

"Then go stay with Angel and send Rex in here to help us," Andrew retorted.

Lisben walked away mumbling under his breath.

Thirty minutes later, Rex, Andrew and Monahan had checked every drawer and had retrieved the Snake, Big Mike, Chase and Sophia and had all of them laying in a row with their body bags unzipped. They also found the two Venturini men, each with a bullet through his head. They didn't find his father, Tony's father, Salvatore or Olga and the pit in Andrew's stomach grew deeper and more sour.

"What do you want to do now, Boss?" Rex asked him.

Andrew tried to separate his concern for his father and think logically. "I want to get them out of here as quickly and quietly as possible." Andrew thought for a moment. "Rex, I want you to get in touch with Giovanni's men at the Towers. Explain the situation and let them know we're bringing Angel, Sophia, Chase, Big Mike and the Snake in. I want one room designated as a medical unit, so they're going to have to move beds in there." Andrew turned to Monahan. "I need ambulances to transport these people."

"Well, all right then," Monahan said and smacked his hands together. "I can do that."

"I'm going to go upstairs and make some calls. You two keep this place locked down until I get back." Andrew started toward the entrance when the whirring sound of a silencer made him draw his .45 and flank against the side of the coolers. He motioned for Rex and Monahan to flank left and right and check the rest of the morgue while he made his way to the entrance. Scanning the area, Andrew saw Angel, still unconscious on the gurney. He passed her and headed toward the examination room, where he found Ian, still handcuffed to the table, but slumped over in a pool of blood. He had taken a bullet through his neck.

Lisben was nowhere to be found.

CHAPTER 7

It took several hours, but Andrew finally managed to get Sophia, Chase, Big Mike, the Snake and Angel moved to the Towers, where a special medical unit was set up in the secret meeting room. The large wooden conference tables were moved to the far side of the room by the windows and five beds placed along the wall, to the immediate left of the entrance. Monahan remained at the hospital with the task of locating Lisben and keeping tabs on the Mayor.

Andrew had instructed Rex to locate Dr. Harold Rainer and bring him to the Towers, by force if necessary. Dr. Rainer was familiar with the Towers, as he was the one Angel had brought in to keep Giovanni sedated after Olga had Tasered him. Dr. Rainer arrived dis-shelved and in his pajamas.

"Dr. Rainer, so nice of you to come," Andrew said and extended his right hand.

"It's the middle of the night and I've been thrown in a trunk and had my life threatened!" Dr. Rainer's eyes flashed anger from beneath his black rimmed glasses. "Your men wouldn't even allow me the decency of getting dressed!"

"We'll get you any clothing and supplies you need," Andrew assured him. "All you have to worry about is taking care of these people."

Dr. Rainer's eyes darted around the room and landed on the beds to his left. "The pub victims?" He gasped and took a step back. "We don't know the nature of the gas they've ingested. We should be in hazmat suits. You might have contaminated all of us!" His dark, beady eyes danced wildly with fear.

Andrew held his palm up to indicate Dr. Rainer should be quiet. "You'll be well compensated." He nodded his head at Rex, who opened a small case filled with hundred-dollar bills. "You get them well and the money is yours."

"Money doesn't much matter to a dead man," Dr. Rainer mumbled and then licked his lips and adjusted his glasses with a sigh. "I'm going to need supplies..." he began and Andrew cut him off.

"Rex will see to it that you have whatever you need. Do we have a deal, Doctor?" Andrew extended his right hand a second time and this time Dr. Rainer begrudgingly shook it.

Andrew explained what they knew of the CoBroGas and that they had found Sophia, the Snake, Big Mike and Chase inside the morgue. "They were all in body bags and temperature-controlled drawers," he said. He also told him that Angel had not been exposed to the CoBroGas, but was sedated with an unknown agent and locked in a cooling drawer. Dr. Rainer grimaced at the details.

While Dr. Rainer examined Angel and her family, Andrew called Sal and asked him to pull up video surveillance from the hospital. Then he went outside to the elevator and spoke with one of Giovanni's men, named Alberto Basilio. He was tall, dark and muscular with spikey hair that stood straight up. He instructed Alberto to work with Rex and assemble a team of trusted men.

"What are our orders?" Rex asked.

"We need to get our people out of that hospital. They're sitting ducks in there," Andrew answered. "And we're going to need someone to assist Dr. Rainer." His plan was to move everyone to the Towers, but Andrew knew that Dr. Rainer could not handle that many patients alone.

"Like a nurse or something?" Alberto asked.

"A nurse would be perfect," Andrew nodded. "Yes, get me a nurse or two." Alberto and Rex started for the elevator when Andrew hollered to Rex. "Try to avoid throwing them in the trunk this time."

"Got it, boss," Rex grunted and they disappeared into the elevator.

It was 4:00am by the time the final shipment of medical supplies had been delivered and Dr. Rainer began getting answers. Chase, Sophia, the Snake and Big Mike were all getting IV fluids and receiving oxygen. Angel was getting only oxygen, but no fluids. "I believe Ms. Maratinzano has been injected with a drug called Midazolam. It's a common benzodiazepine used prior to many surgical procedures. Her vital signs are stable."

"How do you know?" Andrew asked.

"Here," Dr. Rainer pointed to the right side of Angel's neck. "There's a puncture wound here and I found Midazolam in the tissue sample I took."

"How long will she be unconscious?" Andrew questioned. "Is there anything you can use to wake her up?"

"Flumazenil is a benzodiazepine antagonist drug that is used in overdose situations or to reverse sedation, but it isn't recommended," Dr. Rainer explained.

"Why not?"

"It can trigger seizures in some patients, so as long as her vital signs are normal, I think we should let her awaken naturally."

Andrew pondered that for a moment and dragged his top teeth over his bottom lip. If tables were reversed, if he were the one sedated and there was a way to wake him up, he'd want Angel to do just that. On the other hand, he didn't want to jeopardize her health.

"We'll come back to her. Were the other four injected with Midazolam as well?" Andrew asked.

Dr. Rainer shook his head. "No. I'm not finding any sedatives in their systems. The fact that they remain unconscious might be a side effect of the carbon monoxide poisoning or a combination of the poisoning and the cooling." He shrugged. "It is all speculation and difficult to find concrete evidence without a full lab at my disposal."

"Is there any drug that can wake them up?" Andrew asked.

Dr. Rainer shook his head. "Not any I would feel ethically responsible using."

"How long do you think they'll remain unconscious?"

"I don't know." Dr. Rainer removed his glasses and rubbed his eyes before settling the glasses back onto his nose. "If we were only dealing with carbon monoxide gas, we could administer oxygen and it would take four to six hours for the body to expel the gas through the lungs." He shrugged. "Like I said before, I don't know what we're dealing with. This CoBroGas is a different beast and we're just going to have to watch closely, learn as we go, and hope for no long-term neurological problems."

Andrew walked in front of the beds. Angel's was closest to the door, then Sophia, then Chase, Big Mike and the Snake. He studied each one. The blue tint of their skin was gone and they now appeared normal. Sophia had dried blood in the corners of her mouth, as did the Snake, but other than that, they looked like they were peacefully sleeping. Stopping in front of Angel's bed, Andrew exhaled. "Give her the drug to wake her up," he said.

"But, I don't know her medical history and it could trigger sei..."

"Give her the drug!" Andrew ordered, his eyes piercing through Dr. Rainer. Andrew cleared his throat and lowered his voice. "Please."

CHAPTER 8

After about twenty minutes, Dr. Rainer administered the drug and Angel felt groggy but otherwise okay. After all, it was almost five o'clock in the morning, so she had every right to be tired. Andrew filled her in on what had transpired in the morgue and Angel felt grateful for having been sedated. She knew that if someone would have placed her in a body bag and cooling drawer while she was awake, she would have freaked out. Angel moved to sit on the edge of Sophia's bed. She tenderly stroked her mother's hand, willing her to wake up, but Sophia didn't stir.

Dr. Rainer was busy working in the temporary lab which they had set up in the far left corner of the room. He was engrossed in analyzing blood samples which he had taken from each of them, when Rex and Alberto returned with young, blonde, blue-eyed, Nurse Emily in tow.

"She was just getting off the night shift," Rex said. "We met her in the parking lot."

"Good to see you again," Andrew greeted her and Angel noted how Emily's eyes widened almost as if she were surprised to see him. She was wearing a pair of blue scrubs and clutched a clump of computer papers in one hand and her purse in the other.

"They didn't throw you in the trunk, did they?" Dr. Rainer piped in with a bit of sarcasm.

"No," she said in a faint, small voice.

"We asked her nicely if she would be willing to join us," Rex said.

77

"At gun point," Alberto confessed. "We asked her at gun point."

Angel dropped her head and sighed. Poor Emily. She probably had the life scared out of her. Angel slid from Sophia's bed and outstretched her hand toward Emily. "You're in no danger," she said. Emily reached to shake Angel's hand, dropping the papers she had been holding. Andrew immediately squatted down to retrieve them. "I apologize that my men felt the need to coerce you at gun point. They obviously lack some social graces." Angel shot Rex and Alberto a disapproving glare.

"You said bring a nurse, we brought a nurse," Alberto shrugged.

Scanning the papers, he handed them back to Emily. "I'm sure you have questions," he said, motioning her toward the laboratory table where Dr. Rainer was working. "Dr. Rainer will fill you in."

Andrew turned and made a beeline toward Rex and Alberto. "Did she have those papers with her when you picked her up?"

"Nah," Alberto sarcastically chided. "After flashing my piece, I sent her back inside to print out some recipes for me." Alberto visibly cowered beneath Andrew's glare. It was obvious that his sarcasm was unappreciated. "Sorry," he stammered. "It was a joke."

"She had the papers when we grabbed her," Rex interjected.

"You mean when you nicely asked her to join you," Andrew corrected.

"Right, boss, that's what I meant," Rex said.

Andrew shook his head and Angel could see his exasperation.

At that moment, Chase began to stir and opened his eyes. Angel rushed to him, as did Dr. Rainer, Emily and Andrew. Before Chase could speak, Dr. Rainer began examining him, shining a light in his pupils, checking his throat and ears, feeling around his neck, listening to his heartbeat and lungs and checking reflexes.

"Crazy ass thing, man," Chase uttered in a dry, raspy voice. "But my chest feels like I smoked a whole bunch of weed and my mouth is like sandpaper."

"Cottonmouth is a symptom of the gas," Dr. Rainer responded.

"Can I have a drink?" Chase asked and Angel motioned for Alberto to get him a glass of water.

"Do you know your name?" Andrew asked and Chase narrowed his brows.

"Have you been smoking some crazy-ass grass?" Chase joked and Angel smiled. It was nice to hear his wit again.

"What is your name?" Andrew repeated.

"Ch-a-se," he said slowly and then looked at Dr. Rainer and pointed toward Andrew. "I think you're examining the wrong dude, doc."

Angel shook her head and sighed. It would take a while to fill him in on everything that had happened; but now that he had awakened, she felt hopeful that the rest of them would too.

Andrew gave him a cliff-notes version of what happened at the morgue and Chase swung his legs over the side of the bed and sat up. At his request, Emily removed the IV from his arm and he stood.

"How do you feel?" Emily asked him.

"Like I've got a good-ass buzz on," Chase grinned, walking slowly toward the conference table where his computer equipment sat. He pulled out a chair and sat down, opening his laptop and sticking a pencil behind his ear. "We're gonna need surveillance feed from the hospital morgue," he said and began clicking on his keyboard.

"Sal's already on it and should be uploading it to us soon," Andrew explained.

Chase grimaced. "You're making me feel easily replaceable, man."

Angel ran her hand across the back of his shoulders. "No one could ever replace you, Chase."

He grinned gleefully at Andrew. "Did you hear that? Boss Lady says I'm crazy-ass irreplaceable." Chase bounced his knee up and down as he navigated around the computer. "I wish we had a list of patients," he mumbled to himself.

"Can't you hack into the hospital system and get one?" Angel asked.

"Yep, but it'll take time."

Despite the fact that Emily had given him a list at the hospital, Andrew walked briskly toward her. "We do have a list," he said. "Emily arrived with a current patient list, room numbers and all." Emily looked startled. "You dropped them on the floor and after I handed them back to you, you put them in your purse." Emily nodded slowly and without a word, retrieved the list from her purse and handed the papers to Andrew. "I'll need to know why you were taking this information home with you," he said.

Angel saw Emily swallow hard. Andrew was obviously onto something, something that made Emily visibly uncomfortable. Angel turned her attention back to Chase and his computer but made a mental note to question Andrew about it later.

With the list of patients in hand, Chase began to hack into the hospital security system and one-by-one, locate the rest of their people on surveillance video. Andrew had been correct in assuming that the John Does listed were their men. Giovanni was still in ICU, as were Salvatore and Olga. Angel could barely bring herself to look at them on the screen. They were all deathly pale and were connected to heart monitors, oxygen machines and IVs. Charlie Andriachini, Joseph Venturini, Chef Alortini and two of the four bodyguards who had been stationed at the doors, which separated the back room from the rest of the restaurant, were in rooms on the second floor and Tony and bartender, Johnny were in first floor rooms.

"Where are the other two bodyguards?" Angel asked.

Chase shrugged. "They're not in the hospital."

"Check the deceased records," Emily quietly interjected. "They might be in the morgue."

"That ain't possible," Rex huffed. "We checked every drawer."

"Did you check the slab room?" Dr. Rainer piped in and Angel shuddered. Just the sound of it created a visual in her mind that made her want to vomit.

"Slab room?" Angel asked.

"It's sort of like a giant cooler," Emily explained, as if this were just a normal, everyday topic of conversation. "When bodies are slated to be autopsied they're usually placed in the slab room."

"Is there a list that would tell us who's in the slab room? Andrew asked.

"No, it would just show them as deceased on the list," Emily shrugged and turned her attention back to Dr. Rainer and the lab table.

"See if there's a camera in the slab room," Andrew told Chase.

"I'm on it." Chase pulled the pencil from behind his ear and twirled it wildly between his fingers.

Big Mike stirred and Dr. Rainer made a beeline toward him, immediately checking his vitals. The Snake awakened next and finally Sophia opened her eyes and cleared her throat. Angel rushed to her side.

"Water," Sophia moaned with a dry, crackling voice. "I need water."

Alberto quickly poured a glass of water and handed it to Angel, who held it up to Sophia's lips. Her mom took a sip and moaned. She was obviously in worse condition than Chase, The Snake and Big Mike. Dr. Rainer confirmed that the effects of the CoBroGas were harder on older individuals, just as Andrew had warned. The good news was that Sophia knew her own name, her skin was fleshy and pink, but her eyes were glassy and she complained of a headache.

Chase announced that there was no surveillance camera in the slab room. "We'll have to send someone in to check it out," he said, and went back to searching the individual rooms. A picture of Johnny on the big screen grabbed everyone's attention. "This is from the surveillance camera in Johnny's room," Chase explained. "He looks way-ass worse than any of us."

Dr. Rainer adjusted his glasses and neared the screen, as if to get a closer look at Johnny's symptoms. "Where was this man in relation to you at the pub?"

"Johnny is my bartender," Angel answered. "He was in the main area of the restaurant."

"In what room was the gas released?" Dr. Rainer asked.

"We're not sure," Andrew said, and then turned to Chase. "We haven't been able to pull up the camera feed from the pub because you have it encoded."

"Ha!" Chase burst. "Old Sal couldn't crack my code?" Chase bounced up and down in his chair, clicking rapidly across his keyboard, and smiling wickedly. "Looks like I am wild-ass irreplaceable after all." A few seconds later, Johnny's face disappeared from the big screen and was replaced by a picture of the inside of the bar area at Tetterbaum's pub.

"We're looking for anything suspicious from 9:00pm on," Andrew said.

As Chase leapt from camera angle to camera angle, they all studied the faces of the pub patrons. Angel noted how everyone appeared relaxed and happy. No one looked suspicious, not even the Galante and Cullato bogata brothers about whom she had warned Johnny.

Switching to the surveillance feed in the hallway and kitchen area, Chase scanned the feed in fast motion. At 9:25pm one of the bus boys sauntered down the hall and opened the back door to the pub. He was handed a clipboard, which he signed and handed back to the gentleman standing outside.

"Who is that?" Andrew asked, pointing to the bus boy.

"His name is Ricky Dente. He's a bus boy and washes dishes," Angel answered.

"Do your bus boys always sign off on deliveries?" Andrew chided.

"No, normally Johnny signs off on everything, and usually our deliveries are during the day," she said, crossing her arms over her chest.

Chase switched the feed to show the alley outside of the back door. A white distribution van, with coke product emblems painted on it, was parked outside in close proximity to the door. "Looks like it was a soda delivery," Chase said. "Would Johnny have ordered extra tanks because of the grand re-opening?"

Angel shook her head. It was possible, but doubtful. Besides, most people who came to Tetterbaum's came for a stiff drink or a frothy beer; they rarely served non-alcoholic beverages. Ordering more soda products for the grand re-opening didn't make any sense.

"Does Johnny handle purchase orders for the bar?" Andrew asked Angel.

"Yes, but like I said, all of the deliveries are made during the day." Something didn't add up. All of a sudden Angel remembered talking to Johnny in the hospital and how he had said, "so...da." Angel thought he was thirsty but she now realized he was trying to tell her that the attack had something to do with the soda delivery. "Soda!" Angel burst aloud. "Johnny was trying to tell me that the attack had something to do with the soda." She explained what had happened when she saw him at the hospital.

"How well do you know Ricky Dente?" Andrew asked and Angel shrugged.

"Not well. His references checked out and he seemed like a good kid."

Chase chuckled. "Hiring with the heart can make for some wild-ass excitement."

Andrew scowled at Angel and she could tell what he was thinking. How many times had he told her to double-check with him before she hired anyone? How many times had he warned her against trusting people? Too many. Logically, she knew what he said made sense, but when she interviewed people she couldn't help but go by her gut instinct. How could her gut have been so wrong?

Chase maneuvered his way around the surveillance feed and isolated the face of the delivery man. "He's got beady, bad-ass eyeballs," Chase remarked, magnifying the picture. He did the same to the face of Ricky Dente. "I'm sending their mugs to Sal to see if they are linked in the FBI data system with any known groups."

They returned to the pub video surveillance feed and watched as Ricky Dente signed the clipboard, handed it to the delivery guy and then stepped out into the alley. Ricky and the other man unloaded two, aluminum soda tanks from the back of the truck and placed them on a cart. Ricky then climbed into the driver's seat of the truck and the other man wheeled the cart inside the back door of the pub, and down the hallway toward the bar. Johnny was busy mixing drinks, but obviously saw the man and motioned with his head for him to place the canisters behind the bar. The man placed each canister on the floor to the right of the bar, between the bar and the two men guarding the door to the private party room. The delivery man then walked briskly toward the front doors, turning on his heels and firing two shots, one into each canister.

"Those were the shots we heard," Andrew said to Angel and she nodded.

Chase jumped to the surveillance camera outside the front door at the same time frame. They watched as Ricky pulled the truck up to the curb and then slid out of the driver's door and disappeared across the street, leaving the door open. The delivery man rushed out of the front doors, jumped into the truck and sped away.

"Smooth," Chase uttered. "That was smooth as a well-ass oiled engine."

Andrew gnawed on his bottom lip. "I don't like it," he mumbled. "It was smooth but not cohesive." Andrew walked toward the windows and stood facing them, with his hands on his hips, peering out over the city. "They never spoke and they parted ways. Why didn't Ricky stay in the truck and ride with him?" He shook his head. "It makes me think they didn't know each other. They weren't working together on the attack but were merely assigned a task by someone else."

"Like they're just two separate bolts in a bigger engine," Big Mike interjected with a raspy voice and then took a sip of water to clear his throat. It was obvious he was still struggling to clear the gas from his vocal chords.

"A well-ass oiled engine," Chase repeated.

Angel sank into a chair next to Sophia. She couldn't escape the "what if" feeling that had she not hired Ricky, this might not have happened.

"Chase," Andrew turned and neared Chase's computer. "Get Ricky's picture and the driver's picture out to the Cobras and tell Chito and Trig we want them alive and able to talk."

"They're gonna want some hard-ass cash for it," Chase quipped.

"Tell them this is payback time. I'm calling in a favor," Angel gritted. Chito ran the Cobras, which was one of the two main street gangs in the city; of which Trig was a member. The Cobras had taken in Big Mike after his mother had been murdered; overlooking the fact that he would be the only white member of the group. Angel had encountered the Cobras and the other main street gang, the Knights, when a bounty was placed on her head by Carl Cusanelli's grandson, Salvo. Angel paid the two gangs one million dollars to help flush Salvo out, and even though the money hadn't come from her personal account, it nevertheless had been paid and she felt they owed her for her generosity. "Tell Chito and Trig if they find these men to bring them to the Towers," Angel instructed.

"They're gonna wanta know why," Chase said.

"Tell them it's damage control," Angel exhaled.

CHAPTER 9

At Dr. Rainer's request, Chase hacked into the hospital reporting system and pulled up patient information on the CoBroGas victims. Dr. Rainer spent hours studying their charts. He barely stopped to eat the breakfast burritos, donuts, coffee and orange juice Rex and Alberto had delivered for everyone.

At 8:30am Andrew left to go to his father's house in the city and meet with his brothers, leaving Rex at the Towers to assist with everything going on there. Sophia went upstairs to the Penthouse to lie down and Angel began contacting the other families for help. The Andriachini Underboss agreed to send two men to help in relocating Charlie and Tony Andriachini from the hospital to the Towers. Their names were Enzo and Jessie. Both men had been with the Andriachini family for many years and were well respected and trusted members. Angel would expect no less, considering they were going to be held accountable for the well-being of the Andriachini Boss. In addition, she spoke with Giovanni's life-long Compare, Carl Cusanelli, in New York and he agreed to send two of Giovanni's most trusted men.

"I will send you Gunther and Tino. They have both been with your grandfather for many years and they have my full confidence. They will be on my jet and en route as soon as we hang up. I have some things to take care of here, but will follow them shortly," Carl told her but Angel objected.

"My grandfather will feel more secure in knowing you are in New York handling matters for the family in his absence. I promise to keep you informed of his progress." She explained and Carl begrudgingly agreed.

It was a little after noon when Gunther and Tino arrived from New York and met Angel and what little manpower they had in the second-floor conference room. The room was much smaller than the secret meeting room upstairs and a rectangular, wooden table filled the center. Chase had printed out a hospital floor plan for everyone and had marked where each one of their people was located. The plan was to divide and conquer. Every man would be assigned a person to retrieve and load into the vehicles that Chito and Trig were currently working on acquiring.

Angel stood at the head of the table and around the table to her left sat Chase, The Snake, Big Mike, Alberto, Rex, Enzo, Jessie, Gunther and Tino.

"There are nine of you," she began, making deliberate eye contact with each man. "And we have more than nine people to bring home."

Enzo immediately rose to his feet. "Our Underboss wants Don Andriachini and Tony brought back to his house in the city," he blurted. Enzo was five foot, ten inches tall and built like a bull-dog, stocky and broad. He had short, light brown hair and dark brown eyes and his black t-shirt was stretched to the point of ripping around his biceps.

"Since we already have a temporary medical unit set up, we will transport everyone here first. After that, each family can decide whether they want to relocate their members." Angel spoke briskly and motioned with her hand for Enzo to take his seat. He dropped into his chair and slammed his elbows against the table.

"The Underboss ain't gonna be happy," Enzo grunted.

"Hey, how come there ain't no Venturini's here?" Jessie asked. "They should be here to carry their own Boss home."

"Yeah," Enzo agreed. "I ain't lugging no Venturini Boss."

Rex, who was seated at the end of the table, rose slowly and cleared his throat. "I'm with the Venturini family and I'd be proud to carry my Boss." He then lowered himself back into his chair.

Angel couldn't help but notice the shock on Enzo and Jessie's faces. If they were long-term Andriachini men and Rex was a long-term Venturini man, it seemed reasonable that they would, at the very least, be familiar with one another; but Enzo and Jessie's expressions spoke otherwise. It appeared as if they had never seen Rex before. *How odd.* Angel tightened her lip and glared. She could tolerate no division and no traitors among them. For all they knew, whoever tried to murder them in the pub was waiting at the hospital to try again. She needed the assurance that her team was secure and could be trusted.

"Andrew Venturini will be joining us shortly," she explained. "He will attend to his father."

"How come you and Andrew weren't hurt by the gas?" Jessie blurted.

"Yeah, that's strange ain't it?" Enzo added.

"Almost like maybe you and he were in on it," Jessie sneered and before Angel could open her mouth to retort, Big Mike leapt to his feet, drew his .45 and took aim at Jessie.

"You owe the lady an apology," Big Mike said, setting his jaw and readying his weapon.

When the Snake saw Enzo reach slowly down beneath the table, he drew his gun and took aim. "I wouldn't do that if I were you," the Snake told Enzo. "Big Mike's a good shot and I'm even better, so keep your gun in your pants and put your hands where I can see them." Enzo slowly returned both hands to the top of the table.

Chase shook his head spastically, while bouncing his knees up and down, grinning. "I wish I had a dollar for every time someone told me to keep my gun in my pants," he snorted and raised his eyebrows far up into his forehead. "You know what I'm sayin'?"

Alberto chuckled, a smile spread across Rex's face and Angel bit her lip to keep from grinning. This was so Chase. He could find a penis reference in any sentence. As tasteless as it was, it lightened the mood and Big Mike and the Snake put away their guns.

"My apologies," Jessie mumbled under his breath, his words lacking sincerity.

Just as Chase began explaining the plan again, Andrew arrived and the moment he stepped through the door, Angel could tell he had showered and changed clothes. He was wearing black jeans and a black collared shirt and smelled of musky aftershave. Despite how good he looked she could see concern and exhaustion on his face. She wanted to ask how the meeting with his brothers had gone and if there was any word on Lisben, the two things she knew weighed heavily upon him; but now wasn't the time. He pulled a chair next to Rex and sank into it.

Sliding a copy of the hospital floor plan across the table to Andrew, Chase continued outlining the whereabouts of each member in the hospital, the names of those assigned them, which exists were to be used and which vehicle would transport them.

"What about hospital equipment?" The Snake asked. "If they're hooked up to an IV, heart monitors, oxygen... do we unhook them or bring the equipment with them?"

Angel shot Chase a glance telling him to explain the plan. "The members in ICU will need to remain hooked up to everything, so plan on bringing the IV and the heart monitor with them. The oxygen isn't mobile but we will have individual tanks ready in your assigned vehicle. Once you get your person inside, open the tank and place the mask or nose tube back on them."

There was general nodding around the table which gave Angel the impression that everyone understood what they had to do. "In the top left corner of your floor plan you'll see the name of the person or persons you will be responsible for retrieving, followed by a number to the exit door and a letter which indicates the vehicle you are to use for transport," Angel explained. "Are there any questions?"

Gunther held up his hand. "I got a question," he rasped with a voice that sounded like he had been a life-long smoker. "Say our person is awake, can we put 'em in a wheelchair or carry 'em or do we gotta wheel the whole damn bed out?"

"We'll leave that to your discretion," Angel answered.

Andrew stood up and joined Angel at the end of the table. "Our biggest challenge is that we don't know who we're up against or how many are watching. We're going to need to do this quickly and quietly." He paused and looked around the table. "You guys know what I mean by quietly, right?"

"Yeah. We ain't allowed to shoot nobody," Jessie mumbled.

"What if somebody draws on us first?" Enzo added.

"You do what you have to do to get our people and yourself safely to the Towers," Andrew answered in a tone that seemed perturbed.

"What about cops?" Gunther rasped. "You want we should take 'em out so we don't have any problems?"

"No," Andrew and Angel answered in unison.

"We don't want any unnecessary killing," Angel sighed.

"The place is crawling with cops and media right now because the Mayor is there, but we anticipate his release within the next couple of hours. We'll coordinate our rescue with his release time," Chase explained. "The cops will be so wild-ass intense about making sure he's escorted safely away that they won't even notice us coming and going."

"Keep your eyes open for anything or anyone suspicious," Andrew instructed.

"More suspicious than the group around this table?" The Snake joked. "I don't think you're gonna find that anywhere."

When Chito and Trig stuck their heads inside the door, Jessie and Enzo immediately leapt to their feet and drew their weapons.

"Looks like we have some trash to take out," Jessie sneered.

"Allow me," Enzo added. "I love taking out street trash."

Trig threw his long dreadlocks over his shoulder and puffed out his muscular chest. If the tattoos down each arm weren't enough to make someone take pause, the mean snarl across Trig's face and Chito's narrowed eyes and tightened jaw should have done it. "You want to rumble, fat boy?" Chito taunted Enzo. "I'll roll you like a dough boy."

Within a matter of seconds, the room erupted and every man was on his feet with a weapon drawn. Angel put her fingers in her mouth and whistled a shrill, screeching pitch. They all stopped talking and stared at her. "Sit down!" She ordered. "Chito, Trig, please come in and find a seat."

"Wait a minute," Jessie sneered. "We ain't workin' with no street thugs."

"Whatever your relationship with the Cobras or the other families has been in the past, forget it," Angel seethed and paced around the table. "Right now, we are working as a team. Right now, we have a common goal, to get our people to safety. I don't care about your personal preferences, who you love or who you hate. We have one mission. If for any reason you feel you cannot perform the task at hand, leave now." Angel opened the conference room door and glared at the men around the table.

No one moved.

CHAPTER 10

The moment Angel entered the secret conference room with Chase and Andrew in tow, Dr. Rainer rushed toward them. "Ms. Maratinzano," he gasped. "I've got it! I've got it!" His face was flush with excitement. Before Angel could respond, he took her by the hand and pulled her toward the lab equipment located near the back of the room. Chase and Andrew followed closely behind. "When I compare the lab results of your group from the morgue with the results of those still at Northwestern, there is a vast difference in cell deterioration."

"What do you mean?" Angel asked and then realized almost immediately that that was the wrong question. Dr. Rainer went into a lengthy definition using medical terminology that went way over Angel's head. Thankfully, Chase cut him off before she had to admit her ignorance.

"Layman's terms, doc," Chase said. "Otherwise I'm gonna have to look up every crazy-ass word you just said."

Dr. Rainer took a deep breath and exhaled slowly, his exhaustion ever-apparent on his face. "I have sufficient evidence to suspect that the people who were retrieved from the morgue have suffered less cell deterioration than those not placed in the morgue."

"Why?" Angel asked. "They were all exposed to the same gas. Why would there be any difference?"

94

"The only difference I can determine was temperature," Dr. Rainer answered, pulling his glasses from his face and raising his eyebrows.

"Temperature!" Chase snapped his fingers in an a-ha fashion. "Cold slows the metabolic rate thereby slowing the negative effects of the gas on the central nervous system. That's brilliant, doc. Freaky-ass brilliant." Chase sat down at his laptop, his fingers darting wildly across the keyboard.

"How did you get so knowledgeable about the central nervous system?" Andrew asked him.

Bouncing his knees spastically up and down, he explained how he had studied nerve gases during his short career in the U.S. Military. "That crazy-ass shit stays with you, even if you don't want it to. You know what I'm saying?"

"So, are you saying that we need to put all of our people in the morgue?" Angel asked Dr. Rainer.

"Yes, or into some similar form of cooling environment, and the sooner the better."

"That means we have to re-do the rescue plan," Angel mumbled more to herself than to anyone else.

"We can have everyone grab their person as planned and wheel their wild-ass down to the morgue before taking them out to the vans," Chase interjected, but Andrew didn't like the idea.

"We're sitting ducks at the hospital. We've got to get our people out of there," Andrew clenched.

"How long do they need to be cooled?" Angel asked Dr. Rainer, who settled his glasses carefully back upon his nose and shook his head.

"There's no way for me to know. Every person is different and it may already be too late for some."

95

This wasn't what Angel wanted to hear. Andrew brushed his hand against the small of Angel's back and motioned with his head for her to follow him so they could talk privately. "Let's talk upstairs," she said and then turned her attention to Chase. "Keep an eye on our team downstairs. Nobody leaves until we have a new plan in place."

"Roger, that," Chase nodded.

Angel and Andrew stepped into the elevator and headed for the Penthouse. The doors had just closed when Andrew turned to Angel, a stern glare in his eyes. "Sweetheart, we need to get our people out of the hospital NOW."

"That could be a death sentence for some of them," Angel argued. Her greatest concern being Olga, Giovanni and Salvatore.

"And leaving them there any longer could be a death sentence for all of them."

"We have no evidence that they are in danger right now," Angel rebutted. "For all we know the people behind the CoBroGas are long gone." Andrew tilted his head and gave her a look that said, *really?* She exhaled. Even she didn't believe that argument. Chances are whoever is behind the attack is still close, watching and waiting to make his next move.

Andrew took her by the shoulders and turned her to face him. His eyes softened. "I know you're worried about your grandfathers and Olga. I'm worried about my dad, too. But, Monahan says their releasing the Mayor within the next couple of hours…"

"So?" Angel cut him off.

"So, that means the extra security and all of the heightened awareness and protection in and around the hospital will be gone, making it easier for someone to walk in and ice any one of our people," Andrew explained. "Sweetheart, we're running out of time."

Angel gnawed on her index fingernail. She wanted to do the right thing, the best thing for everyone; but that was beginning to feel impossible.

The moment the elevator doors opened, Angel froze. Something was wrong. The Penthouse door stood slightly ajar, which was strange because Sophia had always been a stickler for locking doors. One didn't spend a lifetime in the mafia and not take extra precautions. Angel and Andrew both drew their guns and cautiously approached the Penthouse.

"Why don't you stay here," he whispered, "and let me go in first." She knew what he was thinking. If something terrible had happened to her mother, he didn't want Angel seeing it.

"No," Angel shook her head. "I'm going in with you."

Andrew nudged the door further open and they both stepped quietly inside. Turning to her left and holding her 9mm steady, Angel scanned the dining room and the family room, but there was no sign of Sophia. The kitchen was clear and so was the sitting room outside of Angel's bedroom. Pushing open Angel's bedroom door, Andrew glanced inside. The room was dark and Midnight and Moe looked up from the bed, their yellow eyes glowing.

"Geese, those hell cats give me the creeps," Andrew whispered and Angel narrowed her eyes at him. They weren't hell cats, they were her furry little kids and she loved them.

After checking her bedroom and bathroom, they headed down the hallway toward Sophia and Olga's rooms. Sophia wasn't in her bedroom or bathroom. Stepping through Olga's doorway, Angel saw Andrew's face flush red. She peeked around him and there was Sophia, crouched in the corner, buck naked with Olga's Taser gripped

97

tightly in her hands. In a heap on the floor in front of her was an unconscious man whom Angel immediately recognized.

"That's Stephen Manucci!" Angel blurted and then rushed toward her mother, lifting Olga's Big Bird colored robe from the back of the bedroom door and covering Sophia.

"How do you know him?" Andrew questioned.

"He was the dead guy I saw being wheeled toward the elevator at the hospital." The memory replayed in her mind. "I came out of Tony's room and I saw the orderly wheeling this guy into the elevator. I was worried that he was one of ours so I asked to see him. The orderly lifted the sheet and read the name from the clipboard, Stephen Manucci."

Andrew bent down and checked Manucci's pulse. "How many times did you Taser him?"

Sophia didn't answer. She was visibly shaken. Her hair was wet and Angel surmised she must have been in the shower when he arrived.

"Sophia?" Andrew said. "I need to know how many times you hit him with the Taser."

Holding the robe up for her mother to slide her arms inside, Angel took the Taser from her and set it on the bed. "Four," Sophia said quietly, slipping her arms through, wrapping the robe around her and fastening the tie. "Or maybe five." She had a faraway look in her eyes. "I don't remember."

Andrew pulled Manucci's arms behind his back and cuffed them. Then he telephoned Chase and told him to meet them in the Penthouse right away. "Call down and have the Snake and Big Mike join us," he said.

"On my way," Chase said and hung up.

Moments later, the Snake and Big Mike dragged Manucci to the family room and set him in

one of the dining room chairs which they had
pulled away from the table. Sophia got dressed
and then joined them in the dining room. She told
them how she had just stepped into the shower,
when she thought she heard voices in the hallway.
Turning off the shower, she stood there listening,
but didn't hear anything else. Just to be on the
safe side, she retrieved Olga's Taser from the top
dresser drawer and set it on the bathroom counter.
She was just about to step back into the shower
when Manucci came through the bedroom door.
"Before I even thought about it, I grabbed the Taser
and zapped him," Sophia explained.

"Olga would be wild-ass proud," Chase
grinned, setting his laptop on the dining room
table, angling the camera and taking a picture of
Manucci.

"Every time he started to get up, I zapped
him again." Her eyes widened. "I didn't know
what else to do. I was afraid if I left to get help, or
even to get the phone, he would get me."

"You Maratinzano chicks got balls, man,"
Chase quipped, shaking his head and grinning ear-
to-ear. "Big 'ol crazy-ass kahunas, man."

"You said you heard voices? Plural, as in
many voices?" Andrew asked her.

Angel could tell by her expression that
Sophia was trying hard to remember exactly what
she had heard. "No, I just heard talking, but not
necessarily multiple voices."

"Like he could have been talking to himself
or on a cell phone?" Andrew questioned.

Sophia shrugged. "I suppose so."

Manucci was still unconscious and Andrew
wanted him revived immediately, so Big Mike went
downstairs to retrieve Dr. Rainer. While waiting for
them to return, Andrew checked Manucci's
pockets, pulling out a wallet, car keys and a cell
phone. He tossed the phone to Chase. "Find out

who the last call came from or who he called,"
Andrew instructed and Chase immediately started
searching for data. Opening Manucci's wallet,
Andrew pulled out a driver's license that read:
Stephen Manucci and tossed it to Chase. "Have
Sal run this through the FBI database. I want to
know every alias attached to it."

"Right on," Chase said.

Big Mike returned with Emily, who
promptly listened to Manucci's heart through her
stethoscope and checked his pulse. Tilting his
head back, she opened his mouth and pressed
down on his tongue using a long, wooden tongue
depressor. "Can someone get me a glass of water?"
Emily asked and Big Mike brought her one from
the kitchen. "His vital signs are stable, but I'd like
to pour a little water down his throat and make
sure his reflexes, like swallowing, are working
before I use smelling salts to awaken him." She
poured a little water into his throat and then
pushed his mouth closed and brought his head
forward to open the passageway. He swallowed.
"Perfect," she said, and then tore open the package
of smelling salts and waived it beneath his nose.

He took a deep breath and then began to
cough. "That should do it," Emily said, matter-of-
factly, and then handed the package of smelling
salts to Andrew. "Here, in case he passes out
again." Walking briskly toward the door, Emily
said she needed to hurry back to help Dr. Rainer
prepare for the next round of patients.

"Escort her downstairs," Angel said to Big
Mike and he and Emily left.

Andrew held the smelling salts under
Manucci's nose again and his face contorted. "I'm
awake. You can stop putting that in my face," he
growled.

"Good," Andrew remarked and dragged over
a chair from the dining room so he could sit

directly in front of him. "Let's start with your name."

"Are you a cop?" Manucci asked and Andrew reached into his pocket, pulled out his badge and held it up.

"Actually, I'm a special investigator. Is your real name Stephen Manucci?"

"You don't know what you're doing," the man shook his head. "You got no idea who you're dealing with."

"Then why don't you tell me," Andrew seethed. "Who am I dealing with?"

"I'm not your problem. You've got to let me go." The man's face started to turn a darker shade of red and he began to visibly sweat.

"Why did you break in? Who were you after?" Andrew asked and Manucci grit his teeth and shook his head. "Why were you playing dead at the hospital?"

"I'm telling you, you've got to let me go. I'm not your problem."

"Then inform me. Who is my problem?" Andrew's eyes were piercing. They never strayed from Manucci's face and read every single expression for clues. Angel found it intriguing to watch Andrew in his cop interrogation mode.

Wincing, Manucci broke into a gritty, wheezy cough. "You're all dead men; you just don't know it yet. They're here and it's clean up time."

"Who's here? Who do you work for?" Andrew demanded.

"The same guy you do," he spat.

Rolling up his sleeves and clenching his hands into fists, the Snake stepped closer. "Would you like me to incentivize him to be more forthcoming with his information?" He asked Andrew.

"Not yet," Andrew answered without taking his eyes from Manucci.

Manucci's coughing spell worsened and he sent blood sputtering down his chin and speckling his shirt. "The stars," he gasped. "The stars..."

Chase immediately leapt to his feet, "Son of a ...." He didn't finish his sentence, but pushed Manucci forward, gripped around his chest and then thrust backwards and upwards.

"What the hell are you doing?" Andrew yelled.

"The Heimlich!" Chase hollered and the Snake pushed Chase out of the way and took over. The Snake was bigger and stronger and could maneuver Manucci's body a lot easier than Chase could.

Chase was panting as he pulled out his phone and dialed Alberto, who was still in the second-floor conference room with all of the other men, awaiting instructions. "Lock down the building now," Chase ordered Alberto. "No one in or out."

"What's going on?" Angel yelled, but Chase didn't answer. He dialed Big Mike's phone just as he walked through the Penthouse door.

Whirling around to face him, Chase yelled, "Where's Emily?"

"In the secret meeting room with Dr. Rainer," Big Mike said.

Chase made a mad dash for the Penthouse door, pulling his Russian made, Pistol Makarova from the back of his waistband and hollering at Big Mike to follow him. "She poisoned him!" Chase yelled and the Snake dropped Manucci's body back into the chair.

Andrew placed his fingers on Manucci's neck, searching for a pulse. "Damnit!" He spewed.

"How did she poison him?" Angel asked. "We were all right here."

"She must have slipped him a cyanide pill when she gave him the water," the Snake answered.

"Potassium cyanide wouldn't have worked that quickly unless she cracked it open and we would have seen that," Andrew objected.

The Snake tilted Manucci's head back and pried open his jaw. In his back right molar was a tiny remnant of a brown rubbery pill casing. "She probably fastened the pill to the tongue depressor, shoved it into his mouth and crushed it against his teeth, then washed it away with the water."

"Get rid of the body," Andrew barked and rushed toward the Penthouse door. "I'm going to find Emily."

Chase and Big Mike stepped out of the elevator with their guns drawn. Rushing through the door into the secret meeting room, they saw Dr. Rainer lying face down on the floor by the lab table, with a syringe sticking out of his neck. Emily was gone.

CHAPTER 11

After Manucci's body and Dr. Rainer's body were disposed of, Angel called everyone into the secret meeting room to tell them that they were carrying out the hospital evacuation as planned except that instead of bringing members back to the Towers, they would be transporting them to the morgue.

"We'll have scrubs for everyone, so do your best to blend in," Angel said and then gave Chase a nod to take over.

"Timing will be crucial," Chase explained. "I'll hack into the system and one-by-one change each patient's status to DECEASED. You've got to wait until I've made them dead before you can move them. That way if anyone gets suspicious and looks into the system, it checks out."

"How are we gonna know when you make each of our guys dead?" Enzo asked.

"With these wild-ass babies," Chase beamed, holding up tiny ear pieces. "You'll each be able to hear me, but you won't be able to talk to me. I'll give you the green light and then you get your person down to the morgue pronto."

"Then what? Do we gotta open a drawer and stick 'em in?" Jessie contorted his face as if he were disgusted by the idea.

"Like you ain't never stuffed a body in tight spaces," Enzo taunted.

"This is different. This body is alive," Jessie rebutted. "And how do we know which drawers are being used already?"

"We're not going to use the drawers," Angel answered. "We'll put everyone in the slab room." Just the sound of it made her shudder.

"We'll have oxygen for each patient, so your part of the plan stays the same, except instead of wheeling them outside and into a van, you take them downstairs and into the slab room; and then you hook them back up to the oxygen," Andrew interjected.

"What if someone tries to stop us?" Gunther asked.

"Yeah, do we ice 'em?" Jessie added.

"Be discreet," Andrew answered.

"Use force only as a last resort," Angel added.

"You'll have two contacts in the morgue," Andrew said. "Both are my brothers; Sammy and Joe Jr. They'll make sure you're not bothered once you get our people downstairs."

Enzo held his hands, palms up. "I mean no disrespect, but ain't Sammy a no-good, skirt-chasing lush and don't Joe Jr. run drugs out of Reno?"

Andrew's jaw tightened and Angel wasn't sure what he was going to do. "My brothers may have had questionable dealings in the past, but I met with them this morning and can assure you that they are of sober mind and body and ready to help rescue our father."

"I heard Joe Jr. snorts more snow than…" Jessie began but the look on Andrew's face stopped him mid-sentence, which Angel deemed a wise choice. Andrew was already on edge and, though he was usually the calm, rational one, it wouldn't have shocked her to see him put a bullet in Jessie.

"Does everyone remember who they are assigned?" Chase asked, and there were general rumblings of confirmation. "I'll have you on surveillance and try to give you a warning if I see a dangerous situation developing." Chase's fingers danced across his keyboard. "Just for my peace of mind, let's go over the list: Gunther, you're responsible for Giovanni. No pressure," Chase joked. "Big Mike, you've got Salvatore and Tino, you've got Olga."

"You should pray she's unconscious or you might have a fight on your hands," Big Mike teased.

"Yeah, she's one feisty-ass lady," Chase added, spinning a pencil between his fingers. "Alberto, you're getting Johnny. Enzo, you've got Tony, and Jessie you're bringing Don Andriachini. Rex, you're getting Don Venturini and the Snake, you're getting Angel's two bodyguards."

"What about Andrew?" Jessie asked. "Why ain't he getting his own father?"

"Because he'll be busy keeping an eye on his brothers," Enzo mumbled under his breath and Jessie laughed.

"Because I'll be meeting with the Mayor," Andrew answered, with his jaw tightened. "As soon as the Mayor is released, his security team and all of the extra officers are going to leave, making it easier for anyone to get in and hit our families."

"So, what are you gonna do, sit and have tea with the Mayor?" Jessie snorted and Enzo laughed.

Andrew strode toward Jessie and Enzo, towering over them. "I'm going to keep the Mayor in the building long enough for you two brainless thugs to get in and get your people downstairs," he gritted.

"The fact that Andrew is a cop works in our favor," Angel interjected, trying to diffuse flared tempers. "He'll be able to create a distraction or intervene should any of you get in a tight spot with the police."

Enzo and Jessie mumbled to one another as they dressed in their scrubs, took their ear pieces and left.

"They're like two of the three stooges," Chase quipped.

"Only dumber," Big Mike interjected and they all laughed.

"Can we trust them?" Angel asked Andrew, who gave a nod.

"As much as we can trust anybody else," he uttered.

After all of the men left, Angel followed Andrew to the elevator, stepped inside and pressed the stop button immediately after the doors had closed.

"What are you doing, Sweetheart?"

"I wanted to talk to you and this is the only way to get you alone. Are you okay?" She asked.

He shook his head and exhaled. "I'm losing my touch." He ran his hand quickly through his hair and bit his bottom lip. She had never seen him so intense. "I knew Emily couldn't be trusted. She had the lists of our people and room numbers when Rex and Alberto grabbed her in the parking lot. Where was she taking that list? Who was she supposed to give it to?" He shook his head. "I knew something was wrong and I let it go."

"I did, too." Angel weaved her fingers between his. "For some reason I didn't trust her, but we can't go around suspecting everyone because ninety percent of the time we'd be wrong."

"Maybe, but Dr. Rainer would still be alive and we'd have gotten valuable information from Stephen Manucci."

Angel inched closer to him and reaching her hand up around the back of his neck, she pulled him toward her. "Kiss me," she whispered.

"Sweetheart," he sighed, and before he could say anything else she pressed her lips against his. For a moment his lips felt firm and un-engaging and then, as if a dam of emotion burst, Andrew pushed her backwards against the wall and passionately kissed her. He gripped her hair with one hand and then reached down, and pulled her pelvis firmly against his with the other. She didn't know why, but there was something about Andrew's kiss that could momentarily make the world melt away. She kept waiting for him to stop, to pull away in typical Andrew fashion and tell her why they couldn't do this here or now; but he didn't. He stopped kissing her only long enough to pull the scrubs shirt over her head. Moments later she was naked in his arms, with her legs wrapped around his waist and her back bumping gently against the elevator wall as she welcomed Andrew with every forward motion. This was more forceful passion than she had ever seen or felt from Andrew. It was unprecedented and she loved it. She didn't want it to end. When it did, she slid breathlessly from the wall, wanting to linger in his arms, but knowing they both had a job to do.

"Did that jog your memory?" He teased, a sparkle gleaming in his eyes.

"Oh, I don't remember it being like that," Angel said, while sliding on the scrubs pants and shirt. "I don't think it was ever quite like that."

He pulled her toward him and she looked up at his flushed cheeks and tussled hair. "There's more where that came from."

A warm sensation traveled up the back of her neck and she smiled. *I hope so!*

CHAPTER 12

After everyone left, Angel ran upstairs and changed into a pair of blue jeans, a black cashmere sweater and black boots. It felt good to get out of those scrubs. She wanted to shower but didn't think she'd have enough time since the men were already en route to the hospital. She peeked in on Sophia, who was sleeping peacefully and then returned to the secret meeting room.

Pacing in front of the big screen, she felt suddenly helpless and wished she had gone on the rescue mission with everyone else. She had wanted to be there in case Giovanni or Salvatore or Olga awakened, to explain what was happening; but Andrew thought her presence there would be an unnecessary risk. Big Mike and the Snake agreed and so she stayed at the Towers to give periodic updates to the Andriachini and Venturini families.

Chase sat at the conference table, a pencil stuck behind his ear, bouncing his knees spastically and clicking away at his laptop. Three computers were set on the table and he monitored each one, plus the big screen. He looked like a jittery cat watching several mouse holes at once. Everyone else, except for Sophia and the two guards stationed at the Towers' front door were gone.

"Here it is!" Chase exclaimed and Angel looked up at the big screen, where Chase was playing a surveillance video feed taken from the garage level cameras of the Towers. "There," he blurted. "She took the elevator to the garage."

The video showed Emily exiting the elevator and walking briskly across the underground garage, up the ramp and out.

"You've got to have an access code to go straight to that level from here," Angel said and Chase shrugged.

"Well, then she knew the code." Chase's fingers danced across the keys. "I can pull up the elevator camera and see if she actually punched in a code or if maybe we have a system glitch and she got lucky and didn't need ..."

"No!" Angel blurted so loudly that Chase looked up from his computer with an expression of genuine surprise. She hadn't realized that there were cameras inside the elevator, and the thought of Chase seeing what had just happened with Andrew was more humiliation than she could bear.

"You don't want me to check the elevator camera?" Chase puzzled.

"No," she said and cleared her throat. "It's not necessary. I think our time is better spent trying to figure out where Emily went after she left the building." Angel was a terrible liar and she knew it. Her hands shook and she got flustered whenever she tried to tell even the tiniest fib. She could feel Chase's analyzing eyes pierce through her and then her worst nightmare came true, his eyes lit up and a grin spread across his face, from ear-to-ear.

"Right on, Boss lady." He smiled. "I guess Emily wasn't the one who got lucky in the elevator." He teased. "Boss lady's been taking a wild-ass ride in the el-e-va-tor." His over-enunciation and sing-song, teasing tone was about to make Angel come unglued.

"You're not funny," she snapped.

"Boss lady's been getting' busy in the el-e-va-tor," he chanted.

"Knock it off!" Angel spat.

"You know what they say. If the elevator's a rockin' don't come a knockin'," Chase chuckled and Angel drew her 9mm from the back of her jeans and pointed it at him.

"Are you done?" She glared.

Chase held up his hands in surrender position and wiped the smirk from his face. "Okay, come on now, I'm just teasing. Put the gun down." Angel exhaled and slid the gun back into her waistband. "Seriously, though... exactly what time was it?"

"Chase!" Angel hollered.

"Okay, okay, Boss Lady, I'm just having a little fun. I mean evidentially not as much crazy-ass fun as you've been having..." Angel narrowed her eyes and reached for her gun. "I'm done," he said and redirected his attention to his laptop.

Angel turned back around and faced the big screen. She could feel her cheeks burning. *This is so embarrassing!*

"You know," Chase spoke hesitantly, "if you'd let me know next time I could pipe in a little mood music."

Angel bit her lip and didn't turn around. "I will shoot you," she said, and Chase shut up.

Moments later, they watched on the big screen as Enzo and Jessie walked through the Northwestern Emergency entrance and the rescue plan commenced. Chase put on his headset and spoke into the microphone. "Tony and Don Andriachini are deceased." Even though she knew it was part of the plan and Chase's way of letting Enzo and Jessie know they could proceed, it still made her stomach twist into a grimacing knot. Just the thought of Tony being dead was unbearable.

Next to enter was Gunther, Tino and Big Mike. They were all headed to ICU and would undoubtedly meet with the biggest challenge. Only family members were allowed in the ICU and only with proper identification and during pre-determined visiting hours. Angel was worried that the ICU staff would know that they weren't really hospital personnel and trouble would ensue. She chewed on her index fingernail, listening to the sound of Chase's fingertips traipsing across the keys, and waiting.

"Giovanni is deceased. Salvatore is deceased," Chase spoke into the microphone. "Olga is..." he paused.

Angel whirled around to face him. "Olga is what?"

His face grew somber and suddenly ashen. "Deceased," he said quietly.

Angel rushed toward the computer screen. "What do you mean?" Her heart was thumping wildly and her eyes darted across the laptops. Chase pointed to the screen and Angel read: "Jane Doe. ICU. Deceased." She suddenly felt as if she could hardly breathe. "We don't know if that's our Jane Doe. We don't know if that's Olga."

Chase sat up straighter and spoke into the microphone. "Gunther, Big Mike, proceed. Tino, assist them and ask for clarification at the desk. Tell them you were told to remove a Jane Doe but weren't given a room number."

Angel looked at Chase. "Are you certain Olga was in ICU?"

He nodded. "As of an hour ago, she was the only Jane Doe in ICU."

Angel pulled her cell from her jean pocket and dialed Andrew, but her call went to voicemail. She paced in front of the big screen, watching and listening as Chase coordinated the entrances of the rest of the team. "Did you want to get the Chef's out?" Chase asked. "I just realized we didn't assign anyone to them."

"No." She didn't mean for it to sound cold-hearted, but she wasn't worried about anyone coming back to murder her Chefs.

"Weird-ass thing is," Chase said without looking up from his keyboard, "I show Chef Alortini in a room on the second floor, but Chef Conaletti isn't in the hospital."

"He has to be," Angel said. "Everyone from the pub was taken to Northwestern." She leaned over Chase's shoulder and stared at the listing of names on the screen. "Maybe he had no identification on him. Could he be labeled a John Doe?"

"It's possible..." Chase's voice faded with skepticism. "No. I've got three John Doe's on the second floor. Those are our bodyguards that the Snake is retrieving and Charlie Andriachini that Jessie is moving." He scrolled down the list. "I've got a John Doe on the first floor. That's Tony. Everyone else has a name."

"Is there a list of people in the morgue?"

Chase maneuvered through hospital files. "Bingo! Here it is." Angel leaned in closer and scanned the list. "Wait a tick," Chase uttered. "Something isn't right."

"What?"

He fed the morgue list to the adjacent laptop and pulled up the current hospitalized list onto his main laptop so they could easily compare the two. "See how the current list says there is a Jane Doe in ICU that is deceased?" Angel nodded. "There is no Jane Doe registered in the morgue." Chase went on to explain how the system was designed to work. If a patient dies they are marked deceased in the main computer and then transferred to the morgue. They are then registered in the morgue database upon arrival. "It ensures that no bodies get lost," he quipped and Angel grimaced. "Family members tend to get their panties in a wad when their loved ones are misplaced." His fingers flew across the keys.

"So as we mark our people deceased and move them to the slab room, are they being logged into the morgue database as well?" Angel pondered.

"Yep. Joe Jr. is entering their information as they arrive downstairs. That way, we know they're safely there and anyone else who hacks into the system will think they're really dead." Chase raised his eyebrows. "That way if a contract is out on anybody, the hitter will think his work has already been done for him."

"Brilliant," Angel uttered and Chase beamed. This sort of stuff was his element and it was obvious that he felt right at home.

"Look here," Chase said, pointing at the morgue list. "Tony and the Andriachini Boss have been checked into the morgue."

"You're saying that Olga was marked deceased but was never taken to the morgue?" An alarm began to sound in her head.

"That's what it looks like," Chase answered. "Though, we could always be dealing with a system glitch or human error... there could be lots of factors."

Angel pulled out her 9mm, checked the clip and shoved it back into her jeans. "Give me one of those ear pieces," she ordered.

"Whoa, whoa, Boss Lady, where are you going?" Chase's eyes widened.

"To find my aunt. Now, give me an ear piece, please." She held out her hand and Chase dropped the device into her palm.

"I want to go on record as saying this is a bad idea, a very bad idea," Chase grumbled, following her to the elevator.

"Noted." The elevator door opened and Angel stepped inside. "Have Trig come to the

Towers and be ready if we need the chopper." She pushed the button for the garage level. "Oh, and tell Andrew to text me when he's done talking to the Mayor."

"What are you gonna do if you can't find her?" Chase called out as the door was closing.

"That's not an option."

CHAPTER 13

While she drove to the Towers, Angel replayed everything in her mind. Her bus boy, Ricky Dente, had obviously been working with the man who delivered and administered the CoBroGas, the man presumably contracted with the hit. But who had sent him and who was the target? It could have been any one of them. What really plagued her was the fact that so many key mafia players being at the pub last night was not common knowledge. Only Chef Alortini and Conaletti knew. Even Ricky and Johnny had not seen the private party invitation list. Not even wait staff was allowed in the room. When her family arrived, they were escorted from their vehicles directly into the back room through the alley door, which had no surveillance cameras. Thus, there was no way anyone could have hacked into the city-run surveillance and seen who had come to the pub. Was there a traitor in her family?

Another bothersome thought was the notion that Nurse Emily was a pre-determined part of it, as if they knew that the CoBroGas wouldn't kill anyone right away and that everyone would end up in the same hospital wing. Was it Emily's job to compile a list of patients and their room numbers so that a contracted hitter would know exactly where to go to make his mark? Why else would she have had a printed list with her when Rex and Alberto picked her up this morning?

Why would Stephen Manucci have pretended to be dead? Was that his only means of getting into the morgue, and if so, why would he have wanted to be in the morgue? Why did he instruct Ian Flanko to put her in a body bag and cooling drawer?   Why would he instruct Ian to keep her alive and let no one else inside the morgue? And why would he show up later at the Penthouse? Was he working with Emily or against her? Was he a contracted killer come to hit his mark? Was the CoBroGas used to flush out the mark? Was the mark someone usually so obscure and protected that it became necessary to gas an entire restaurant to get to him or her? And what happened to Chef Conaletti? Was he somehow involved? Angel shook her head. There were too many unanswered questions and unfortunately anyone who could fill in the blanks was either dead or suddenly missing. Of one thing she was certain, Andrew was right, they were sitting ducks in the hospital.

CHAPTER 14

Monahan met Andrew just outside of the elevator on the fourth floor of Northwestern Memorial hospital. "What took you so long?" He chided. "They're getting ready to release him right now."

"Can you get me in to talk with him?" Andrew asked, as he flashed his badge at the security guards and walked briskly down the hallway toward room 486.

Two armed guards stood on either side of the Mayor's door. "The guy on the right is my buddy. He thinks the Mayor will see you, since you've been assigned specifically to his case." Monahan gave Andrew a wink.

"I've been assigned to his case?" Andrew raised an eyebrow and shot Monahan a sideways glance. Andrew knew he hadn't been assigned to anything. In fact, he still hadn't met with the Captain to explain why he had called the police to the scene of the crime at Tetterbaum's and then wasn't there when they arrived; not to mention the fact that he was the one who gunned down two of the three men in the cellar and watched a mob Boss shoot the other man and the Mayor. Hopefully, that sordid detail would never surface. "Why'd you tell them I was assigned specifically to this case?"

"Because they weren't going to let you in unless they thought you were sent by Captain Senalli himself," Monahan explained. "So I sort of made them believe that you were."

"Nice touch," Andrew said and Monahan beamed. "Does the Captain know this?"

"Nah, I thought we'd cross that ugly bridge later," Monahan replied.

"E' bello vedere ancora una volta, amico," Monahan's friend said, extending his hand to Monahan.

"È stato troppo a lungo," Monahan replied as they shook hands.

Andrew found himself both amazed and intrigued by the fact that Monahan spoke fluent Italian. After a brief introduction to the hallway security detail, Andrew and Monahan were told to wait outside.

"I would have never guessed you spoke Italian," Andrew commented.

"Yeah, most people are freaked out by it. They don't expect a big, Irish oaf to be fluent in other languages," he quipped, and Andrew got the feeling that Monahan had overheard Lisben calling him an "oaf" and was tired of being stereotyped.

"Lisben doesn't mean anything with the 'oaf' comments. That's just his way." Andrew defended. "He's a grouch but a good hearted one." Monahan nodded but said nothing. "So, where'd you learn Italian?"

"My mom died birthing me and my dad was never in the picture so I was eventually adopted by an Italian couple in the city. Puccio's their name but they let me keep my mom's maiden name of Monahan. They said I looked a lot more like a Monahan than a Puccio." He smiled fondly. "My dad never did learn English so I had to learn Italian just to be able to talk to him."

"Was your dad from Italy?" Andrew asked.

"Sicily originally, but he came to the States for a new life and new opportunities." Monahan leaned in closer to Andrew. "The mob made things rough over there," he whispered. "My dad used to say, 'Destra e sinistra sarà fatto a te.'"

"Do right and right will be done to you," Andrew translated aloud.

Monahan nodded. "Not exactly mob philosophy, though."

Andrew was escorted into Mayor Tompkins room where two more security guards stood. The Mayor was a large man, standing an even six foot with a round middle. He wore a dark gray, pent-striped suit, black wing-tipped shoes and a silver tie, which complimented the silver streaks in his dark, short hair. He had a square-tipped nose, thin upper lip and dark eyes. Despite his landslide victory in the last election, the Mayor's support had dwindled and it was no secret that he needed nothing short of a miracle to be re-elected.

"Detective Venturini I presume," the Mayor bellowed and outstretched his right hand. "I've checked your record. Outstanding service and one of Chicago's finer, finest."

"Thank you," Andrew said.

"I hear you've been assigned to my case, so let me tell you everything I know." The Mayor motioned for Andrew to sit in the chair by the window as he leaned against the side of his bed, crossing his left foot over his right and folding his arms over his chest. "I received an anonymous letter telling me to come to a meeting at the address where I was shot. Upon arriving, I was gunned down in the alley." He unfolded his arms and raised his palms into the air, as if to motion that his statement was complete. "That's all I know."

"Mr. Mayor, why didn't your security detail accompany you into the alley?" Andrew asked, and the Mayor appeared visibly uncomfortable with the question. He shuffled his feet and pressed his lips together.

"I asked them not to come," he reluctantly answered.

"Why?" Andrew scooted to the edge of his seat. "You obviously felt that there was a possibility of danger because you wore a bullet proof vest, so why not take your security team with you?"

The Mayor moved toward the door and asked his security guards to wait outside; then he closed the door and turned to face Andrew, taking a deep breath and exhaling slowly.

"I had an indiscretion prior to the time that I took office. As indiscretions go, it was short-lived and I broke it off when I was elected. My wife doesn't know and I'd very much like to keep it that way." He slowly paced the length of the room with his hands clutched behind his back.

"The anonymous letter you received was from this woman?" Andrew posed.

"Yes. She demanded that I see her and threatened to go to the media with evidence of our affair if I didn't show up." He dropped his head. "Surely you can understand why I had to go alone. What choice did I have? She could destroy my marriage and my career."

"Or take your life," Andrew interjected.

The Mayor let out a lengthy sigh. "I didn't see that coming. I never thought she was capable of killing me."

"I'm going to need that letter," Andrew told him.

"I destroyed it...burned it. I couldn't risk it being found."

Andrew paused momentarily and studied the Mayor's face. "Tell me, was it this woman that shot you or someone else?" Andrew probed.

"I didn't see the shooter," he answered briskly. "I simply opened the door and that was all I remember."

"Do you think it could have been her?"

"I don't know who else it could have been." A smirk tempted the corners of his mouth. "As they say, hell hath no fury."

Andrew studied him, trying to ascertain whether there was any truth in what he was saying or if the entire story was contrived. It was possible that some anonymous woman had lured him into the alley alone and had three men there waiting to do him in. His story wasn't out of the realm of possibility; however, something wasn't adding up for Andrew. The timing of it was off. The fact that it happened precisely at the same time as the CoBroGas attack made Andrew doubt the Mayor's innocence.

"Mr. Mayor, why do you think she asked you to meet her at this particular location?" Andrew questioned.

"I don't know," he answered flatly.

"Don't you find it strange that she would want to meet you in a dilapidated cellar? I mean, typically a scorned lover will return to a familiar location, a place where affection was shown, somewhere that prompts a positive memory…"

The Mayor cut him off. "I don't know why she chose that spot!"

"Are you aware that three men were found dead where you were supposed to meet this woman?"

"Yes, I was given that information." He pursed his lips together and bounced his head slightly up and down. "I don't know how that is relevant to me."

"Maybe it's relevant because you were really going to meet these men and not because you received a letter from a past indiscretion?" Andrew posed and could see that the Mayor was ready to come unglued.

"I don't know those men. The fact that they were shot in close proximity to my location was purely coincidental and believe me, the driving effort of my office will be to take whatever action is necessary to lower the crime rate in this city." The Mayor's hands were clenched into fists and his jawline tensed. The Chicago crime rate was the highest in the country and still rising and Andrew knew the Mayor was taking a lot of heat because of it. It was the hot media topic and obviously got Mayor Tompkins hot under the collar.

"I'm going to need to speak with this woman," Andrew said, calmly.

The Mayor's eyebrows lifted into his forehead. "That won't be necessary, Detective Venturini; I'm not pressing any charges."

"Sir, if your account is true then this woman either tried to kill you or arranged to have you killed. We call that attempted murder or conspiracy to commit murder, and it really doesn't matter whether you want to press charges or not," Andrew explained. Though he knew Angel was the one who had fired the shot, he needed to press the Mayor and see what other truths might leak out.

The Mayor's face reddened. "Perhaps you do not understand," he uttered through clenched teeth. "This matter is closed."

Andrew stood up. "I understand." He strode toward the door and then turned around. "If you have a change of heart, you know where to find me. In the meantime, I'd keep that vest handy."

"Are you threatening me?" Mayor Tompkins barked.

"No sir. I'm simply suggesting that someone tried to take you out and failed which means they'll probably try again." The Mayor's eyes widened and Andrew got the distinct feeling that that thought hadn't previously crossed his mind. Andrew took a step closer. "Statistically speaking, if someone takes the time to lure you to a remote location to kill you, and their attempt fails, there will be a second attempt."

Mayor Tompkins looked stunned. He teetered on his heels and then lowered himself onto the bed, his shoulders slumping forward.

"Is there something else you'd like to tell me?" Andrew asked.

"No," the Mayor sighed. "I find myself uncertain of where to go from here."

"I'd increase your security detail and lay low for a while. If you absolutely have to go out, wear a vest, move quickly and don't schedule any outings in advance. The harder you are to find, the harder you are to kill," Andrew explained and then inched his way back toward the door.

The Mayor exhaled a big sigh. "Perhaps I will remain here for a while longer."

"That's not a bad thought," Andrew agreed. "You're safe in here and it buys us more time to locate the shooter."

"You're probably right." Mayor Tompkins stood up and outstretched his right hand. "Thank you, Officer Venturini. You've given me some clarity." They shook hands. "In return, I will give you the name of my...indiscretion." He cleared his throat. "But I need to know it will be kept confidential."

"You have my word," Andrew said.

"Her name is Martha Craden." A sense of sadness filled his face as he spoke her name. "Please handle questioning her with the utmost discretion. I am still having difficulty believing that she could have arranged to have me murdered."

"If you don't mind me asking, how did Martha handle the news that you were ending your relationship?" Andrew asked.

"That's what doesn't make sense," the Mayor answered with genuine confusion. "We both knew our relationship wouldn't last forever." He shook his head side-to-side. "She knew if I were elected that it meant the end for us, romantically speaking." A smile curled in the corners of his lips. "She used to tease me and say she wouldn't vote for me because of that."

"How long were you together?"

The Mayor's shoulders sank lower as if regret or remorse enveloped him. "We go way back," he muttered, sinking down onto the bed. "We were in love in college, but as fate would have it, we went separate ways. We dated other people but kept in touch and then when my girlfriend at the time conceived, I married her and that was the end of my contact with Martha." Mayor Tompkins glared up at Andrew from beneath his eyebrows. "That information is confidential as well. I don't need to see the morning headline: Mayor and Wife Had Love Child." Andrew sympathetically nodded. "My wife and I wed immediately after finding out she was pregnant and when I told Martha about the engagement and the baby she said she would never forgive me."

"So, when did you reunite with Martha?" Andrew asked.

"About four years ago. I was campaigning heavily for the election and we ran into each other at a restaurant downtown. She was with her husband so we didn't banter beyond a polite hello and brief introduction. The next day she called my campaign office and we talked for over an hour." His eyes beamed. "It felt good just to hear her voice after so many years. We met for coffee later that week and every week for about a year, well, until I won the election. That was three years ago."

"And you haven't seen her in three years?" Andrew asked with a hint of skepticism.

"No." The Mayor shook his head. "Well, yes and no. We haven't been involved since I took office three years ago." He made quotation marks with his fingers around the word "involved." Exhaling as if his shoulders bore the weight of the world, Mayor Tompkins explained. "We tried to remain in contact platonically, you know, meet for coffee, talk about our spouses and kids, pretend we didn't want to grab ahold of each other and never let go; but it was too difficult for both of us. Sometimes severing ties completely is the only way to move beyond the pain of letting go. Out of sight, out of mind, but never out of heart."

"Why do you think she contacted you now?"

Mayor Tompkins shrugged. "I don't know. I heard she was widowed and I guess I thought maybe she was just lonely and needed an old friend."

This didn't make sense. If he thought he was going to meet an old friend, why would he wear a bullet proof vest? In addition, he had originally stated that the woman threatened to go to the media with their relationship if he didn't meet with her. This didn't sound like the Martha he was describing now. Was she a scorned lover or a lonely woman needing a friend? Something didn't add up, but Andrew knew it wasn't the right time to point this out. He wanted to do some investigating first and made mental note to confront the Mayor with it later.

Leaving the Mayor's room Andrew felt satisfied. If the Mayor's story about Martha was true, then he had a lead upon which to follow-up; a lead that might trace all the way back to the person who stole the CoBroGas. More importantly, by convincing the Mayor to remain in the hospital he was able to buy Angel and her team more time to get their family members to safety. The longer the Mayor stayed, the longer the extra-security and media hovered around the building, making it more difficult for a contracted killer to sneak in unnoticed and hit his mark.

Andrew left the room and hurried toward the elevator, where Monahan joined him. "We got trouble," Monahan spurted the moment they stepped into the elevator and the door closed. "The Captain is looking for you and he's not happy. He wants to know why you were talking to the Mayor and why you led the Mayor to believe he assigned you to the case." Monahan grimaced. "Sorry."

"Who told him I was talking to the Mayor?" Andrew gritted.

Monahan shrugged. "Beats me, but the only people who knew were you, me and Mayor Tompkin's security."

CHAPTER 15

By the time Angel arrived at the hospital, all of their people had been transported to the morgue, with the exception of Olga. Joe Jr. had entered everyone's names in the computer and Sammy coordinated their positioning in the slab room. This was the first time she had ever met Andrew's brothers and she instantly understood why Joseph did not want to leave the family in their hands. Joe Jr. resembled Joseph Venturini in outward appearance but when he spoke he reminded Angel of a slimy used car salesman. Sammy looked a lot like Andrew but oozed with a womanizing vibe. He made a beeline for Angel the moment she entered.

"Angel Maratinzano!" Sammy blurted, taking her hand to his lips and giving it a lingering kiss. "You are absolutely stunning; way more beautiful in person than even I imagined; and I have quite an imagination," he said with a wink. "It is an honor to meet you."

"Thank you," Angel answered quietly and withdrew her hand from his grasp. "I'd like to see everyone now."

He led her to the slab room and Angel peered inside. Tony was sitting up in a wheelchair with oxygen in his nose, as were the two bodyguards; everyone else was lying down. Angel scanned the room and let her eyes linger on Giovanni and Salvatore, willing them to fight. They were both such strong men, at least in spirit; but Angel wasn't sure how much their bodies could withstand. After saying a silent prayer for each of

128

them, she pulled herself away and went to find the rest of her team. She was going to need help locating and moving Olga.

The Snake, Big Mike, Gunther, Tino, Alberto, Enzo and Jessie were all in the examination room, waiting for Chase to give them the go ahead to load everyone into the vans.

"How long do we gotta keep 'em here?" Enzo barked the moment he saw Angel. "Our underboss ain't gonna be happy."

"Chase is reviewing Dr. Rainer's notes and will let us know," Angel explained. "For now, we sit tight and wait."

"Ms. Maratinzano," Joe Jr. said from the doorway. "May I make a suggestion? Your men in there are freezing their junk off; you know what I'm sayin'? The ones who are unconscious, well, they don't know nothin's happenin', but the ones who are awake have gotta be shriveled to the size of a..."

"I get the picture," Angel interrupted. She couldn't get over how thug-ish Joe Jr. spoke and what a contradiction it was from how educated and charming Andrew sounded. Case in point, Andrew would have never used the expression, 'freezing their junk off.' "What is the temperature in there?" Angel asked and everyone shrugged except Big Mike.

"Post-mortem temperature is anywhere from 35.6 to 39.2 degrees Fahrenheit," he said.

Angel grimaced. "What is the temperature in the refrigeration unit drawers?"

"Depends on whether they are set to be positive cooling environments or negative ones. With this many drawers, each unit could be set for something different," Big Mike explained. "Positive units will run 35.6 to 39.2 degrees Fahrenheit and slow decomposition for a couple of days. Negative units will run anywhere from 5 degrees to a -13 degrees Fahrenheit and will stop decomposition altogether, completely freezing the body."

Angel instinctively shivered. She wished she knew which was better under the circumstances, morgue drawers or the slab room. The only thing she knew was that according to Dr. Rainer's theory, cooking and oxygen would slow and even possibly reverse the negative effects of the CoBroGas. "Let's get a blanket for Tony and anyone else who is awake and explain to them why they need to stay in the cooler," Angel instructed Sammy and Joe Jr.

"Tony already threatened to kill me as soon as he gets his gun back," Sammy said. "So, I ain't taking him a blanket and telling him he's got to stay in there longer."

"Get me the blankets," Angel ordered. "I'll talk to Tony."

Sammy scurried off to find blankets while Angel pulled the Snake and Big Mike aside to give them one very specific assignment: Find Olga. They immediately left the morgue and then Angel instructed Gunther and Tino to check every cooling drawer in every refrigeration unit. Then she retrieved a picture of Olga in her cell phone camera feed and held it up. "If Giovanni's sister is already dead and in one of these drawers, I need to know now; before he awakens," she said, fighting the lump of emotion rising in her throat. They both nodded in agreement and immediately went to work opening drawers one-by-one, unzipping body bags and peering inside. According to Carl, Gunther and Tino had been with Giovanni for a long time and were two of his most trusted men. They, of all people, would know the importance of locating his sister.

When Sammy returned with the blankets, he and Angel opened the slab room door and stepped inside. It was even colder than Angel had imagined and she hurried toward Tony while Sammy covered both of the bodyguards.

"B-Ba-Babe," Tony's teeth chattered and Angel wrapped a blanket around his chest and draped another one over his head, covering his ears and dangling down around his shoulders. She massaged his muscular arms hoping to cause friction and warmth.

"How are you feeling?" She asked.

"Cold."

Angel studied his face, analyzing his skin color and the whites of his eyes. She didn't know if it was her imagination or wishful thinking, but the yellowish tone seemed to be fading. "You're looking better," she said and Tony grabbed her hips and pulled her onto his lap.

"You could warm me up, babe," he said in a tone that was raspier than normal, but otherwise typical of Tony.

"Do you know who I am this time?" She asked, hoping he could come up with the correct answer.

"Sure I do," he grinned. "Tu sei l'amore della mia vita, il mio angelo." She had no idea what he said but it melted her heart nonetheless. His eyes were beaming with affection and she suddenly felt overwhelmed with the all-too familiar confusion of a heart torn between two men. "You're the love of my life, my Angel," he translated and pulled her closer. Angel buried her face in the nape of his neck. She wanted to shriek with delight and weep at the same time. So much was going wrong and out of her control, and yet Tony's arms made her feel safe, like everything was going to be all right.

Giving the appearance of strength meant everything in the mob world so Angel fought the urge to cry. She needed to focus on the orchestration of their safe return to the Towers, after which she promised herself a hot shower and a good cry.   Planting a tiny kiss on Tony's cheek, she whispered, "I love you back."

As she slid from his lap, Tony let his eyes run the length of her body and smirked. "Even in freezing temperatures, babe, you still make me hot." Angel rolled her eyes and smiled. It was nice to see that Tony was back to his old self again.

After checking on his father, Tony asked Angel to wheel him out of the slab room and into the examination room, where he got a drink of water and began to warm up. He appeared a little woozy but otherwise fine. Angel brought him up to speed on everything that had happened, and watched the anger etch itself across his face.

"What's our next move?" He clenched.

Enzo tossed him a .45. "Our next move is to get you and Don Andriachini home safely."

"Yeah," Jessie blurted. "Otherwise things ain't lookin' so good for us, capisce?"

Tony gave Enzo and Jessie a nod, slowly rose from the wheelchair, slid the gun in the back of his pants and took Angel by the arm, leading her out of the examination room, out through the morgue doors and into the hallway.

"Ms. Maratinzano," Joe Jr. belted, "it ain't advisable for you to be standing outside the morgue. We can't protect you out there."

"I got this, Ace." Tony scowled at Joe Jr., who quickly raised his palms up as a gesture of surrender.

"Her blood's on your hands." Joe Jr. stepped away from the doors and they closed behind him.

Tony spun around to face Angel, anger flashing in his eyes. "What the hell are you doing? How the hell did you get hooked up with these thugs?" He pushed her back against the wall and leaned in closer. "Do you know that Joe Jr. is a

132

no-good drug dealer that would be dead already if he wasn't the Boss's son and Sammy can't be trusted at all? He'd sell his soul and every family member for a quick lay." He drew in a deep breath but before Angel could speak, he went off again. "And Enzo and Jessie are the lowest of the low. If my dad knew that they were responsible for his well-being, he would not be resting peacefully right now!" His voice escalated and Angel motioned for him to calm down. "Who's running this rescue operation?"

Indignation rose in her throat. "I am!" She barked.

"Oh, that's right, you and Andrew, who just happened to escape moments before the nerve gas was released." Tony shook his head and Angel couldn't believe what she was hearing.

"You think Andrew had something to do with this?" Angel gasped.

"Look at the bigger picture, babe. Andrew's like a lovesick pup around you, but he can't have you unless he can figure out a way to change the rules and the only way to do that is to get rid of the old way and pave a new one." Tony leaned in closer. "Who's next in line to be Boss of the Venturini family when Joseph dies?" Tony raised an eyebrow. "Who has FBI contacts, making it easy to learn the whereabouts of lethal nerve gas, arrange to have it stolen and brought here and then cover his tracks? You, yourself, said you thought it was strange that Andrew already knew the nurse that was brought to the Towers. Maybe that was because Rex was instructed to bring a particular nurse, a nurse working for Andrew."

Angel shook her head. This was ludicrous. Andrew would never betray her or his own family like this. He would never attempt to kill innocent people. "You're talking crazy," she said.

"Am I?" Tony sneered. "Am I, babe? Or am I making so much sense that it scares you?"

The truth was Tony's words were beginning to cause Angel to have doubts, doubts a year ago she would have dismissed as irrational; but now, in her current position as a Mafia Boss, she could not ignore. She stared at Tony, confusion sweeping over her and her mind racing to justify every move Andrew made. "He knew Nurse Emily because he saw her in the hospital earlier that evening, and even if Joseph died and Andrew quit the police force and took over the family, which he wouldn't do, he still couldn't marry me," she defended.

"He could if Giovanni and Salvatore and my father were all dead too." Tony took a piece of Angel's hair and tucked it neatly behind her ear. "Don't be naïve. It doesn't suit you anymore, babe."

"I'm not naïve!" Angel seethed. "You're being jealous and paranoid."

"C'mon Angel, you know he would kill to have you and so would I!" Tony hollered and Angel froze. She couldn't believe what he had just said.

"Don't say that," she scolded gently. "Don't ever say you would kill people just to be with me." Angel shook her head. "That's not right."

Tony dropped his head and exhaled, his expression softening. "All I want you to do is look at the facts. In an ironic coincidence Andrew and you disappear right before a deadly nerve gas is released in the pub. If the gas killed everyone as it was probably intended to do, Andrew would then have the power to re-write the rules. He could marry you, combine the Venturini and Maratinzano families and probably even become considered for the position of Capo di Tutti Capi. There would be no one to stop him."

"The Galantes and Cullatos would ...." she began but he cut her off.

"They wouldn't care. They're in disarray as it is and would love to see Giovanni, who does not trust them, gone forever." He took several steps backwards and leaned wearily against the wall. "Just think about it."

Chase's voice suddenly filled Angel's ear piece. She pushed the ear piece further into her ear and listened intently. "Angel, I've got video confirmation that Andrew and Monahan have left the Mayor's room and are on their way now. Plus, we got a big-ass problem. After he took Joseph Venturini to the morgue, Rex left the building and got into a car with a woman. I couldn't see who she was, only caught a glimpse when he opened the passenger door to confirm that the driver was female; and there were no plates on the vehicle. I think we need to assume Rex is a bad-ass traitor and move our people out sooner than later."

Angel glanced up at Tony. This conversation would have to wait. For now, she had to trust Andrew and dismiss Tony's theory as a paranoid delusion caused by the CoBroGas. What choice did she have?

The morgue doors flew open and Gunther hollered, "Ms. Maratinzano, come quickly! We've found Lucia!"

Angel's heart stalled as she knew this meant Olga was most assuredly dead. Tony gripped her hand and squeezed tightly. "I'm right here, babe," he uttered and they followed Gunther through the doors and toward the refrigeration units.

CHAPTER 16

Angel's heart began to thump wildly as she walked past the first two refrigeration units. Her knees felt as if they would buckle at any moment as they approached an open drawer on the bottom level with a black, unzipped body bag peaking over the edge. Scared to death, she gripped Tony's fingers tighter. The prospect of looking down and seeing Olga dead was more than she could bear.

"She's right here," Tino said. "Her skin's a little blue but she don't look half bad."

Angel grimaced. *What an inappropriate thing to say.* She tightened her grip on Tony's hand and drew closer to the drawer. Time slipped into slow motion. Angel tried to slow her breathing and hold back waves of nausea, as she crept closer and peered down at her aunt. Tino was right, she didn't look awful; she looked peaceful, as if she were sleeping. As Angel dropped to her knees, big, crocodile tears filled her eyes and cascaded down her cheeks. *Olga! Not you. I'm so sorry. I'm so sorry.*

"Ms. Maratinzano," Tino said and Tony shushed him.

"Show some respect," Tony muttered.

"But, Ms. Maratinzano," Tino repeated and Tony grabbed him by the scruff of his neck and slammed him backwards against the refrigeration unit.

"I said give the lady some space, Ace!" Tony gritted.

"But she's alive," Tino sputtered.

"Yeah," Gunther interjected. "She's got a pulse. She ain't dead."

Angel's eyes widened and she pressed her index and middle finger against Olga's neck. Sure enough, she could feel a tiny pulsation against her fingertips. Olga was alive! Angel's spirits were so lifted that she felt like she could fly. "Get her out of there!" She ordered and Tino and Gunther lifted the bag out of the drawer and gently laid Olga on the floor. "We need some warm blankets," Angel said and Tino stepped over Olga as he hurried to find them.

"How long do you think she's been in there?" Gunther asked.

There was no way of knowing. Hopefully, it had been long enough to stop the effects of the CoBroGas, but thankfully, it had not been long enough to kill her.

Angel jumped as Chase's voice suddenly filled her ear piece again. "Smile for the camera," he said and she instinctively looked around to see if she could locate the surveillance camera he was using. "Bend over again, Boss lady, that's a sweet-ass view," he teased and she whirled around, looking up at the ceiling. "Almost as good as the elevator porn I watched a few minutes ago."

Her face instantly flushed a bright red and Tony grabbed her. "Babe, Are you okay?" He placed his palms on her cheeks and gazed into her eyes. "You look all red and sweaty. You're not going to pass out, are you?"

"Awwwkkkkwwward," Chase sang into her ear piece.

"I'm fine," Angel sighed, pushing Tony's hands away. "I'm listening to Chase," she explained, pointing to her ear piece. Being able to hear Chase and not being able to respond was maddening. Narrowing her eyes, she ran them the length of the ceiling. *You just wait!*

"Damn, Boss Lady, if looks could kill," Chase grunted. "Seriously, though, I see you've found Olga and judging by your expression, she's alive. Give me two thumbs up if this is correct." Angel held both thumbs in the air. "Right on!" Chase cheered. "She's one tough-ass, old lady. It'll take more than a little gas to knock her crazy-ass lights out." Angel smiled. She couldn't argue with that.

"I'm notifying Big Mike and the Snake to stop their search now and return to the morgue," Chase told her and Angel gave a nod. "According to Dr. Rainer's notes, you should be able to start moving people within the next fifteen minutes, keeping oxygen on those that are still unconscious."

Angel gave another nod.

Olga was covered with blankets and moved into the slab room with the others, while the two bodyguards from the pub came out and joined the men in the examination room. Their voices were raspy, but their skin looked normal and the whites of their eyes were white again. They assured Angel that they were able to help transport the others back to the Towers.

"If you're feeling up to it, I'd like you two to head to the Towers now and secure that location. No one, except us, comes into the building," she explained and the two body guards left immediately, taking one of the unmarked vans Chito and Trig had waiting directly outside of the morgue exit.

Angel watched as they climbed into the van and then closed the steel doors, ensuring she heard the lock click. Just as she turned, an enormous explosion rattled the steel doors, causing every muscle in her body to tense.

"What the hell was that?" Tony rushed toward her. "Are you okay, babe?"

"It sounded like it was right outside," Angel uttered and reached toward the doors. The moment her fingers gripped the door handle, Chase screamed into her ear piece. "Don't open it!" Angel released the handle and stepped back. "Don't open the door," Chase repeated quickly. She could hear his fingers racing across his computer keyboard. "The explosion was our van."

"Our van exploded," she relayed to Tony, who clenched his fist and spewed obscenities.

Angel stood momentarily frozen, staring at the steel doors. She couldn't believe what had just happened. She didn't even know the names of the two men she unknowingly sent to their death. Did they have family? Wives? Children? Surely someone would be waiting for them to come home and their worst fears would manifest with a visit from the police telling them that their loved one was never coming back. She remembered that day all too well. It was the day she learned that her father was never coming back. To this day she could close her eyes and envision the officer standing on their front porch. She was too little to remember what was said, but she would never forget the tears in her mother's eyes or the expression on her face. Empathetic remorse tugged at Angel's heart and she vowed in the quiet of her mind to find their families and offer some form of restitution. Pushing sorrow aside, she swallowed hard and drank in a deep breath. There was a frightening truth she and the others had to face. Any one of them could have gotten in that van. Any one of them could have died in that moment. Fear threatened to immobilize her, as this definitely confirmed her worst suspicion. Someone was indeed watching and waiting for the next opportunity to kill them; but she knew better than to let fear win. Angel forced back the emotion, her lips tightening as bolts of hot anger shot up the back of her spine. Retrieving her 9mm from her waistband, she turned to see that her team had assembled behind her, each with his weapon drawn. They were obviously feeling the same way. This was war and they were determined to win. Sammy and Alberto stood in front of the slab room entrance, guarding the door. Enzo and Jessie stood in front of the morgue doors, guarding the entrance. Gunther and Tino were positioned as back-up should anyone get passed Enzo and Jessie. Joe Jr. was at the desk by the doors, staring at the computer.

"We're set up here. If anyone tries to come in, they won't get very far," Tony said, approaching her.

Angel looked around at the faces of the men before her. They were a motley crew indeed, but each one was armed and willing to die to save his Boss. In a backhanded sort of way, there was something noble about their cause; they were like knights ready to ride into battle.

"Ms. Maratinzano," Joe Jr. hollered. "Somebody wants to talk to you."

Confused, Angel approached Joe Jr. and looked down at the computer. It was Chase's face. "I Skyped you," he said.

"So, you can hear me now?" Angel asked.

"Yep," Chase nodded. "We don't have a lot of time. There are two black SUV's, unmarked, no plates, waiting outside the morgue exit doors. These are not our vehicles. Exiting those doors would be walking into a deadly-ass ambush." Chase fidgeted in his chair.

"Then how do you propose we get out of here, Ace?" Tony blurted.

"Why can't we take out the men in the SUV's?" Enzo posed.

"Yeah, we gotta enough manpower to take them down and then load up our people," Jessie agreed.

"Tell Tweedle-Dee and Tweedle-Dum to shut their traps and listen," Chase barked. "Even if you could take out the guys in the SUV's and load our people up, who's to say our vans outside aren't crazy-ass rigged to blow like the last one?"

That was a good point. "So, what's your plan?" Angel asked.

"We've got Andrew, Monahan, the Snake and Big Mike upstairs. I've told them to hold their positions until they hear from me. I say we use them to help clear a path to the rooftop helipad and chopper our people home."

"We've got six unconscious older people down here," Tony said, leaning down toward the screen so Chase could see him. "Even if we can get them into a sitting position and load two in at a time, we're still talking three chopper trips back and forth."

"I know," Chase's spikey haired head shook back and forth. "It's not ideal, but it's all we got."

"I don't like it," Tony grimaced. "If these people have government issued nerve gas, don't you think they might just have a grenade launcher handy to blast our chopper right out of the sky?"

Chase stopped wiggling and stared into the screen. "Trig is a damn good pilot. I served with him, man, if anyone can do this, that wild-ass brother can." They stared at each other through the computer screen. "I know it's risky..." Chase began.

"Not for you, Ace," Tony interrupted and Angel shot him a scolding glance.

"Agreed. I've got the easy part."

"At lease you acknowledge it," Tony uttered and Angel shot him another glance, this time narrowing her brows and scowling.

141

"What, Babe? It's true." Tony shrugged.

"My job is to get you guys home the quickest, easiest way possible, and that's what I'm trying to do," Chase argued.

"All right," Angel interjected. "Send Trig and we'll start getting our people to the roof."

"Right on, Boss Lady," Chase quipped. "I'll be in touch with everyone through your ear pieces."

Tony shot Angel a disapproving glare. "We don't even know who we can trust and you're willing to wheel our people out into the open? That's my dad in there," he gritted. For the first time in a long time, Angel saw fear in Tony's eyes and she now understood why he was being so hard on Chase and edgy with her and everyone else. He was worried about his dad and Angel knew that feeling all too well.

Weaving her fingers between Tony's, she gazed up at him. "What choice do we have?" Obviously he didn't like the plan, but no one had a better one and Angel guessed that he felt as trapped as she did. Tony wasn't the type of man easily backed into a corner and Angel knew that shooting his way out was more his style than sneaking into a chopper and hoping to fly away unnoticed.

It took several moments to re-organize the men, but by the time Chase gave them the go ahead, Angel had everyone in place. Joe Jr. would bring his father, Joseph Venturini. Alberto would bring Salvatore. Gunther would bring Giovanni. Tino would bring Olga. Enzo would bring Johnny. Tony would bring his father, Charlie Andriachini. That left Jessie, Sammy and Angel to provide coverage if needed; although Angel hoped it wouldn't be necessary.

Jessie and Sammy opened the morgue double doors, checked to make sure the hallway was secure and proceeded toward the elevator. The plan was simple. Jessie would ride with each group to the top floor, where the Snake and Big Mike would be waiting to help them get to the rooftop. There was no elevator access directly to the roof, so the men would have to carry their assigned individual up a flight of stairs. Andrew and Monahan were standing by on floor one and floor two, which appeared to have the busiest flow of elevator users. Their job was to discourage the use of one particular elevator and direct traffic flow to the others.

Gunther wheeled Giovanni down the hall with Alberto and Salvatore right behind them. They were operating under Tony's theory that whoever was responsible for the attacks against them, might not notice the first chopper flight; thus, the most prominent members needed to be moved first. There was no higher standing than the Capo di Tutti Capi and Head of the Costa Nostra. Each man would then accompany his assigned individual into the chopper and be responsible for getting them safely to the Towers.

Giovanni and Salvatore were loaded and shuffled away without a problem and Angel began to breathe a little easier. *Just two more trips,* she told herself.

Next were the other bosses, Joseph Venturini and Charlie Andriachini. "Take them up to the top floor," Chase instructed, "but don't move them to the roof until you get confirmation from me that the chopper is in route."

Angel relayed Chase's message to Tony. "The Snake and Big Mike will meet you on the top floor," she said, as Tony, Jessie and Joe Jr. stepped into the elevator. "Good luck."

Tony planted his foot in front of the elevator door to keep it from closing. "Get in," he told Angel.

143

"I'm staying here to make sure everyone gets loaded. I'll come with Olga," she rebutted.

Tony instructed Jessie to hold the door open, and then he stepped out of the elevator, pulling Angel down the hallway so that they couldn't be seen or heard by those inside the elevator. "You're a Boss, Babe, and that means your butt needs to be on this chopper."

Technically, he was right. Her position was next in the line of importance, but Angel didn't see things that way. She wasn't going to leave Olga. She shook her head and Tony moved in closer, towering over her.

"If I have to, I will throw you over my shoulder and apply to your more logical side in front of Joe Jr. and Jessie," Tony whispered, and Angel knew it was not an idle threat. Tony had slung her over his shoulder and slapped her on the ass before; albeit, never in front of anyone and always playfully. She narrowed her brows, glaring up at him. Before she could argue, Tony continued, as if he had read her mind. "Being the last group up, Olga will have plenty of coverage. She and Johnny will have Enzo, Tino, Jessie and Sammy, not to mention Andrew, the Snake and Big Mike watching their back."

Angel bit her lip. Wanting to be with Olga was only part of the reason she didn't want to go, the other part was that she was afraid of being blown out of the sky; but she couldn't admit that aloud. She was a Mafia Boss. She wasn't supposed to be afraid of anything. She knew all too well that fear was a sign of weakness and in the mob world weakness was the fastest way to get killed. Tony slid his hands around her cheeks and gazed down at her. "Don't be afraid, mio amore," he said. "I'll be with you."

Every time Tony spoke Italian, even the tiniest word, Angel melted into a pool of mush. "Okay," she nodded. "Okay, I'll go."

The elevator started and Angel took a deep breath, exhaling it slowly and willing herself to calm down. Chase's voice came through her ear piece. "Giovanni and Salvatore are safe and the chopper is headed back," he said. She relayed the message to Tony and Joe Jr., neither of which had ear pieces.

Suddenly, the elevator jolted to a stop. Angel drew her gun, as did Jessie, Tony and Joe Jr. No one spoke because they were all straining to hear any hint of trouble either above or below them. The only sound Angel could hear was her heartbeat thumping so wildly that it sounded as if her heart had moved into her ears. She retrieved her cell phone from her jeans pocket and text Chase: Elevator stopped.

His voice instantly filled her ear piece, "I know. I'm working on it, Boss lady, and don't get any kinky-ass ideas this time...not that I wouldn't mind watching another wild-ass elevator ride, if you know what I'm sayin,'" he teased and Jessie snickered aloud.

Angel's eyes darted to Jessie. Had he heard what Chase just said to her? Had Chase accidentally transmitted his comment to everyone wearing an ear piece? She didn't have to wonder for long. "You got a thing for doing it in elevators, huh?" Jessie sneered and Angel felt her face burn with humiliation.

Without understanding why Jessie made this remark, Tony slammed him face first into the side of the elevator. "That's disrespectful, Ace!" He seethed. "To me and to her. Apologize!" Tony demanded.

"I'm sorry, but it wasn't me. Chase said it," Jessie squirmed beneath Tony's grip and Tony begrudgingly released him.

Turning to face Angel, Tony asked, "What's he talking about?"

It was as if all moisture left her mouth and Angel was stunned into absolute silence. "I...I don't ...know," she stuttered. "You know how Chase is, always making perverse comments..." her voice faded. She was a terrible liar and she knew that Tony saw right through her. She also knew if they lived through this day, the subject would be brought up again. That was a conversation she was already dreading.

"Give me your ear piece," Tony said to Jessie, who immediately pulled it out and dropped it into Tony's palm. Tony glared at Angel and shoved the ear piece into his ear.

"Did you do something with Chase in an elevator?" Tony's jaw tightened. Anger and jealousy oozed from his eyes.

Angel couldn't help but crack a smile while trying to stifle a laugh at the mere thought of her and Chase sharing some form of sexual relationship. "Oh my gosh, no," Angel giggled. "Chase? Really?" She shook her head at Tony. "I think you know better than that."

"Who was it?" He asked, his nostrils flaring like a bull.

Angel shook her head. This wasn't the place or the time to have this discussion. What's more, it wasn't any of his business. "No one," Angel blurted.

The elevator jostled unexpectedly and Tony put his finger to his lips, signaling everyone to be quiet. He then pointed upward, toward the panel that led to the elevator shaft. Joe Jr. and Jessie aimed their guns upward. "You want me to take 'em out through the panel?" Joe Jr. whispered.

"It's too dangerous," Tony warned. "Elevators are made of steel and if you can't penetrate it, the bullet's going to ricochet."

The elevator car jostled again. "Somebody's definitely up there and they ain't up to something good," Joe Jr. quipped.

"Yeah, what if they're putting a bomb on us or somethin'?" Jessie added. "A bomb in the elevator shaft would make us plummet like a lead balloon."

Angel thought she was going to throw up. A lump of fear lodged so tightly in her throat that she felt like she couldn't breathe. They were trapped and listening to the men discuss options and outcomes made it seem like the walls were slowly closing in around her.

"I'll climb up on the gurneys and open the panel, and then when I duck down, you guys fire and nail the bastard," Joe Jr. said.

"You better duck fast," Jessie warned. "I don't want to have to blow your head off to hit my mark."

They moved Charlie Andriachini's gurney against the far right wall and Angel stood in the corner between his feet and the elevator control panel. Joe Jr. climbed up on the edge of Joseph Venturini's gurney while Tony and Jessie stood below, taking aim. On the count of three, Joe Jr. lifted the panel and quickly ducked down. There was no one on top of the elevator, but they did hear something roll across the top and then stop.

"What was that?" Jessie blurted.

"It sounded like a steel ball. I'll check it out," Joe Jr. said and climbed up into the elevator shaft.

Moments later, a gun shot rang out, followed by an immediate explosion that rocked the elevator and sent it on a downward free fall. Joseph Venturini was thrown from his gurney and

147

wedged between the gurney and the far left wall. Charlie Andriachini's gurney smashed Angel against the control panel in the front corner as a wave of fire engulfed the top of the elevator. Jessie dropped to the floor and Tony made his way toward Angel, wedging himself between her and the gurney, and freeing her so she could hit the emergency button. Angel slammed her palm against the red button at the top of the panel and they could instantly hear the screeching sound of metal on metal as the braking clamps fought to do their job. When the elevator finally stopped, Angel was thrown backwards from the control panel, smashing her head into the back wall and landing on top of Jessie. She heard alarms sounding just before she drifted into unconsciousness.

She awakened to Chase's voice in her ear. "The hospital is being evacuated. This is perfect chaos to get our people out unseen. Hurry!" She tried to move, but darkness engulfed her again.

"Angel. Babe. Can you hear me?" Tony's voice cut through the cloud of fuzziness in her head and she pried open her eyes to see him bending over her. His nose was bleeding but other than that, he looked to be all right. "Can you stand up?" He tugged at her arms.

She felt wobbly and lightheaded but fought to scramble her way up; gripping his forearms for support.

"Chase has no visual in here, so we've got to get out. They're evacuating the hospital so now is our best opportunity to leave unseen," Tony explained and Angel could hear him but his voice sounded faint and far away; drowned out by the buzzing in her head. "Can you push Don Venturini?"

Everything felt as if it were moving in slow motion. She glanced over and saw that Andrew's dad was lying on the gurney again, surmising that

Tony must have lifted him from the floor. How long had she been unconscious? "What about Jessie?" She asked, her eyes drifting slowly downward.

Tony quickly took her chin in his hand, directing her eyes upward to meet his. "Don't look down, Babe," he said sternly. "Jessie didn't make it. He was hit by shrapnel from the bomb."

"What about everyone else?" Angel's eyes widened as concern flood her.

"We're all on our own now." Tony handed Angel her 9mm and then took Jessie's gun and laid it on top of the gurney, sliding it underneath his father's right shoulder so it couldn't be seen. Leaning down, he pulled off one of the brake handles from the gurney. "I'm going to wedge this between the elevator doors and force them open. I need you to have your gun ready the second the doors open." He licked his lips. "I don't know what might be waiting on the other side of these doors, so shoot first and ask questions later."

Angel nodded and held her gun steady.

The opened doors revealed that they had stopped between the first and second floor, which presented a challenge for wheeling the gurneys out. Near as Angel could tell, both floors were a bustle of people and no one took any notice of them.

"I see you now!" Chase's voice came booming into Angel's ear, startling her. "I'm sending your location to the Snake and Big Mike, so sit tight."

"Easy for him to say," Tony mumbled. "He's not the sitting duck in here."

Angel watched the feet of people scurrying on the second floor and the determined expressions on the faces of those on the first floor. There were a lot of policeman on the first floor and she assumed things were extra frenzied because the Mayor was still in the building. Chewing nervously on her index fingernail, she was hoping the Snake and Big Mike would get there soon, as she knew it was only a matter of time before the killer would try again. Her head was pounding and she fought the urge to close her eyes and drift back into darkness.

When Big Mike and the Snake appeared below them, Angel breathed a little easier. They were like a beacon of hope in a dark, stormy sea. A quick assessment left them no choice but to separate the Bosses from the gurneys in order to lower them out. Tony quickly lifted his father from the gurney and laid him on the floor of the elevator, next to Jessie's bloody body. He then folded the gurney's wheels and slid it through the opening and down to the Snake and Big Mike. They did the same for Joseph Venturini's gurney. They then had to lower each Boss head first because it was the only way to be sure that their heads wouldn't crash onto the floor on the way down. Tony held his father's legs, dangling his torso low enough for Big Mike to get a secure grip under his arms; making it possible for the Snake to catch his legs the moment Tony released them. Once he was repositioned on the gurney, Tony picked up Andrew's father and slid him through the opening.

"You better be thankful they're unconscious," Chase snorted into their ear pieces. "Because this is not exactly what I would call class-act handling of the merchandise. I'm not exactly feeling the respect if you know what I mean."

"You got a better idea, Ace?" Tony gritted.

"He can't hear you," Angel reminded him and Tony rolled his eyes.

All of a sudden Angel glanced upward to see a pair of men's black boots walking directly toward

150

the elevator. When the boots stopped so did
Angel's heart. She drew in a breath to say
something to Tony, but it was too late. The nose of
a .45 semi-automatic appeared in the opening and
Angel screamed, diving into Tony and forcing Don
Venturini's legs to slip from Tony's grasp. The
Venturini Boss plummeted downward onto Big
Mike.

"One shooter, male, Caucasian, on the
second floor, east wing!" Chase relayed into all of
their ear pieces. "Repeating: One shooter, male,
Caucasian, on the second floor, east wing!"

Right then, the assailant opened fire and,
without hesitation, Tony threw Angel out of the
elevator and then dove head first after her.

The Snake had broken Angel's fall and Tony
landed atop them, knocking the wind out of her.
"Holy shit!" Chase yelled in their ears. "Get up!
Get out of there! Get out of there!"

The shooter continued to fire and bullets
ricocheted off of the steel elevator, filling the first
floor with panic and drawing police attention. Big
Mike had slung Joseph Venturini on top of Charlie
Andriachini and was already half way to the
automated Emergency doors, when Tony and the
Snake swept Angel off of her feet and dashed after
him.

"Gunther is right outside in an ambulance
to your left, get in it and get the hell out of there!"
Chase hollered into their ear pieces.

Angel heard more gunfire as they left the
building and hurried into the back of the
ambulance. Big Mike slammed the doors, climbed
into the passenger seat and Gunther sped out of
the parking lot. After catching her breath, Angel
looked over at Tony, who was bent forward with his
head between his hands, obviously trying to catch
his breath as well. The Snake leaned his head
back and closed his eyes. She was certain that

they were all trying to process what had happened and to recover from the adrenaline surge that comes with a near-death experience. No one spoke. After about a minute, Angel let her eyes drift to the two Bosses, stacked like flapjacks on the gurney; Joseph Venturini atop Charlie Andriachini.

"Oh, no," she uttered, the sound catching in her throat. "No, no, no, no, no," Angel repeated, shaking her head and moving closer to the gurney. Blood filled Joseph Venturini's white tuxedo shirt where a bullet had pierced his chest.

CHAPTER 17

There was no time to get Joseph Venturini across town to another hospital. Finding supplies in the ambulance, the Snake placed compression packs on the wound, but Joseph was losing blood quickly and his pulse was weakening. "We need to get him to a doctor, now!" Angel screamed into her cell phone and listened while Chase's fingers skated wildly across his keyboard.

"I've got a place less than one minute from your present location," Chase said. "It's crazy-ass unorthodox, but there will be doctors there."

"Where?" Angel blurted.

"It's called God's Creatures and it's on Huron." Chase gave the address to Gunther through his ear piece. Gunther immediately made a sharp left turn and headed in that direction.

"That's an animal hospital," Angel said, stunned by Chase's recommendation. "I've taken my cats there."

"You've heard the expression, 'beggars can't be choosers'? Well, we're living proof," Chase rebutted. "There will be doctors there and no cops. Hopefully they can get him stabilized and as soon as Trig gets back with the chopper, I'll send him to airlift Joseph to a real hospital."

Angel hung up and looked at Tony, who was working with the Snake to lift Joseph's body and roll him onto his side. "What are you doing?" She gasped, as the ambulance swerved and Joseph's body almost fell from the gurney.

153

"I want to see if the bullet exited," Tony explained, running his fingers down Joseph's back. When he held his hand up, it was covered in blood. "That's good news, Babe," Tony said and the Snake nodded in agreement. Even though she knew it was better to have a bullet exit the body than to have it lodged inside, it still made her grimace. With Joseph Venturini covered in blood, it certainly didn't look like good news.

The ambulance squealed into the God's Creatures parking lot, Gunther spun it around and backed up to the front door. Big Mike quickly leapt out of the passenger side, raced to the back and opened the doors.

"Get my dad to the Towers and then come back for us," Tony told Gunther, who gave an acknowledging nod. This was a wise decision, as there was no reason to risk Charlie Andriachini's safety by keeping him out in public. They were in damage control mode and right now the most important thing was to do whatever necessary to protect the Bosses.

Within seconds Tony, the Snake and Big Mike lifted Joseph from the ambulance and carried him toward the clinic. Angel slid from the ambulance and raced in front of them, pulling open the clinic door and holding it while they shuffled inside. She watched through the glass door as Gunther sped from the lot.

A wide-eyed receptionist stood behind the front desk. "This is an animal hospital," she gasped.

"Not today," Tony uttered. "Get the doc."

"Sir, we don't treat people," she mumbled, her face draining of all color as her eyes ran the length of Joseph's bloody body. Tony released Joseph's leg, letting Big Mike and the Snake pick up the slack, pulled his gun from his waistband

and took aim at the young woman. "Get the doctor NOW!" He raged.

The woman was visibly shaken and Angel imagined that this was the first time she had ever had a gun in her face and probably the first time she had ever seen a shooting victim up close. The mere fact that she hadn't fainted or vomited was commendable.

"Doctor Woodard!" The woman hollered. "Doctor Woodard, come quickly!"

Tony slid his gun back into his jeans, walked over to the front door and locked it. "You're closed," he said to the woman. "Capisce?"

She nodded spastically.

When the doctor appeared, Angel remembered him as having been the one who neutered Midnight and Mo several years earlier. He was in his early fifties, had dark hair speckled with gray, a clean-shaven, tanned face and caramel colored eyes. Panic filled his face when he saw Joseph. "Gentleman, this man needs to be in a hospital," he reprimanded.

"That's where he was shot," Big Mike said.

"We're out of time and we need you to stabilize him until we can get him to a hospital," the Snake explained. "The bullet passed through and I've attempted to apply compression to the wounds but he's bleeding through."

"We've got a chopper on the way," Big Mike interjected.

"Follow me," Dr. Woodard uttered and led them through a swinging door, down a narrow hallway and into a small examination room. Angel could hear dogs barking from further down the hallway. "Lay him on the table, face up," Dr. Woodard instructed the Snake and Big Mike, and then he placed his stethoscope on Joseph's chest, just to the left of the wound. "Nancy!" He hollered and the young receptionist appeared in the doorway. "Call 9-1-1."

"No!" Tony and Angel blurted in unison, stopping Nancy in her tracks.

"9-1-1 will alert the police," Angel explained and she watched as recognition spread over Dr. Woodard's face like a shadow of fear.

"I know you," he said slowly. "You're head of the Maratinzano crime family."

"Yes," Angel said. "We don't need police intervention. All we need you to do is stabilize this man."

Dr. Woodard nodded and re-focused his attention on Joseph. "I don't have the equipment to help him," he stuttered.

"Let me help you, doc," Tony spewed, drawing his gun. "If he dies, you die." Tony aimed his gun at Dr. Woodard's head and Angel saw the doctor swallow hard.

"Nancy, I'm going to need to get an IV started right away," he uttered, while turning a knob on an oxygen tank, shoving a small green tube up Joseph's left nostril and attaching it with white tape. "We're also going to need some working room in here," he said to Angel and she motioned for Tony, the Snake and Big Mike to wait in the lobby. Over the course of the next fifteen minutes Nancy scrambled from room to room, retrieving everything Dr. Woodard requested and assisting him in trying to stabilize Joseph. Sweat droplets formed on his forehead as he worked to stop the bleeding. With his white lab coat now covered in blood, he glanced at Angel and shook his head. "I've slowed the bleeding as much as I can. The bullet missed his heart, but I think there is damage to his left lung. He needs blood and I don't have it here. You've got to get him to a hospital." There was fear in his voice and in his eyes and Angel knew his plea was as much to save his own life as it was to save Joseph's.

Angel dialed Chase.

"Trig is already on his way, and so is Andrew," Chase explained.

Andrew. Angel breathed a sigh. It was a relief to know he had made it out of the hospital alive, but he had yet to learn that his brother, Joe Jr., had been killed and his father was fighting for his life which made Angel feel very sorry for him. "Any word on the rest of our people?" Angel asked.

"We have your family. Olga is awake and Sophia is trying to calm her spunky-ass down. She insists that it was a cop who took her to the morgue."

"A cop?"

"Between you and me, I think she's got some screws lose upstairs, if you know what I mean. Maybe the effect of the gas..." Chase's voice tapered off. "Anyway, Giovanni and Salvatore are still unconscious but they're on oxygen and their vital signs are good, near as I can tell. It would help if we had a doctor here." Chase explained. "Boss Lady, you better get your wild-ass back here before Giovanni wakes up, or we're all gonna be on his hit list, and being that I'm the first guy he's gonna see when he wakes up, I'm not feeling too comfortable."

"I'll have Trig fly me home once we get Joseph to a hospital."

Chase informed her that Charlie Andriachini and Gunther had arrived safely and that Enzo, Sammy and Johnny escaped the hospital unscathed and had returned to the Towers. This was all good news and yet Angel's heart couldn't rejoice, knowing the anguish Andrew would be feeling when he learned of his family's loss.

Disconnecting the call, Angel turned to Dr. Woodard. "The chopper will be here any minute."

"Andrew's here!" The Snake hollered and Angel raced from the examination room to the front lobby just in time to see Tony unlock the glass door and let him in.

"He's in the back, Ace," Tony told Andrew and gave him a supportive pat on his shoulder.

Andrew rushed passed Angel without a word and then stopped abruptly in the examination room doorway, his eyes falling upon his father.

"What happened?" Andrew mumbled.

"He took a bullet in the elevator. We didn't know until we were in the ambulance," Angel answered but Andrew didn't acknowledge her response.

"What happened?!" Andrew repeated a little louder, this time drawing his .45 and gritting his teeth.

Angel peeked around Andrew, saw Nancy sniveling in the corner and then heard Dr. Woodard apologize. Looking at Dr. Woodard's face, she knew instantly that Joseph was gone.

"We did everything we could," Dr. Woodard muttered. "He lost too much blood." Dr. Woodard held his palms up. "There was nothing else we could do here. We treat animals. I don't have the equipment for human patients. He needed blood."

"Andrew..." Angel said softly, but he didn't acknowledge her. His eyes were aflame with a rage she had never before seen in him. He pressed his lips together and breathed heavily through his nose. "Andrew, put your gun down."

"What happened?" Andrew hollered and the sheer volume of his voice made Nancy fall to her knees on the linoleum floor and weep; her body shaking violently.

"I couldn't save him," Dr. Woodard yelled. "It isn't her fault. Let Nancy go. It's my fault."

Tears pooled in Andrew's eyes and Angel watched as he fought to maintain emotional control. His face was bright red and a vein on the right side of his neck protruded, divulging his pulsating rage. Angel slid passed Andrew and stepped in front of Dr. Woodard, blocking him from Andrew's aim. "Put your gun down," she said calmly.

At that moment, Tony strutted through the doorway. "Yeah, put your gun down, Ace. I got this one for you." Tony's gun was drawn and extended toward the doctor.

"Tony!" Angel gasped, but he ignored her.

"I told you, doc, if he dies you die," Tony spewed.

Dr. Woodard was trembling. "I'm sorry," he said. "I did everything I could. I swear I did everything I could."

Tony cocked his gun. "You give me the go, bro, and I'll get rid of this no-good piece of crap," he said to Andrew, who blinked slowly.

The whirring of the chopper overhead was heard by all and it felt for a moment as if time stood still. Angel was looking down the barrel of both Tony and Andrew's guns and it felt surreal. Her heart beat wildly, and though she knew neither of them would shoot her, she thought they might take Dr. Woodard out despite the fact that she was attempting to block their shot.

"No," Andrew finally uttered, holstering his piece. "Get Angel home."

Angel breathed a sigh of relief, thankful that Andrew's sense of logic prevailed once again. Stepping toward his father, Andrew bent over him, lifted his left hand and kissed it tenderly. He then slid a gold ring from Joseph's finger and whispered something in Italian.

Tears pooled in Angel's eyes, as she could hardly bear to see Andrew in so much pain. She reached for his hand, but he moved away from her. "These people cannot talk," he said to Tony and then stormed out of the exam room, walking toward the front door. Angel wanted to chase after him but she was afraid that the moment she stepped from the room, Tony would kill Dr. Woodard and Nancy.

"Well, Babe," Tony smirked. "We either keep 'em or kill 'em. We can't have them running to the police or selling their story to the National Inquirer. It wouldn't be respectful toward the deceased." Tony shifted his weight and held his aim steady. "What'll it be?"

Angel exhaled. She knew they couldn't risk Dr. Woodard or Nancy running to the police; and she couldn't let the press have a field day with Don Venturini dying on an examination table in a veterinary clinic. She didn't know all of the unspoken mafia rules, but she was pretty sure that that would be viewed as one of the highest forms of disrespect. Tony was right, they had to keep them or kill them. Deep despair gripped her. She knew what had to be done, even though she didn't like it. "Kill them," she whispered, turning toward the door.

"We won't talk," Dr. Woodard begged. "We won't tell anyone. I swear we'll do anything you say."

Angel turned on her heels and held up her hand, motioning Tony to pause. "Anything I say?" She stared at Dr. Woodard.

"Anything," he gasped. "Please."

"I have some people that need medical attention." Angel neared him. "I could use a doctor and a nurse for a few days." Dr. Woodard's eyes were glassed over and Nancy's shoulders shook up and down as she silently wept. "I'm not asking for charity. You'd be on my payroll, of course, and once my people are better you'd be free to go."

"Provided that you never breathe a word of this to anyone," Tony added. "If this hits the papers, I hit you. Capisce?"

"Yes," Dr. Woodard exclaimed. "Whatever you say."

Angel smiled internally. This was the first time she had ever played good cop, bad cop and got to be the bad cop. It felt simultaneously powerful and scary; nevertheless, it got her a doctor and that's what she needed. While Big Mike and the Snake loaded Nancy and Dr. Woodard into the chopper, Tony waited for Angel to pay her last respects to Joseph. "He was a good man," she whispered. "My mom is going to be devastated."

Tony draped his arm around her shoulders. "Your mom is a strong lady. She'll be okay in time."

Angel stared at Joseph's body. His black suit jacket was torn and his white shirt, which had been ripped open to give easy access to the gunshot wound, was saturated in blood. A year ago, staring at death would have sent her into the throes of nausea, but, now, death had become as much a part of life as breathing, eating and sleeping.

She leaned down and planted a tender kiss on Joseph's forehead. "May God bless your soul," she whispered, and then noticed something poking her left shoulder. Rearing back, she ran her hand over his sport coat until she found the hard object. Reaching inside his right interior pocket, Angel pulled out a small, black, velvet box. With trembling fingers, she cracked open the box and gazed at the beautiful, five carat, emerald shaped diamond ring set in a white gold band. With the sinking realization that Olga had been right about Joseph's intention to propose to her mother, emotion overtook her and Angel clutched the velvet box to her chest and wept.

CHAPTER 18

The Venturini family held a double funeral service for Joseph and his son, Joe Jr. Despite Giovanni's arduous attempts to keep her locked in the Towers, Angel attended the service, partly to support her mother and partly with the hope of seeing Andrew. He had been missing in action for the past two days and she couldn't erase the image of his anguished face from her mind. She had text him and called numerous times but he never responded. It was as if he would allow no one to walk with him through the shadows of grief and mourning.

The service was held at St. John's Cathedral on the north side and the burial took place at St. John's Cemetery, where her father was buried and her ex-lover, Grayson Galante, and probably every other mafia boss throughout Chicago's history. Charlie Andriachini attended the service, though still in a wheelchair, as did a representative for the Galante family and Carlo Cullato, Boss of the Cullato crime family. Giovanni made a brief appearance, offered words of condolences to the family and then quickly left. He believed, with the assassin still at large, that it was foolish for all of the family heads to be in the same location. Angel knew his concern was valid and agreed to make her appearance brief as well.

After the service, as everyone shuffled past the family and out of the front doors, Sophia sat staunch-like in the pew. Angel was amazed by the fact that her mother didn't cry during the service. She simply sat, stone still, staring at Joseph's casket. Angel sat next to her, wanting to say something, anything that would ease her mother's pain; but words failed her. How many loves had Sophia buried? How deep was her heartache? Angel couldn't imagine.

Olga waddled up the aisle and plunked her rounded hips into the pew next to Sophia. "We've got to skedaddle," she said. "Big Mike says we should leave right now, and he was downright bossy about it," Olga scowled. "I've got half a mind to take my Taser to him if he cops that attitude with me again. Humph!"

Sophia didn't move or in any way acknowledge what Olga had said.

"Merciful Heavens," Olga exhaled. "She's gone deaf with grief." Angel shot Olga a puzzled look. "It's a real syndrome. It's called Grief Deafness. Elsa, down at the hair salon, had a customer who had a sister who suffered a tragic loss and she went temporarily deaf from the grief." Olga widened her eyes and nodded her head slowly up and down. "It's true."

"Well, if Elsa said it, it must be true," Angel teased.

"Don't sass your old aunt, and especially not in the house of our Lord." Olga shook her finger at Angel. "You better watch yourself, missy." Olga rose from the pew, made the sign of the cross over her body and then announced that she was going to tell Big Mike and the Snake to give Sophia a few more moments.

"I'm not deaf," Sophia whispered after Olga waddled away. "And I've never heard of grief deafness."

"I know, right?" Angel answered, feeling relieved that Sophia had spoken. It was the first words she uttered since receiving the news of Joseph's death. For two days she had laid in her bedroom, weeping. Angel gave her mom's hand a tender squeeze. "I don't know what to say," she choked.

Sophia returned the squeeze. "That's because there isn't anything to say." She turned slightly and faced Angel. "Death is a part of life. We must learn to face it and then quickly move on." Sophia released Angel's hand and rose slowly, running her hands over the front of her black, straight skirt. "We should leave now before Giovanni sends in the troops to forcibly remove us."

Angel couldn't help feeling shocked by her mother's sudden lack of emotion. Was she masking her heartache or was she as inwardly strong as she outwardly appeared? Angel studied her. "Mom?" She slid out of the pew and joined Sophia in the aisle. "Are you okay?"

Sophia smiled and looped her arm in Angel's. "Joseph loved me and not even death can take that away."

CHAPTER 19

It was eleven o'clock and Angel couldn't fall asleep. She was worried about Andrew. She had only caught a glimpse of him at the funeral and by the time she left the service, he was no longer standing with the rest of his family. Sammy was there, but Andrew had disappeared again. Knowing he was in agony and being unable to help him was driving her crazy. He hadn't returned her calls nor responded to her texts and it was becoming difficult not to take his silence personally. She wanted to know what he was thinking. Was he considering quitting the force and taking over as head of the Venturini family?

Angel could hear Olga snoring from down the hall as she crept from her bedroom into the kitchen to make a cup of hot tea. With tea in hand, she moved into the living room, sat down on the couch and text Andrew again. PLEASE TALK TO ME.

Angel waited, but there was no response. After twenty minutes, compassion and sympathy dwindled. The fact that he had ignored her for two days was beginning to piss her off. After all, even in despair, one could take a moment to text back. Was he angry at her for some reason? Her expectations weren't unreasonable. She wasn't expecting him to drop everything and run to her side. She merely wanted to know that he was all right. She hadn't even been able to give him a hug since his father's and brother's deaths. Grabbing her phone, she text again: IF YOU DON'T RESPOND IMMEDIATELY, I'M COMING OVER!

Forty minutes later, Angel was behind the wheel of the Tank with the Snake in the passenger seat and Big Mike in the back. The car phone rang and then Chase's voice was heard through the Tank's speaker system. "Where is your crazy-ass headed, Boss Lady?"

"To see a friend," Angel answered curtly.

"Booty call," Chase teased. Angel grunted and disconnected the call.

The Snake shot her a sideways glance but said nothing while Big Mike failed miserably at trying to stifle a chuckle. Upon seeing Angel's scolding expression in the rearview mirror, he cleared his throat and apologized.

A second later the car phone rang again and Angel begrudgingly pushed the answer button. "I take it you're not alone, which is a good-ass thing because if you were out there alone right now, Giovanni would kill all of us; starting with me."

"I've got the Snake and Big Mike with me," Angel gritted, hoping that would be enough to curtail Chase's sexually charged jokes.

"Destination?" Chase asked and Angel could hear his fingers tapping across his keyboard.

"Andrew's house on the north side."

"His father's house?" Chase posed.

"No." Angel sighed. She knew there would be a lot of people at Joseph's house and she didn't want to just show up there, unannounced. "I want to see if he's at his own house first," she explained. "I'll let you know if I decide to go anywhere else."

"I'm tracking your wild-ass, so I'll know anyway. Giovanni's long-standing orders." Angel rolled her eyes. Would she ever have any privacy again?

Disconnecting the call, Angel saw Big Mike smirk from the rear view mirror. "It's not funny," she said to him.

"Be thankful you have a family who cares about you," Big Mike uttered, his smile fading.

He was right. As annoying as Giovanni could be, his actions were motivated by his love for her and for that, she was grateful.

Angel pulled the Tank into Andrew's driveway, killed the engine and turned in her seat to address the Snake and Big Mike. "I'd like to go in alone," she said. "That is, if he's even home."

"Negative," the Snake rebutted. "We'll check the premises, escort you inside and secure the home; then, we'll leave you two alone." She started to object, but the Snake cut her off. "We're the ones that will have to answer to your grandfather if something happens. We do this my way or we go home now."

She had only previously seen this authoritative side of the Snake once and it was just before he strapped himself to her and hurled her out of a plane 18,000 feet above an Iowa cornfield. Angel gawked at him, a smile hinting at the corners of her lips. "Whatever you say, Sean," she said, emphasizing his real name, partly in sarcasm to let him know that he was being bossy, but also to let him know that she remembered what happened in Iowa and completely trusted him.

His eyes softened at the sound of his first name, as if he, too, recalled their conversation in the cornfield. "Thank you, Angel," he said, intentionally using her first name as well.

Exiting the Tank, the Snake led Angel to Andrew's front door, while Big Mike brought up the rear. Upon seeing that the front door was slightly ajar, all three of them drew their weapons. "Ms. Maratinzano," the Snake whispered. "Return to your vehicle and lock the doors."

"Negative, Sean," Angel retorted. "I'm going in." He shot her a disapproving glare but Angel wedged her foot in the door and pushed it open.

The Snake slid through first and flanked right. Angel followed him while Big Mike entered behind her and flanked left. The family room was dark, except for a small lamp on the end table that cast a dim glow over the couch. Angel gasped when she saw a man lying face down on the sofa, with a .45 dangling from his left hand.

Big Mike closed the door and locked it. "Do you know him?" He asked Angel.

"I know of him, but we've never been formally introduced. His name's Lisben. He's Andrew's partner on the force, has been for a long time. He disappeared the other day from the morgue."

The Snake crept toward Lisben and quickly retrieved the gun from his hand. Lisben didn't move.

"Is he dead?" Angel asked.

Placing his fingers on Lisben's neck, the Snake searched for a pulse. "No. He's alive."

Big Mike strode to the left of the couch, which led into the kitchen. Flipping on a light, he chuckled. "Holy..." he stopped his sentence short. "He might not be dead, but it looks like he was trying to drink himself into oblivion."

Angel peered into the kitchen and almost couldn't believe her eyes. The table was covered in liquor bottles, most of which were empty. There were several vodka bottles, two gin bottles and two bottles of tequila; one of which was still half full. The kitchen smelled of vomit and urine and Angel guessed that Lisben had been too drunk to make it to the bathroom. Grimacing, she covered her nose with her forearm. Andrew obviously hadn't been back to his house since the CoBroGas attack. *Where has he been staying the past couple of days?* Angel wondered and then surmised that he was probably at his father's house in the city with Sammy and the rest of the family. It was probably easier to stay there while making funeral arrangements.

They searched the rest of the house, and being satisfied that it was secure, they returned to the family room to awaken Lisben, a task they quickly realized was more daunting than anticipated. When shaking, talking and getting him into a sitting position didn't do the trick, Big Mike and the Snake scooped him up by his armpits, dragged him down the hall and threw him into a cold shower. Angel waited in the family room and text Andrew again: FOUND LISBEN. CALL ME!

CHAPTER 20

She had never heard from Andrew and now her anger was beginning to morph into worry. Was he okay? Had something happened to him? It was 6:00am when Angel showered, blew her hair dry, pulled it into a low pony tail and got dressed. She slammed down a few gulps of hot coffee and took two bites of one of Olga's homemade, left over Cannoli; and then sneaked quietly from the Penthouse. She wanted to go down to the secret meeting room and check on Lisben. They had been unable to sober him up enough to acquire any useful information last night, so they opted to bring him to the Towers and let him sleep it off. The only thing Lisben had repetitively mumbled in his drunken stupor was, "you'll never believe it" and "I couldn't believe my eyes." Angel was anxious to hear what was so shocking.

"Ms. Maratinzano," Gunther said as she stepped into the hallway, dropping his head slightly in a gesture of respect.

"Gunther, did you work the night shift?" Angel was surprised to see him. She was certain that Giovanni had mentioned sending both Gunther and Tino back to New York.

"Yes, ma'am."

"Where's Alberto?" Alberto typically worked the night shift so the change seemed odd.

Gunther shrugged. "He wasn't feeling well. He left last night around midnight and Chase asked Giovanni if Tino and I could fill in his shift, so here I am." Doubt must have shown on her face because Gunther paused momentarily and then opted to explain more thoroughly. "Giovanni told us to inform you but you weren't home." Angel's stomach grew instantly hollow. Did this mean that Giovanni knew that she had left the Towers last night? Hot shivers traveled up her spine and made her face flush. Was she in trouble?

"And?" Angel bit her lip.

"And when we couldn't find you, we told Chase and he said he would make sure you were informed of the change." The elevator door opened and Gunther escorted Angel inside.

Whew! So Giovanni doesn't know I left. Angel punched in the code to the secret floor and the elevator door closed. All of a sudden, her face flushed as thoughts of Andrew flood her mind. As soon as she exited the elevator and stepped into the secret meeting room, she saw Chase grinning ear-to-ear like the Cheshire Cat from Alice in Wonderland. "Pleasant thoughts while you rode the elevator, Boss lady?" He teased.

"Don't make me shoot you first thing in the morning," she growled. "And stop calling me 'Boss Lady'!" Chase chuckled and headed back to his laptop while Angel surveyed the room.

Lisben was asleep in the first hospital bed, with his right arm handcuffed to the railing and his ankles duct taped together. "Has he said anything else?" Angel asked.

"Just that he's a dead man," Chase said.

"Why would he say that?" Angel pondered.

"Call me crazy, but it might have something to do with the fact that he got picked up by the Mob and woke up handcuffed to a bed." Chase shrugged. "That might make me think I was as good as dead." *Good point.*

Johnny was in the bed next to Lisben and Nancy was curled into a little ball in the third bed. Dr. Woodard sat in the far corner of the room, near the lab equipment that Dr. Rainer had set up. He was facing the windows, staring out at the waking city below.

"Good morning, doctor," Angel said as she approached him. "Can I get you some coffee?" He shook his head and continued to stare out of the window. Dragging a chair next to his, Angel pulled an envelope from the back of her jeans and then sat down. "I like to watch the sunrise over the city. It seems so peaceful in the morning," she said.

"That's because all of the criminals are still asleep," he seethed. "Well, not all." He shot Angel a sideways glance.

Ordinarily, Angel would have been angered by his sarcasm, but instead she felt compassion for him. After all, he had been threatened and basically forced to come to the Towers and help Johnny, Charlie Andriachini, Olga, Giovanni and Salvatore get better. He was completely out of his element, up against a neurological gas he knew nothing about and treating human beings when he was only licensed to treat animals. And to top it off, a crime family Boss had died on his table and he now feared for his life. Stress etched deep, dark gray circles beneath his eyes.

"Do you have any family?" Angel asked.

Dr. Woodard shook his head. "No."

"Does Nancy have family? Is there anyone that might be concerned that you or she has disappeared?"

"No. Her family is out of state. Why? Are you looking for collateral? Something you can hold over our heads to keep us here longer?" Dr. Woodard seethed.

Angel pursed her lips together and felt her jaw tighten with anger. "Have you been in any way mistreated, Dr. Woodard?"

"I'd call having a gun waved in my face, mistreated!"

"I apologize for that. Back at your clinic my men were only doing what they thought was necessary for the greater good," she explained. "Since you've come here, have you or Nancy been in any way mistreated?"

Dr. Woodard dropped his chin to his chest. "No."

"Has your clinic, your staff or your family been jeopardized in any way?" She asked and studied his face as he rubbed his eyes and shook his head to indicate they hadn't. "Good." Angel handed him the envelope. "Here is your money. You can choose to pay Nancy whatever amount you deem appropriate."

He took the envelope and for the first time since they were at the clinic, he looked Angel in the eyes. "You mean we're free to go? You're not going to kill us?"

Remorse tugged at Angel's heart. She hated that people thought she was a cold-hearted killer. "I was never going to kill you," she sighed.

"But at the office, you told one of your guys to kill us..." his voice cracked and he quickly cleared his throat. "And I heard some of your men talking about how the last doctor that was here is now dead."

Angel had been so wrapped up in worrying about her mother and Andrew that she had completely forgotten about what she had said while in his office. It never crossed her mind that he was feeling like a prisoner and fearing for his life. Angel leaned in closer. "Dr. Woodard, back at your clinic Tony and I were sort of playing good cop, bad cop," she tried to explain. "I needed you to agree to come here and the only way to do that was to make you think you would die otherwise."

"So, you made me an offer I couldn't refuse," he murmured.

"Yes." She hated using that cliché tactic, but it was often the only one that worked. "But I never had any intention of hurting you or Nancy." She thought she saw him exhale a sigh of relief. "Dr. Rainer, the one who was here before you and set up all of this equipment, was killed by a nurse named Emily. We're not sure why she murdered him."

Dr. Woodard looked down at the envelope. "So, you really are going to let us walk away from here, even though we could tell people what we've seen and heard?"

"Geeze, doc, it's like you're trying to convince her to ice your ass," Chase blurted, having walked up behind without either of them noticing. "If I were you, I'd take the money and run." Turning his attention to Angel, Chase said, "Boss lady, I thought you might want to know that Lisben is starting to stir and I finally made contact with Andrew."

Angel's stomach leapt upward at the mention of Andrew's name. "You did?"

"Yep. He's on his way over. I, uh, thought you might want to go meet him in the elevator." Chase grinned and sauntered away singing, "Boom-chicka-wow-wow-Chicka-wow-wow."

Angel glared at Chase and shook her head. "I swear I will shoot you." No sooner had the words left her lips than she saw Dr. Woodard's eyes widen with fear. "No, no, I was joking. It's just a joke. I'm not really going to shoot him," Angel stuttered, but the doctor remained un-amused.

By the time Andrew arrived, Lisben was sitting at the conference table next to Chase, the Snake and Big Mike. He was carefully sipping a cup of hot coffee, as his wrists were handcuffed together and his ankles were still duct taped. He looked as if he had tied one on last night, and they all knew he had. In fact, Angel thought he looked as if he had been drunk for days. His eyes were puffy and red and his shoulders slumped forward. It was an obvious struggle to even lift his head.

Tino had replaced Gunther on guard duty and Nancy and Dr. Woodard were in the far corner talking low.   When Andrew stepped through the door, Angel's heart rate increased. She watched him cross the room, hoping to make eye contact, but he never looked at her.   He appeared different somehow. His jawline looked more chiseled than normal, his eyes set a little deeper and his gaze was more intense. His stride was forceful and his presence demanded attention. It was as if any softness, tenderness or gentleness about him was gone. Angel reached for his hand but he strode quickly past her. "Andrew?" She muttered, but he ignored.

"Let's go," he said to Lisben and the Snake and Big Mike immediately stood up.

"Don't you have some questions you'd like to ask him?" Angel said to Andrew.

"Yes, I do, but they are none of your concern," he answered without turning to face her.

Angel couldn't believe the coldness with which he was treating her. What had she done to deserve this? "We would like to be a part of your interrogation," Angel spat.

"And I'd like my father and brother back, but we don't always get what we want, do we?" Andrew spun on his heels and faced Angel, glaring down at her with what could only be described as rage. His hardened demeanor literally took her breath away.

"Andrew..." Angel began but he quickly turned his back toward her.

"Lisben, we're leaving now," Andrew barked.

"You'll have to cut my legs free," Lisben muttered and then calmly picked up the cup in front of him and took a sip.

"What's your hurry, Ace?" Tony's voice came from the doorway. Walking toward the table and motioning with his head for Big Mike and the Snake to stand guard at the door, Tony made it obvious that Andrew wasn't taking Lisben anywhere.

"This is none of your business," Andrew scowled.

"Is it police business?" Tony sneered. "Oh, wait a minute, it can't be police business because you're no longer a cop, are you, Ace?" Tony got right in Andrew's face.

"Back off," Andrew gritted.

"Is that true?" Angel asked, but Andrew didn't answer her.

"What's the matter? Why don't you want us to know what Lisben has to say?" Tony paced closely around Andrew. "Are you afraid something he says might incriminate you?"

"Incriminate him?" Angel scoffed. "Incriminate him in what?"

"The murder of his father," Tony spat. "That wasn't your first plan, though, was it, Ace?" Tony circled Andrew like a shark coming in for the kill. "Oh, no, your first plan was to wipe out all of the crime families, including your own. Wipe them out so you'd be the hero on the force, the next Elliot Ness." Tony hissed and Angel couldn't believe what she was hearing. "To single-handedly clean up the city would be quite an accolade; probably enough to put you in a viable position to run for public office, like, maybe the Mayor's office."

"Omigod," Angel gasped. "Tony, knock it off."

"Can you explain it better, Babe?" Tony scoffed. "Why was the Mayor walking alone in a dark alley mere moments after almost all of the crime family heads in Chicago were suffering from a deadly nerve gas attack?"

"I don't know," Angel groaned.

"Did he pay off Andrew to arrange the attack and kill all of us? Or was Andrew planning on taking out the Mayor the whole time?" Tony backed away from Andrew and shrugged.

"Stop it!" Angel blurted. "Andrew didn't shoot the Mayor!" Angel hollered and then stopped abruptly, sensing all eyes were on her. She cleared her throat. "Someone else did."

"C'mon Babe, don't you think it's a little strange that you and he were the only two to escape the gas?" Tony's face turned bright red with anger.

"What are you implying?" Angel demanded.

"Don't you think it's odd how his guy, Rex, and your guy, Alberto, just happened to be the ones that brought in the killer nurse, and that she poisoned Stephen Manucci right in front of Andrew and he didn't even notice?" Tony scoffed. "He's a trained cop, a special investigator with years on the force, and standing inches away from Manucci. C'mon!"

"That's enough!" Angel yelled, but Tony didn't listen.

"And now ironically it's Rex and Alberto who are mysteriously missing?" Tony seethed. "Doesn't this seem a little too coincidental to anyone else?" Tony spun around to face the Snake and Big Mike, as if to ask if they suspected foul play. The Snake momentarily locked eyes with Angel and Big Mike lowered his eyes to the floor and shrugged.

"What are you saying?" Angel asked. "Are you accusing me of something?"

"Only of falling for the wrong guy, Babe." Tony's face softened as he looked at Angel and then hardened quickly when he returned his focus to Andrew. "He's been playing you from the beginning."

Angel didn't know what to think or what to say. Tony's questions were valid and she could see how some of the evidence could appear incriminating; however, she knew Andrew and she knew he didn't possess some dark, hidden, evil motive. Was Tony speaking purely out of jealousy toward Andrew or did he know something that she didn't?

"Nobody's been playing me..."

"Not even in the elevator?" Tony's eyes pierced through Angel and she shot Chase a horrified glare. Chase's eyeballs bulged and he shook his head rapidly, as if to indicate he had not shown Tony the surveillance feed from the elevator nor told him anything about it.

Though her gut told her that Tony's comment was nothing more than speculation, she was nervous and felt her mouth go instantly dry. What was she supposed to say? Tony knew her so well that if she tried to lie, he would see right through her; but she wasn't ready to publically announce her private intimacy with Andrew, especially after the cold manner in which he was now treating her. Clearing her throat, Angel looked Tony in the eyes. "We all make mistakes. The elevator was one of mine."

Tony's expression shown complete surprise and Angel wasn't sure whether he was more shocked that she admitted to something happening in the elevator or that she deemed what had happened a mistake. Lowering his gaze to the floor, Tony looked as if the wind had just been kicked out of him. Guilt swept over Angel. She looked at Andrew and saw that his shoulders suddenly appeared weighted down and his head hung downward. With one sentence she had crushed both of the men she loved.

Andrew stood motionless, his brows narrowed and his eyes transfixed, as if he were trying to define his own thoughts. He didn't respond to Tony's accusations nor did he acknowledge Angel's spiteful words. Everyone stared at him as he pulled out the chair across from Lisben and sank down into it. Licking his lips and running his fingers through his hair, Andrew took a deep breath, exhaled slowly; and then looked Lisben squarely in the face. "Tell me what happened," Andrew said.

"Is it true?" Lisben mumbled. "Did you leave the force?" Andrew didn't answer. "Are you taking over your family?" Lisben labored. "Are you gonna kill me after I talk?" Andrew stared at his friend and Angel could only imagine the mental battle that was raging in his mind. If Lisben confessed to betraying Andrew and the families in some way, it would be Andrew's duty to kill him. Remorse didn't remove guilt and the guilty had to pay. That was the unspoken mafia law. All of a sudden it dawned on Angel why Andrew didn't want to interrogate Lisben in front of anyone. If Lisben was guilty of some form of betrayal and no one else knew about it, Andrew could let him live. She suddenly understood that Andrew wasn't concerned about Lisben implicating him, he was scared to death Lisben was going to implicate himself and then he'd have no choice but to murder him. Compassion tugged at Angel's heart.

"It doesn't matter," Lisben muttered. "I'm a dead man anyway."

"Andrew," she interrupted, moving quickly toward where Lisben was seated. He looked up and met her gaze, this time with pain-filled eyes. "You're right. This interrogation doesn't involve us. You and Lisben should go." Their eyes locked momentarily in silent conversation. Unspoken words transmitted heart to heart... *"I'm sorry."*

"I understand."

"I didn't mean what I said."

180

"Wait a minute..." Tony began but Big Mike chimed in before he could finish his sentence.

"I will escort Andrew and Lisben from the building," Big Mike said, making a beeline for Lisben and cutting the tape from his ankles.

"Unbelievable!" Tony barked.

"Snake, will you and Tony escort Dr. Woodard and Nancy home?" Angel asked. "Their services are no longer needed."

"I don't work for you, Babe," Tony uttered belligerently, and no sooner had the words left his lips when Giovanni and Salvatore appeared in the doorway.

"No, but you can do that favor for me, can't you?" Giovanni uttered.

Tony whirled around to face them, immediately lowering his head in respect. "Yes."

Andrew rose and kept his eyes on Angel's. "Thank you," he mouthed silently and though tears were threatening to form in the back of her eyes, Angel forced a smile and slowly blinked an acknowledgment.

Don't make me regret it.

Salvatore asked to speak with Tony privately while Big Mike escorted Andrew and Lisben to Andrew's SUV that was parked out front and the Snake led Nancy and Dr. Woodard to the parking garage beneath the Towers into one of Giovanni's SUV's.

"You have your doubts about this Lisben character, no?" Salvatore asked.

"I have my doubts about a lot of people being allowed to walk out of here," Tony grunted.

Salvatore wrapped his arm around Tony and led him toward the elevator. "Your instincts are good. Follow Andrew and this Lisben, let them talk and as soon as they part ways, kill him."

Turning to face him and placing his hand on Tony's right shoulder, Salvatore leaned closer. "He is a loose end that must be tied up. Capisce?"

"Capisce."

CHAPTER 21

Alberto walked briskly past the first-floor motel windows until he reached the staircase that led to the second floor. Chomping wildly on a piece of gum and skipping every other step, he raced upward, turning left at the top and heading anxiously toward room number 218.

He had been with Giovanni long enough to know that suspicious activity meant you were guilty and if you were guilty, you were dead. The catch twenty-two was that if you noticed someone else behaving suspiciously and brought it to a Boss's attention, both you and the guy you ratted on usually wound up dead; guilty by association. Alberto had seen it happen more than once and he knew, in his current situation, the only way to stay alive was to bring Angel concrete evidence of his suspicions. Maybe he should have let her in on his thoughts before he sneaked from the Towers, but it was too late to think about that now. He was in too deep.

Stopping just before room 218, Alberto flanked his back against the wall and took a deep breath. He had only one shot to prove his suspicions correct. The curtains were drawn so Alberto crept quietly passed the window and to the door, taking the gum from his mouth and placing it over the peep hole. It had taken him all night to confirm the whereabouts of the person he believed to be on the other side of the door; and he couldn't mess things up by being seen now. Pulling a black ski mask from his jacket pocket, he placed it over his head, adjusted it for an unobstructed view; and then removed the keycard from his right pants pocket and his .45 from his waistband. Holding the gun steady, he slid the keycard into the scanner and pushed open the door.

"What the hell!" The man's voice rang out, while the woman screamed and pulled the bed sheet up to her chin.

"Don't move!" Alberto yelled, as the naked man reached for his gun on the night stand. "You move one muscle and you're dead." Alberto flipped on the light switch and let the door close behind him. "Get your hands in the air! Both of you!" He seethed.

"You're making a big mistake, bro. You don't wanta rob me. You have no idea who I am," the man growled.

Alberto snatched the gun from the nightstand and shoved it into his waistband; and then he took the man's wallet and shoved it into his pocket. After taking both of their cell phones, he ripped the hotel phone from the wall and smashed the receiver.

"You look like you've done this before," the man sarcastically spewed. "Like you're almost a pro."

Alberto paused for a moment, wondering if it were possible that he had been recognized, but he quickly dismissed the thought. It didn't matter. He had the evidence he needed to stay alive and that was all that mattered. As he turned toward the door, the man lunged at him and Alberto whirled around, instinctively pulling the trigger and shooting him in the upper, left thigh. The man flew backwards, gripping his leg, writhing in pain and spewing obscenities. The naked woman left the confines of the sheet and scrambled to help him.

"Call an ambulance," she begged.

"I think you can handle it. You're a nurse, right?" Alberto couldn't help but grin as his retort brought an expression of shock to her face. He closed the door behind him and was down the staircase and in his car before the door opened again. The woman rushed out wearing only a towel and yelling for help.

Alberto sped out of the motel lot, down the side street and back toward the Towers. Removing the ski mask from his face, he set it gently on the seat beside him. "Did you get all that?" He said aloud, and a few seconds later his cell phone buzzed.

"Got it loud and clear," Chase said. "Nice work, but next time could you aim the camera more on the sweet-ass, naked girl?"

"You know she's a killer."

"I'm not looking for a long-term relationship, man," Chase laughed. "Just a little T and A at the end of the day."

CHAPTER 22

Gunther and Tino escorted Alberto into the building and up to the secret meeting room, where Giovanni, Angel and Chase were waiting. As they entered, Giovanni stood and glared at Alberto, while Gunther carried the two cell phones, the wallet, two guns and the ski mask over to the table and set them down. "This is all he had on him," Gunther announced.

Tino pushed Alberto onto his knees and placed the barrel of a .45 caliber on the back of his head. "You want me to do him up right here?" Tino grunted.

"I can answer that," Chase piped in. "I wouldn't pull that trigger until you see what's on this video."

Giovanni motioned for Tino to lower his weapon and then, turning to Chase he asked, "What is this all about?"

As he spoke, Chase removed a small camera from the front of the ski mask. "This," he answered, holding up the camera. "Alberto had a suspicion that one of our guys wasn't on the up and up, so he left last night to find him and see if his suspicions were true."

"To whom are you referring?" Giovanni asked.

"I could tell you, sir, but it'd be a helluva lot more fun to show you." Chase raised his eyebrows and grinned like a kid in a candy shop.

Returning to his seat, Giovanni sighed heavily and gave Chase a nod of approval. Angel could tell what her grandfather was thinking. He

was unaccustomed to computers and spy cameras
and surveillance feeds. To Giovanni, technology
was something that slowed down conversations
and got in the way of business. Just as she was
offended by the practices of old, he was equally
puzzled by the way the world now ran. Dancing
his fingers across the keyboard Chase brought up
the video feed and directed them to the big screen,
where they all watched in amazement as Alberto
burst into the motel room, catching Rex and Emily
in bed. Chase paused the video on the part where
Emily dove forward after Rex was shot, exposing
her breasts. "This is my favorite part," he grinned.
"That's one sweet-ass frame right there."

Giovanni's face reddened slightly. "I do not
understand the relevance," he uttered.

"Alberto can answer your questions better
than I can," Chase retorted.

"Very well," Giovanni exhaled and motioned
for Tino and Gunther to bring Alberto closer. They
lifted Alberto from under his arms, carried him
toward the conference table and dropped him back
onto his knees in between Giovanni and Angel.

From his knees, Alberto explained that
when Angel sent him and Rex to get medical
supplies and to bring back a nurse, he noticed Rex
behaving oddly. "He was on his phone in the car
and gave somebody a time. I didn't think that
much of it until I later realized that the time he
gave was the exact time that we then pulled into
the hospital parking lot and Emily just happened
to be right there, as if she was waiting for us."

"I'll play the wild-ass, devil's advocate,"
Chase blurted. "I love this role." He cleared his
throat dramatically. "That could be a pure
coincidence, or some crazy-ass fate," he said to
Alberto.

"I didn't think much of it at the time, but
something else was bothering me. She didn't seem

surprised to see us when we walked up." Alberto squint his eyes, like he was retrieving the memory to create a clearer picture in his mind. "She turned and we were right there. Anybody would have been startled, but she didn't even flinch."

"Then what happened?" Angel asked.

"She touched his hand."

"What do you mean? Like she pushed his hand away?" Angel posed.

"No ma'am. She touched it like you touch somebody you're close to. She took her little finger and stroked it across the top of his hand, flirty like."

"Why did you not report this before?" Giovanni questioned.

"Because I didn't think that much of it at the time. It wasn't until later, when he left that I started to put it all together," Alberto defended.

"Maybe she's just a skanky-ass ho, who gets kidnapped a lot and likes to stroke her captor's hands," Chase blurted and Angel shot him a glance that said *gross!* "What? I told you I was going to play the devil's advocate."

"She might be, but that ain't why she was with Rex," Alberto answered and went on to explain what transpired the day Emily murdered Stephen Manucci and Dr. Rainer. "I was with Rex and all of the other guys in the second-floor conference room when Chase called and told me to lock down the building. Before I could assign positions, Rex left and took the elevator to the garage. It seemed strange to me but I dismissed it, thinking maybe someone had told him to lock down that area."

"Ironically, the garage level is where our sweet-ass Emily exited the Towers," Chase interjected.

"Her relationship with Rex would explain how she had the access code to get to the secret meeting room and down to the garage," Angel added in an a-ha tone.

"With all of these little things adding up, I started to think that maybe Rex was up to no good..." Alberto explained and Giovanni cut his sentence short.

"Why did you not bring this information to us?" He pounded his fist atop the table and watched as fear filled Alberto's face.

"I wanted to bring you proof." Angel couldn't help but notice that his hands were trembling. "If I brought you speculation and you confronted him and he lied and turned it on me, I would be dead."

Giovanni nodded. "I see."

"I went to Chase and told him of my suspicions and he set me up with the camera and helped me track down where Rex headed after he left the hospital."

"Actually, Sal gets more tracking credit than I do," Chase added. "The vehicle was unmarked and had no plates, so that makes things harder on my end; but Sal has some crazy-ass technology on his side." Chase raised his eyebrows far into his forehead and smiled.

"So, what have we gained from this acquired information?" Giovanni asked.

"I've got Sal running Rex and Emily's phones as we speak. Hopefully, we've uncovered more than a kinky-ass love affair, and their calls will lead us to whoever is behind this," Chase explained.

Giovanni rose from the table and motioned for Alberto to get off of his knees. "You have done well, but next time, trust me with your suspicions." Gunther and Tino escorted Giovanni toward the elevator. Stopping abruptly, he turned and uttered breathlessly, "Michelangela, join me upstairs."

"I'll be up in a moment, grandfather," Angel answered.

Once the elevator closed, Angel turned to Chase and Alberto. "If you ever go on another covert operation without keeping me in the loop, I will personally hunt you down!" Her blood was boiling and both men appeared genuinely shocked by her anger.

Chase's Adams apple slid up and down as he swallowed hard and his eyes bulged from his head. "Sorry, Boss Lady," he murmured.

"And why didn't you bring Rex and Emily in?" She demanded.

"Alberto was going to, but I talked him out of it," Chase answered and Alberto shook his head up and down in agreement. "I thought that by planting a seed in their minds that we were onto them, they might panic and start making mistakes... stupid-ass mistakes that might lead us to the person behind everything."

Angel rolled her eyes and exhaled. She couldn't deny that Chase's plan sounded good. "Next time, you keep me in the loop," she scolded and then huffed off toward the elevator.

"She has her grandfather's temper," Alberto said to Chase once Angel was out of earshot.

"You got that right, man," Chase nodded. "These Maratinzano women are fiery-ass mamas. You do not want to piss them off, especially Olga."

"Yeah, I've heard stories about Lucia, I mean, Olga, in her younger days," Alberto confided. "Some men were talking and said that a few months ago Olga Tasered Giovanni. Is that true?"

Chase chuckled. "Don't ever bring up, man. We don't talk about it. The only one who ever mentions it is Olga and you should see Giovanni's angry-ass face when she does."

"Thanks for helping me find Rex," Alberto said.

"It's what I do." Chase shrugged. "Hey, you want to watch the part where Emily jumps out of her sheet again?"

CHAPTER 23

Angel stopped just before entering the Penthouse and took a slow, deep breath. She had no idea why Giovanni had requested to meet with her and she had a gut feeling that she wasn't going to like the topic at hand. Gunther stood guarding the front door. "Any idea why he wants to see me?" Angel asked.

"No, Ms. Maratinzano. Sorry." Gunther said, opening the door and escorting her inside.

Angel was relieved to see that Salvatore, Sophia and Olga were all sitting on the living room couch across from Giovanni. This meant that the meeting was probably something generic and not something specific to her. Giovanni rose from his armed chair. "Michelangela, come and sit," he said.

Dragging a chair from the dining room table, Angel sat down, angling so that she faced both the couch and Giovanni. "What's up?" She asked and then she saw a smile grab the corners of Giovanni's lips.

"Only my granddaughter would ask 'what's up' in the presence of the Capo di Tutti Capi and the Head of the Cosa Nostra," he uttered and it was obvious that her casualness amused him.

"I'm sorry," Angel said with a smirk. "Perhaps I should have said ciò che viene in mente?" Giovanni's eyes widened with delight and a smile tightened his otherwise sagging jowls.

"Michelangela!" Salvatore gasped. "You are speaking your native tongue."

"Ben fatto!" Giovanni said, clapping his hands together and giving her a wink. Angel tilted her head.

"Did you just call me fat?" She puzzled.

This made Olga burst out laughing and she smacked Sophia atop her knee. "Merciful Heavens, that's funny! She thought he called her fat. Whoo-hoo, that's funny! I can't wait to tell Elsa, down at the hair salon, about this."

Giovanni closed his eyes and moaned. "So much hope and then..." his voice trailed.

"Hope is dashed," Salvatore completed his sentence and they both sighed aloud.

Angel rolled her eyes at the level of drama in the room. "Anyway..."

"Ben fatto means well done," Sophia interjected.

"But I take it back," Giovanni teased. "This month we start you in Italian lessons. I cannot have the granddaughter to the Capo di Tutti Capi unable to communicate with the families."

"I'm sorry," Angel huffed. "Had I known about my roots I would have studied Italian in school instead of taking years of Spanish."

"It is not your fault, Michelangela," Giovanni said in a soothing tone. "I blame Lucia."

Olga came off of the couch, shaking her fist in the air. "Now just a minute you old coot!"

Giovanni chuckled and Salvatore and Sophia pulled Olga back down. He took way too much pleasure in taunting his sister.

"Giovanni, there would be no better place for Angel to learn her native tongue than in Sicily," Salvatore added. "Living among her heritage for a few months could do wonders for her."

"Not in Sicilia," Giovanni grunted. "I mean you no offence, but she is to learn of her Italian heritage here..."

Salvatore rose from the couch. "She is half Sicilian!" He scoffed. "She must learn of that heritage as well."

"Merciful Heavens," Olga blurted. "They're going to have a pissing contest right here in the living room."

"Papa, sit down," Sophia scolded. "Enough."

"I'll learn both," Angel interjected. "Now, can we get on with the meeting?"

The topic of the meeting was benign, nothing about which Angel should have been worrying. Salvatore wanted to tell everyone that he was heading back to Sicily in the morning and had requested Sophia join him on the flight. Sophia considered it but changed her mind when Giovanni told them that the Venturini Compare had telephoned him to invite the Maratinzano family to a reception in honor of Joseph Venturini and Joe Jr. The reception was to be held tomorrow evening at Joseph's private estate on the outskirts of the city.

"While the latest attack against our family is still unresolved, I do not believe it would be wise for all of us to attend; so, it is my recommendation that Sophia and Angel go as representatives of the family," Giovanni explained.

"What about me?" Olga blurted. "Why can't I go?"

Giovanni rolled his eyes. "Because you are not the public representation we want."

Olga stood up, scooted her way past Sophia and paraded from the room in a huff, stopping briefly in front of Giovanni. "You better sleep with one eye open," she spat.

"Likewise," Giovanni rebutted with a grin.

They all heard Olga mumbling nasty phrases about her brother as she strode down the hallway and slammed her bedroom door. "You two," Sophia shook her head. "You fight like children."

Giovanni continued the meeting by explaining the new role Sophia would have in the future. Since Angel's father never married Sophia, she was not technically a Maratinzano, which meant her first obligation was toward the Buscetta family and her father, Salvatore. Sicilian mafia rules would never allow a woman to head up a family, so it was imperative that Sophia, being Salvatore's only bloodline heir, return to Sicily and marry a Sicilian man to take over the family. The only other alternative was to denounce her heritage and allow one of the Made members of the Buscetta clan to contend for the higher-ranking position. Denouncing her heritage meant giving up the Buscetta name and associated power. It was equivalent to disowning her family and Salvatore feared that if she chose this path, she would never again be welcomed to return to her home.

"You must return to Sicily," Salvatore implored.

Sophia shifted on the couch and Angel could tell that she was not comfortable with this topic. "Papa," she said to Salvatore. "I've told you a hundred times, I am not going to go back home to marry someone that I do not love."

Angel could certainly relate to that feeling. Several months ago, she and Giovanni had gone round and round on this very topic.

Clearing his throat, Giovanni addressed Sophia. "Your father and I have been discussing viable solutions to allow you to remain in the States without denouncing your familial responsibilities back home."

"Is that possible?" Sophia questioned with a glimmer of hope in her eyes.

Before Salvatore could rebut, Giovanni spoke. "You do not have to go back. We have determined that we, your grandfather and I, as heads of the families on both continents, can come to an agreement to make you our Messaggero."

Angel didn't know what that word meant and she studied Sophia's face to see if she believed the suggestion was a good one. Sophia appeared to ponder it for a moment, as if she were mulling over every detail. The curiosity, coupled with everyone's silence was driving Angel crazy. "Okay," Angel threw up her hands. "Since no one is going to tell me what a Messaggero is... I'm just going to assume that you called her a mess and leave it at that."

Sophia cracked a smile, Salvatore dropped his head to his chest and shook it back and forth and Giovanni rubbed his hand over his jowls and exhaled. "I did not call her a mess. A Messaggero is a liaison between families," Giovanni explained. "There hasn't been one in years..."

"There has never been one between the Sicilian and the stateside families," Salvatore interjected. "It will not be well-received."

"It would give you standing among all of the families, here and in Sicily, and allow you the freedom to come and go as you please," Giovanni added.

Angel thought this sounded like a great idea. It was the best of both worlds, so why did Sophia appear un-enthused?

"Merciful Heavens, that's a death sentence." Olga's voice came from the other side of the kitchen wall. She had obviously sneaked into the kitchen to eavesdrop. Waddling into the living room carrying a half-eaten Cannoli, Olga put her hand on her hip and gave the Cannoli a scolding shake in Giovanni's direction. "There's a reason we haven't had a Messaggero in years...because they were all killed!"

"Is that true?" Angel asked, looking at her mother, who gave a half smile and a tiny shrug, and then reluctantly nodded.

"That was a different time," Giovanni justified.

"Wait a minute," Angel stood up and began to pace. "Why were they all killed?"

"You've heard the expression 'don't kill the messenger'? Well, mobsters don't give a rat's ass about that rule. They ALWAYS kill the messenger," Olga explained as she shoved a big bite of Cannoli into her mouth.

"Then you can't be a Messaggero," Angel said to her mother. "It's too dangerous."

"Ha!" Olga burst. "Merciful Heavens, child, are you the pot or kettle?"

"Whose side are you on?" Angel spat at Olga.

"Nobody's," she rebutted. "Remember, I'm a poor representation so I'm on nobody's side. Humph!" Olga waddled back into the kitchen, once again mumbling under her breath.

Angel sank down into her chair. She understood the position her mother was in, and she hated it. Denounce the Buscetta family and never be allowed to return home again or go back to Sicily and marry someone she probably wouldn't love or take the dangerous position of being a liaison between the families. If she went back to Sicily to marry, would Angel ever see her again? Probably, but not often. All of a sudden Angel understood how marrying Joseph Venturini would have given Sophia a certain sense of freedom. She would have still been a part of the mafia world, but she would have merely assumed the role as a wife and wouldn't have had to be an active player. She could have remained in Chicago, close to Angel and Olga, but still have visited her father in Sicily from time to time without having the pressure of marrying someone there because she would have already been wed. She would never have been forced into denouncing her Sicilian heritage altogether. Joseph had been Sophia's ticket to freedom and now he was dead.

"I need twenty-four hours to consider this proposal," Sophia said.

"Very well. We will meet again after the Venturini reception," Giovanni said.

"Speaking of the reception," Salvatore added. "It may not be my place, but I think you should allow Lucia to attend. If you don't let her go she will be here with YOU all evening," he said with a wink.

"I had not considered that," Giovanni nodded. "That is an incentive." Giovanni rose from the armed chair. "Very well. Michelangela, please inform your aunt that she has my permission to attend the Venturini reception."

Peeking her head around the kitchen wall, Olga let out a loud, low growl. "I don't need your permission, you old coot, I was going to go anyway." She stuck her tongue out at him and then quickly vanished back into the kitchen.

Salvatore shook his head at Giovanni. "Now that is a loose end you will have to tie up one of these days."

"Si," Giovanni agreed.

CHAPTER 24

Andrew drove Lisben to the abandoned strip mall, which housed what Angel referred to as his secret "bat cave." Pulling the Equinox behind one of the dumpsters, he killed the ignition.

"Seems awful convenient to park right next to a dumpster where you can easily dispose of my body," Lisben chided.

"I'm not going to kill you, and even if I was I wouldn't throw your sorry ass into a dumpster where you'd be easily found," Andrew said, opening the driver's door and stepping out. Lisben got out and followed him toward the back entrance to the mall.

"That doesn't sound promising," Lisben mumbled.

Andrew unlocked the steel door and hurried Lisben through it, down the long staircase and through another set of steel double doors. It was dark except for an emergency exit sign hanging overhead. Once through the double doors they entered a sterile looking room, filled with all sorts of equipment and weapons. It was the "bat cave." The floor was light colored tile and the walls were concrete, painted white. Two elongated florescent bulbs hung overhead making the room uncomfortably bright and a black punching back hung in the far corner, next to a set of weights and a black mat. A long table in the other corner was home to a number of different weapons including several .22 and .45 caliber pistols, a couple of automatic rifles, silencers, Tasers, tear gas containers, hand cuffs, and several hand-held

Uzis. On a table next to the weapons sat a computer monitor, keyboard and mouse, as well as recording devices and a GPS tracking system. In the far corner hung two Kevlar vests next to a cot with a white cotton blanket and a pillow.

"Holy cow, you've got quite the set up down here," Lisben uttered.

"It's where I come to think," Andrew retorted and then sat down in front of the computer screen. "Sal was able to pull up the satellite feed from the security camera just outside the hospital morgue exit door," Andrew began and Lisben cut him off.

"Right into business, eh?" Lisben neared the table with all of the guns and ran his fingers over each piece.

"Let me cut to the chase." Andrew said pulling up the camera feed Sal had sent him. "The camera shows you exiting the morgue doors and running into the hospital parking lot a few seconds after Ian Flanko was murdered." Andrew looked up from the computer screen and met eyes with Lisben. "Then you disappeared for two days. The entire Chicago police force has been searching for you."

"They have?" Lisben's eyes widened and Andrew suddenly saw the look of a desperate man.

"Yeah, my phone has been buzzing constantly, and if I hadn't been preoccupied with burying my dad and brother, I'd have been out searching for your sorry ass too."

Picking up one of the Uzis, Lisben shifted the gun from his left to his right hand and back to his left again. "She's a lot lighter than I thought she'd be."

"The handhelds are," Andrew mumbled. "And don't try to change the subject." Lisben set the gun back on the table and sank into a folding chair next to Andrew. He stared intently at the computer, watching the video of himself running from the hospital.

"I really need to take off a few pounds," he casually remarked.

Leaning back in his chair, Andrew crossed his arms and gave Lisben the stare down. They'd been partners a long time and Andrew had seen Lisben in just about every situation, from the proud father at his son's wedding to the mourning widower when his wife lost her battle with cancer. They'd played good cop bad cop more times than Andrew could count and Lisben had risked his life on numerous occasions to chase down an armed assailant. Fleeing a crime scene was something Lisben had never done and Andrew couldn't imagine what could have forced his friend into hiding.

"Did you kill Flanko?" Andrew asked but Lisben didn't answer. "You know you're going to have to confide in me," Andrew said.

"Yeah, I know," Lisben grunted, exhaling loudly and rubbing his eyes with his hands. Andrew could see exhaustion on his face as Lisben sat up straighter and shifted his weight in the chair. "You sure you're done being a cop?" He asked.

"Right now, I'm not sure of anything."

Lisben nodded his head and lightly chewed on the corner of his lip. "You're a damn good cop, the best partner I ever had." Andrew studied his friend and the ever-apparent melancholy that swept his expression. "What I'm about to tell you is going to change everything. It makes no sense. Hell, I've been racking my brains trying to understand it."

"Maybe I can help," Andrew interjected and Lisben nodded again, as if he were still contemplating full disclosure.

"We've known each other a long time," Lisben began. "And you know I consider you to be my family..."

"What the hell is going on?" Andrew cut him off, his patience wearing thin.

"Are you one of them?" Lisben blurted, jolting to his feet. "Are you working with him?"

"Who?" Andrew jumped up and hollered back.

"Because if you are...and you've trapped me here...so help me, I'll kill you!" Lisben reached into his jacket and pulled out a .22 pistol that he had confiscated from the table in the corner; and then aimed it at Andrew. "I don't want to kill you, but I will."

Andrew had never seen him like this. Reaching his hand into his waistband, he slowly retrieved his .45 and offered it, handle first, to Lisben. He then raised his palms in the air. "I'm not working with anyone. I want to find out who killed my father and my brother. I want to know what the Mayor was doing in the alley and who was behind the CoBroGas attack on the families. All I'm doing is trying to connect the dots here..." his voice tapered off as Lisben collapsed back into the folding chair.

"I'm a dead man," he wailed. "Help me, I'm a dead man." Andrew had never seen him in this condition.   Sliding into the chair next to him, Andrew leaned forward so he was face-to-face with Lisben.

"Whatever you saw, whoever you saw, whoever threatened you, I will find them and put an end to this," Andrew seethed. "I'll have your back, but you've got to tell me what we're up against."

Clearing his throat and wiping his face, Lisben pulled himself together. "At the morgue when you told me to keep an eye on Angel while you, Monahan and Rex searched the refrigeration units, I heard a noise from the hallway. I crept toward the door, just as someone unlocked it. I didn't think he saw me, but now that you say the entire force has been searching for me...well, he must have known I was there."

"Who must have seen you?" Andrew licked his lips and watched Lisben intently, but it was as if he was lost in the memory and didn't even hear Andrew's question.

"He walked in so calm, went straight over to Flanko and shot him and then just turned and walked out."

Andrew grabbed Lisben's shoulders. "Who?!"

"The Captain."

Releasing his shoulders, Andrew jolted back against his chair in shock. This couldn't be. Captain Senalli had been with the Chicago force almost as long as Andrew. He was one of the youngest to ever hold the Captain of Police position and was hailed as one of the most driven, ethical and outstanding men in Chicago's history. His record was impeccable. Andrew couldn't believe the accusation and had anyone other than Lisben made it, he wouldn't have even considered the remote possibility that it could be true. "Are you absolutely positive it was him?" Andrew asked.

"Yes, that's why I ran. I panicked. I didn't know if you were working with him or Monahan was working with him. I didn't know who to trust so I got the hell out of there," Lisben confessed and went on to explain that with a lot of help from Jose Cuervo he had finally mustered the courage to talk to Andrew, which was why he ended up slobbering drunk at Andrew's house. "When I woke up handcuffed to a bed in the Towers, I thought my life was over for sure."

If Captain Senalli was involved then this thing went higher up than Andrew had imagined, which confirmed what Stephen Manucci had told him. When Andrew asked who Manucci worked for, he had said, "The same guy you do." Did that mean Manucci worked for Captain Senalli or was he referring to someone in the Mob?

"Why would the Captain want to kill Ian Flanko?" Andrew pondered aloud, trying to ascertain how Ian was connected to the whole thing.

"Maybe he was just a loose end," Lisben shrugged. "Like me."

CHAPTER 25

As soon as Andrew and Lisben left the building and headed toward Andrew's Equinox, a shot rang out, causing both of them to dive behind the nearby dumpster. Andrew pressed his back against the dumpster, retrieved his .45 from his shoulder holster and pulled a 357 magnum from his waistband. Handing it to Lisben, he chided, "This will work better than that piece of crap .22 you stole from me."

Lisben grimaced as he checked the clip and readied the gun. "I'm getting too old for this shit."

Andrew peeked around the side of the dumpster and another shot was fired. "I don't have to miss, Ace," the shooter yelled and Andrew stood straight up.

"Tony?" Andrew gasped. "What the hell are you doing shooting at us?"

"You're not the mark this time, so stand down, get out of the way and let me do my job," Tony yelled, with his jaw tensed and his .45 extended. He approached the dumpster.

Andrew extended his gun toward Tony and walked out from behind the dumpster. "You can't have Lisben," he clenched, taking aim at Tony's head.

"I can make this a two-for-one special, or you can stand down, Ace. The choice is yours," Tony seethed, taking aim at Andrew's head.

"Andrew, do what he says," Lisben wailed from behind the dumpster. "I'm a dead man anyway."

"Who gave the order?" Andrew yelled but Tony shook his head to indicate he wasn't going to tell. "Listen to me. This thing involves Captain Senalli and Mayor Tompkins and it may even go as high up as whoever gave you the order to hit Lisben." Andrew inched closer. "Lisben saw the Captain kill Ian Flanko, who was our only witness as to who wanted Angel in the first place."

"I already know who wants Angel, Ace. You!" Tony sneered. "I've had my eye on you from the beginning. You, the Mayor and the Captain probably set this whole thing up. You knew the gas attack was coming, which is why you took Angel out of the room right before it happened."

"Bullshit!" Andrew hollered. "If you'll think back, it was Angel that asked me to join her because she wanted to show me the rest of the pub renovations."

Tony narrowed his brow, as if he were considering Andrew's words. "You ordered your father's death so you could take over the family and have her all to yourself," Tony seethed.

"This isn't about me and you and Angel. I'm not even sure I'm going to take over the family," Andrew defended and then cursed aloud. "I need a favor. I need you not to kill Lisben."

"I did you a favor, Ace; when I didn't kill you, remember?" Tony chided. "And what's my payback? You were making it with my girl in an elevator." Tony gritted his teeth and his nostrils flared with rage.

"She isn't your girl anymore," Andrew rebutted and then lowered his head and let his gun swing by his side. He was certainly guilty of loving Angel and if that was the source of Tony's hatred than there was nothing he could say or do. Andrew holstered his gun and looked Tony square in the eyes. "If you can tell me that you wouldn't have done the same thing, then pull the trigger."

Tony's face reddened with anger and Andrew could tell there was a part of him that wanted nothing more than to drop him in a bloody heap on the pavement. There was fire in his eyes as they stared at each other for what seemed like an eternity. Finally, through clenched teeth, Tony lowered his weapon and uttered, "You're not my mark."

"What about Lisben?" Andrew asked.

"I'll say I haven't been able to locate him yet," Tony said. "And you better keep it that way."

Sliding his gun into the back of his jeans, Tony turned around and walked toward his black SUV. Andrew hollered to Lisben, telling him to get into the Equinox and then did a quick jaunt to catch up to Tony. "I owe you one," he said, causing Tony to stop abruptly and turn to face him.

"Actually, this is the second favor I've done for you so you owe me two. You can pay up right now, Ace," Tony remarked. "Give me your word that you won't marry Angel."

Andrew's heart stuck momentarily. The fact was Tony had once risked his own life to save Andrew and was now giving Lisben a fighting chance. Andrew did owe him and he knew that calling in the favor was fair, no matter how difficult the outcome would be. Andrew pursed his lips together and ran his hand through his hair. Tony was playing the trump card and in the current situation there was nothing Andrew could do about it. It was a smart play, especially now, before Andrew officially became a Boss.

"If you can't make the deal then give me Lisben," Tony quipped.

"I'll make the deal, if you give me one more piece of information," Andrew negotiated. "Did Giovanni order the hit on Lisben?"

Tony shook his head to indicate no, opened his driver's door and climbed behind the wheel. Rolling down the window, he outstretched his hand to Andrew. "You don't marry her, she never hears about this conversation and we're even. Capisce?"

"Capisce."

CHAPTER 26

It was 3:00pm when Chase burst through the Penthouse door with his laptop clutched tightly in his hand. "Boss Lady, you have got to get a load of this!" He excitedly blurted, causing Olga to rush from the kitchen to the dining room.

"Merciful Heavens, what's all the fuss about?" Olga gasped, wiping her hands on the yellow apron that clung to her rounded hips. She had been in the kitchen for hours making homemade Cannoli and a large pan of her special recipe meatballs. It was no secret that Olga cooked whenever she was upset so Angel knew that she was busying herself to keep from thinking about the fact that Salvatore had left that morning to go back to Sicily.

"What's up?" Angel came from her bedroom, freshly showered, with her wet hair dangling down around her shoulders.

Chase set his laptop on the dining room table and began clicking wildly at the keys as he explained that Sal had been running Rex and Emily through the FBI database while he had been running their phones through the local database. "Believe it or not, Rex is squeaky-ass clean," Chase said with surprise.

"That is surprising," Angel admitted, as she was certain that Rex was one of the main players; but Rex's phone only showed calls to Emily, Andrew and to the Venturini family, which was normal considering he worked for them. Other than the fact that he was sleeping with Emily, there was no cause for suspicion.

"It gets better," Chase said, raising his eyebrows into his forehead and smacking his lips together. "Emily is better known as Amelia Craden, one of the most sought-after hackers in an underground organization called Anonimi."

"What?" Angel scrunched up her face in disbelief. "She's not a nurse?"

"Nope. According to Sal, she has a bunch of different aliases, but Amelia Craden was the one she used when Anonimi hacked into the FBI security database, retrieving secret codes for government funded defense programs." Chase shook his spikey haired head back and forth and chewed on the end of a pencil. "This wild-ass young thing hacked into our government and got the codes which allowed access to the research lab in DC that was authenticating the CoBroGas." A big smile filled Chase's face. "She's not only hot, she's freaky-ass brilliant!"

Olga threw her hands in the air. "Merciful heavens, I think the boy's in love."

"You do remember she's the enemy, don't you?" Angel reminded Chase.

"Yeah, I know, but damn is she impressive." Chase said, making Olga giggle and waddle back into the kitchen. Angel rolled her eyes. *Men!*

"Other than her being hot and freaky-ass brilliant, is there anything helpful you can tell me about Emily? Like, oh, I don't know... where we can find her?"

Chase put the pencil between his teeth and began clicking rapidly on his keyboard. "We're working on that now, but I can give you a list of the numbers she has called within the past several days, which might lead somewhere."

Angel instructed Chase to print out the list of numbers with names and addresses. "Also, get me a list from Sal of every alias Emily has used. There's got to be a link somewhere."

Pulling out her cell phone she dialed Tony and Andrew, leaving them each a message asking to meet her at the Towers at 4:00pm. "We have a lead on the CoBroGas," she explained in her message and then instructed Chase to tell Big Mike and the Snake to join them at 4:00pm.

"Do you want Gunther, Tino and Alberto too?" Chase questioned.

"No. Just my men," Angel responded and then realized the irony that Tony and Andrew would never be *her men.*

Dressed in blue jeans and a black cashmere sweater, Angel pulled on her black and white, Converse tennis shoes, shoved her 9mm in the back of her jeans beneath her sweater and headed toward the Penthouse door. It was almost 4:00pm and she was anxious to get some answers. Not only that, but she was looking forward to seeing Andrew and hoping they could find a few private moments to talk.

Gunther escorted her from the Penthouse to the elevator and into the secret meeting room, where Chase, the Snake and Big Mike sat waiting. Scanning the room, she flushed with disappointment because neither Tony nor Andrew were there. Chase handed out the list of phone numbers from Emily's cell phone and the addresses associated with each number. He then handed each of them a list of Emily's aliases, each name followed by the state or country in which she used that name. The first line read: Amelia Craden, Washington DC

Angel scanned the list but nothing caught her eye. Amelia Craden, Emily Craden, Emily R. Craden, Rose Craden, Rose E. Craden. "Do you think her real name is Rose or maybe that's a middle name?" Angel posed.

"Could be," Chase shrugged. "Sal's running every alias to see if we can narrow anything down to the Chicago area. The only thing we have right now is that she is the daughter of Martha Craden and Rinaldo Rosenalli."

"Does that ring any bells for anyone?" Angel asked but Big Mike and the Snake both shook their head indicating it did not.

"We're at a bit of disadvantage," the Snake pointed out. "I've spent most of my time in New York and Big Mike's been out in the corn fields of Iowa."

Angel exhaled a frustrated sigh. She needed Tony and Andrew. They would know instantly if these names meant something here in Chicago or were connected to one of the five families. Angel paced around the table and chewed on her index fingernail. "Okay, get me everything you know on Emily's parents and we'll start there."

On her way back to the Penthouse, Angel stopped at Giovanni's apartment, located between the secret meeting floor and the Penthouse. Despite the fact that Angel invited him to stay in the Penthouse, Giovanni insisted on having his own apartment when he visited. "That is your home," he told her. "Besides, I could not stand to sleep down the hall from Lucia," he teased.

She wasn't certain why, but she felt like she needed to talk with her grandfather. Having almost lost him in the hospital made a part of her want to cling tighter now; and it also raised some questions to which she hoped Giovanni would have answers. His face lit up when he saw her standing outside his door. "Come in, Michelangela, and sit down," he said, ushering her toward the couch. "Most people do not pay me social visits."

That's because most people are afraid of you, she wanted to say, but refrained. As much as she loved her grandfather, she had no desire to be feared the way he was. What he called respect, Angel called terror.

"To what do I owe the pleasure of your company?" Giovanni asked, sitting down on the couch next to her.

Angel had a million questions bouncing around in her head, all of them vying for priority status. She wanted to talk about her mother and the Messaggero position Giovanni had offered. Would Sophia be in constant danger? She also wanted to know what would have happened to the family had Giovanni died at the hospital. Who would have taken over? Who would be the next Capo di Tutti Capi? Though these things were important, she mostly wanted to talk about Andrew and the prospect of him becoming Boss of the Venturini family. Angel fidgeted nervously with her fingers. "I am some questions," she began.

"And I have some answers," he added. "Let me go first, huh? My answers might make your questions disappear."

Angel shrugged her shoulders. "That seems a little bass-akwards, but okay."

"Humor me," Giovanni sighed. Rising from the couch, he walked to the window behind the kitchen table and gazed outside, as if he were pondering how to begin the conversation. "I have watched you grow up," he began. "Albeit from afar, I was always watching. I knew there would come a day when we would make contact and I prayed you would accept me into your life." Giovanni made the sign of the cross over his body and then kissed his fingertips. "When you did, you made an old man very happy." He smiled and Angel thought back to the day they had met. Aside from having a pillow case thrown over her head and being shoved into a trunk, it was a pretty good first meeting. "There will come a time, Michelangela, when I will not be here to help guide you." Giovanni walked back toward the couch and sat down. "You will have to stand alone in your authority, but you will never be alone. Do you understand?"

Angel narrowed her brow. "I think so."

"What I mean is, I will not be alive forever, but I have taken measures to ensure that you will always have the guidance and the support you require." Angel wasn't sure what he was talking about. Did he mean that her financial future was secure? Or did her mean that he had arranged some type of relationship for her?

"I hope you're not talking about an arranged marriage," she winced. "Because we've been down that road."

Giovanni chuckled. "No, no, I am aware of your feelings on that topic. I'm talking about family security in keeping the Maratinzano name well-known and highly respected." He went on to explain that it was his intention to make certain that the next Capo di Tutti Capi would come from the Maratinzano family.

"How is that possible? There's no other bloodline heir." Angel knew he couldn't have been referring to her taking over the Capo position because a woman would never be accepted in the role, and quite frankly, Angel didn't want the title. She still wasn't sure about bearing the title of family Boss, much less the Boss of all Bosses.

"There is one heir," he said softly and Angel was certain that confusion shown on her face. She remembered that her father had one sibling, a sister, who had been killed by a car bomb; and that her grandmother was gunned down outside of a bakery shortly thereafter. Olga was Giovanni's only sibling and she never bore children, so how could there be another heir?

"I'm not following," Angel expressed.

"Years ago, I knew a woman named Bella Rosalini. You might say she was my Andrew or my Tony." Angel smirked and Giovanni shot her a raised eyebrow, sideways glance. "It is not something I am proud to admit."

"It's no big deal," Angel assured him. "You were widowed and probably just needed to feel the comfort that only a woman could give." Angel shrugged. "It's totally normal."

The corners of his lips curled into a small grin, one which he quickly stifled. "Your generation leaves too many loose ends." He pointed his finger at her. "Loose ends have a way of backlashing and entangling you when you least expect it."

Giovanni's paranoia never ceased to amaze her. Everything had to be buckled up, every I dotted and every T crossed. "So, Bella entangled you?" Angel teased.

"Si, she bore a son named Vanni Rosalini and she raised him alone, never telling me he was my son." Giovanni's face reddened and his jowls pulled tight as he pursed his lips together. "When I found out, I was enraged. Ha scelto di fare lui illegittima quando egli avrebbe potuto essere la mia famiglia!" He bellowed, shaking his fist in the air.

"I have no idea what you just said," Angel quipped. "Can I get that in English please?"

Giovanni rolled his eyes and shook his head. "I said she chose to make her son illegitimate instead of allowing him to be my family."

"Why did she hide him from you?" Angel asked, though she was pretty sure it had something to do with his Mafia position. Bella probably didn't want her son gunned down at a young age by someone seeking revenge against Giovanni. If Angel had to guess, she would have said that Bella Rosalini and Sophia had a lot in common when it came to parenting.

"Bah," Giovanni frowned. "No reason was good enough to hide him from me. I could have given him everything." He shook his finger at her. "Learn from the error of my ways and tie up your loose ends."

Angel couldn't help but feel that her grandfather was subtly implying that Tony and Andrew were her proverbial loose ends in need of being tied. "So, what happened to Bella?"

"She went on with her life and I with mine. The good news is that I have recently connected with Vanni and Carl and I am considering making him a Consigliere to the family."

"A Consigliere? Isn't that the same things as a Compare?" Angel asked and after Giovanni exhaled an exasperated sigh, he explained that a Compare, like Carl Cusanelli, is a trusted friend that remains outside of the family, both in bloodline and in the context of formal representation; but a Consigliere is third in line in the family ranking, behind the Boss and Underboss, and is considered a part of the family administration, having the added responsibility of representing the family in the Boss's absence.

"I have brought Vanni into the family to try him out for a while and if he proves strong, one day I will make him the Maratinzano Consigliere," Giovanni explained.

Angel nodded. "Would you rather have him be Boss here in Chicago?" She tentatively asked, wondering if Giovanni had doubts about her ability and was secretly grooming Vanni to take over. Giovanni took her hand and squeezed it.

"You are the Chicago Boss," he said poignantly. "My job is to give you the tools you need to effectively do your job. A Consigliere is one of those tools."

"Did you reconnect with Bella too?"

"No. Bella passed away, God rest her soul," Giovanni said and Angel saw a flash of sadness sweep over his face. "She was a fine woman."

Rising from the couch, Angel began to pace. Giovanni's confession regarding Bella made her realize that despite his crusty exterior, he understood what it was like to love and to long for someone you loved. If he did, then surely he would understand her wanting to know how Andrew becoming a Boss might affect her relationship with him. She wanted to ask if there was ever a time when two Bosses married, but she didn't know how to bring it up. A part of her felt silly even discussing it, as she and Andrew had never talked about it, at least not officially. For all she knew Andrew didn't want to marry her; and what about Tony? She could feel Giovanni's eyes piercing through her.

"What is churning in that mind of yours?" He asked.

"You once told me that after my grandmother died, you never loved another woman. Now, I find out about Bella. Did you love her?"

Giovanni leaned against the back of the couch and closed his eyes. "Aw, l'amore e le molte domande del cuore," he sighed.

"Si, nonno, l'amore," Angel repeated, having understood only one word from his entire sentence, and that word was l 'amore, which meant love. Giovanni smiled as he did whenever she tried to speak Italian.

"Si, yes, I cared very much for Bella but after the way I lost your grandmother, I was unwilling to allow myself to become vulnerable again."

"Was that because you were afraid something like what happened to grandma would happen to her?"

Looking as if he were pondering her question, Giovanni nodded slowly. "A good leader always fears for the safety of his loved ones."

"Grandfather," she blurted while gnawing on her fingernail. "If Andrew becomes the Boss of his family..." her voice tapered off. "I mean, if he and I were to..." She stopped and exhaled. This was hard. "Have Bosses ever married?" She burst out and Giovanni's expression grew somber.

"No. E' impossibile. It is impossible." A thick silence fell between them. "Michelangela, come sit with me," he said, soothingly and Angel plunked down onto the couch. "You are a beautiful young woman, who could have anyone's hand in marriage. Choose someone with whom you can build your familia together. Tie up these loose ends."

Angel stared down at the carpet. He wasn't telling her anything she didn't already know, but a part of her had wished that he would have said otherwise and promised his blessing if it should ever occur.

Placing his palm on her cheek, Giovanni spoke softly. "You carry on with Andrew and Tony and right now it is okay. You are young yet. But a time is coming when you will have to choose a suitable husband, not someone whose allegiance lies with another family." He gently patted her cheek. "You are passionate like your grandmother, beautiful like your mother and smart like your father. When the time comes you will tie up the loose ends and make the right choice for yourself and su familia." He gave her a quick wink. "I have faith in your strength up here." He pointed to her forehead. "And in here." He pointed to her heart. "Remember, being a leader means balancing your heart, cuore and your smarts, astuto."

"Cuore y astuto," she repeated. Balancing her heart and her head seemed almost impossible. Her head told her that she could not have a lasting relationship with either Tony or Andrew, but her heart wanted them both. Would she ever find the

strength to tie up those proverbial loose ends?
Just walking into a meeting without seeing Tony
and Andrew sitting around the table made her feel
undeniably empty. She couldn't imagine going
through life without them; and yet she knew the
day was coming when she would have no choice
but to let them go.

CHAPTER 27

It was 7:00pm and Angel was putting the finishing touches on her make-up. She was wearing the same black Versace dress she wore the night of the CoBroGas attack with a new pair of black strappy stilettos. Her 9mm was packed neatly in her left thigh holster and her cell phone was strapped to her right thigh. As long as she remembered not to try to cross her legs throughout the evening, everything should be fine. Her hair lay in long, lose curls around her shoulders and diamond stud earrings glistened from each lobe. Though her reflection gave positive feedback, she couldn't shake a blanket of negativity weighing heavily upon her. Neither Tony nor Andrew had bothered to contact her to explain why they hadn't attended the four o'clock meeting. It was out of character for both of them and she couldn't help taking it personally. She felt rejected.

Sinking onto her bed, Angel reached up her dress and retrieved her cell phone. She assumed Tony was still mad at her because of the elevator incident and the fact that she allowed Lisben to leave with Andrew. She started to text him, but quickly changed her mind. There was nothing she could say to fix his jealousy and she didn't want to find herself put into the position of trying to explain her feelings for Andrew. How could she explain something even she didn't fully understand? At least she would get to see Andrew at the Venturini reception tonight. Mustering up courage, she sent Andrew a text: CAN WE TALK LATER?

Within seconds he responded: YES, I'LL SEE YOU AT 8:30PM

Butterflies of excitement fluttered in her stomach. She was going to get to spend some time with Andrew and she couldn't wait. After returning her phone to her thigh strap, Angel flitted from her bedroom into the dining room where her mother, Olga, Giovanni, Chase, the Snake and Big Mike awaited.

"Merciful Heavens, don't you look like a million bucks!" Olga burst as soon as Angel entered the room.

"Damn, Boss Lady," Chase blurted. "Smokin'."

"You look lovely," Sophia added.

"Thank you. You both look beautiful too," Angel said and gave her mother and Olga a once over. Sophia wore a black straight skirt, light gray silk blouse and a black blazer. Her hair was pulled back into a bun and pearls adorned her ears and neck. Olga was dressed in black satin slacks with a yellow satin, high neck blouse that tied into a big bow around her neck. Her hair was slicked back into a bun and she wore a matching clip on the left side of her head.   Sophia was the embodiment of class and Olga of flamboyance.

Giovanni, who had been seated at the head of the dining room table when Angel entered, now stood and grinned. "Michelangela, you and your mother are stunning; and Lucia doesn't look half bad either."

"Humph!" Olga snorted. "Old coot."

Before they headed downstairs, Chase went over some last-minute instructions. "We're not expecting any problems at the reception, but on the off chance that something goes down, you all know what to do, right?"

"Yep. I Taser the son of a ..." Olga retorted.

"Lucia!" Sophia scolded, cutting her sentence short. "A lady doesn't Taser anyone at a reception."

"This wild-ass lady does," Chase said, pointing at Olga.

"Oh, and you're one to talk, missy," Olga retorted with her hands on her hips. "Weren't you the one that was half-naked the other day, Tasering the socks off that Manucci guy?"

Sophia stifled a grin. "Yes, but it wasn't at a reception," she corrected.

Chase elbowed Big Mike. "These are some crazy-ass women. Good luck tonight."

"Ladies, can we get back to business?" Giovanni interjected. "This is precisely why the Mafia has historically been run by men."

"Merciful Heavens, you're a sexist old coot!" Olga barked.

"And you are a nagging hen, constantly pecking," Giovanni rebutted.

Olga narrowed her eyes and gave Giovanni a glare that looked almost powerful enough to vaporize him. Reaching in her handbag she retrieved her Taser and held it up. "Do you want some more of this?"

Giovanni's jowls drooped lower. "Lucia, if you ever advance toward me with your weapon again, I will have no choice but to order you shot," he warned.

"Seriously?!" Angel blurted, grabbing the Taser from Olga's death grip and shoving it back into her purse. "Are you two ever going to get along?" Their bickering, though sometimes comical, was maddening. "Chase, can we please continue with the instructions?"

"Right on, Boss Lady," Chase quipped and reviewed the precautions they had discussed earlier that day. Big Mike and the Snake were going along as their security detail and they were each fully armed. Everyone wore a tiny ear bud inside their right ear which enabled Chase to communicate with them in the event of an emergency. Olga complained incessantly about the ear bud, calling it an ear BUG and moaning that it made her feel like something was crawling around in her head. "Remember," Chase added, "you'll be able to hear me through your ear bud but you won't be able to talk to me."

"Well, what good is that?" Olga objected and Giovanni let out a loud, exasperated sigh and rubbed his eyes.

"You are tiresome, woman," Giovanni said.

"Humph!" Olga crossed her arms and threw her chin in the air.

"Proceed," Giovanni said to Chase.

"Now, you're each wearing a state of the art, tiny-ass camera. Does everybody have their camera?" Chase asked and everyone nodded. Sitting down at the dining room table, he opened his laptop and clicked rapidly across the keys, until five squares displayed on the screen. He held the laptop up so they could all see. "This is what I will be able to see. It's all five of your camera feeds simultaneously." A smile filled his face as he explained the importance of the cameras. "These babies are the only way I can see what is going on inside the house."

"So, don't block the feed," Big Mike summed up.

"Yes," Chase agreed. "And listen to my instructions." Chase set the computer back on the table and twirled a pencil spastically between his fingers. "If I see something suspicious over by Angel, I may ask Sophia to turn toward Angel so that I can get a better view."

"I don't think any of this is going to be necessary," Sophia sighed. "This is a simple reception to celebrate Joseph and Joe Jr.'s life."

"Agreed," Angel said. "So, can we go?" She was anxious to get there and see Andrew.

"One last thing," Chase added. "If you believe you are in danger, work the code word into a sentence and I'll send help."

"What good is saying a code word if you can't hear us?" Olga chided.

"I'll have limited capacity to hear you through the cameras," Chase clarified, "but I'll talk to you through your ear buds."

"What's the code word?" Sophia asked.

"Elevator." A grin filled Chase's face and Angel gawked at him, un-amused.

Big Mike and the Snake escorted the ladies to the main level where Gunther had the Tank running and waiting. They were leaving right on time, as the reception started at 8:00pm and it would take them approximately thirty minutes to get to the Venturini property outside of the city. Big Mike drove with the Snake in the passenger seat and the three ladies were seated in the back. Sophia was directly behind Big Mike, Olga sat behind the Snake and Angel sat between them. While they rode, Angel described the Venturini home, including the central fireplace, Joseph's evident love for sailing and the bookshelf that had a secret doorway.

CHAPTER 28

It was 8:30pm when Andrew pulled his Equinox in front of the Towers and Tino escorted him inside. On the elevator ride up, he loosened the collar on his black, long sleeve shirt and tried to calm his nerves. There had been so much tension between him and Angel that he wasn't sure what to expect upon seeing her. He also knew that he owed her an apology for his cold behavior, and that wasn't going to be easy.

At the Penthouse level, Andrew met Gunther, who was standing guard outside of the door. Gunther appeared surprised to see him. Andrew explained that Angel had requested to meet with him, and Gunther's expression grew more skeptical.

"Ms. Maratinzano isn't in at the moment. Perhaps you would like to speak with Giovanni instead?" Gunther said.

Andrew agreed and Gunther escorted him inside, asking him to wait in the foyer while he spoke privately with Giovanni. When Gunther returned, it was with his weapon drawn and he confiscated Andrew's gun. "What's going on?" Andrew asked.

"That is the exact question the Capo will be asking you," Gunther retorted and nudged Andrew toward the living room and onto the couch across from where Giovanni sat staunch-like in his armed chair.

Andrew leaned forward, placing his elbows on his knees and interlocking his fingers. "Giovanni, what's going on?"

225

"I will ask the questions," he remarked.

Suddenly, a light bulb lit in Andrew's brain. Angel must have lured him here to force him to talk with Giovanni about becoming the next Venturini Boss. *That sneaky little minx.* Exhaling, he leaned back against the couch, crossing his left leg over his right knee.

"What are you doing here?" Giovanni asked.

Andrew licked his lips. "Well, I was under the impression that I was supposed to meet with Angel, but clearly I see that I have been set up for an interview with you."

"Bugiardo!" Giovanni seethed, leaving Andrew genuinely confused.

"With all due respect, sir, I am not a liar," Andrew defended. Reaching into his pants pocket, he withdrew his cell phone. "I'll show you." He clicked on the messaging button and brought up Angel's number. "Here," he said, handing the phone to Giovanni. "She text me and asked if we could talk, wherein I responded that I would be here at 8:30pm."

Andrew watched as Giovanni read the text and his face began to redden. He turned to Gunther. "Get me Chase. NOW!" Without hesitation, Gunther dashed toward the Penthouse door right as Chase came barreling through it with several laptops stacked in his arms.

"Capo, sir," Chase blurted, fumbling with the laptops as he moved rapidly toward the dining room table to set down the equipment. "We've got a big-ass problem." Chase caught Andrew out of his peripheral vision. "Holy shit, man, what are you doing here?"

Andrew was on his feet, making a beeline toward Chase. "You want to fill me in on what the hell is happening?"

Before Chase could begin, Tino burst through the door, his hands and forearms covered in blood. "It's Rex," he uttered breathlessly. "He's in the elevator with Alberto. Says he needs to see Giovanni."

Gunther tossed Andrew his gun and Andrew raced out of the Penthouse and toward the elevator, his gun extended and readied. He had seen a lot of death in his time, but nothing could have prepared him for what he was about to see in that elevator. Rex lay crumpled in a bloody heap with Alberto trying to stop the bleeding. His face was beaten so badly, he was hardly recognizable. Andrew gasped at the sight.

"He drove here like this," Alberto said. "Fell out of his car on the damn pavement and started to crawl towards us." Disbelief rang in Alberto's tone. "Says he needs to tell Giovanni something." Alberto was visibly shaken by Rex's condition.

Andrew knelt down aside Rex. "Can you hear me?"

"B...o...ss," Rex uttered. "The re...cep...tion," Rex gasped for a breath.

"What reception?" Andrew blurted.

"T...r...ap." Rex gasped again for air but this time his body went limp and his eyes, dead.

"Damnit!" Andrew spewed. Any hope of gaining information as to Rex's connection to Emily, Manucci and Captain Senalli was gone. Rising from his squatting position, Andrew turned around to see Giovanni, Gunther and Tino standing in the hallway behind him.

"Clean up this mess," Giovanni uttered and returned to the Penthouse.

"What reception?" Andrew yelled, following Giovanni inside. "Chase, what reception was Rex talking about?"

"The Venturini reception in honor of your father and brother," he answered.

"What!" Andrew exclaimed. "There's no reception for my dad and Joe Jr."

Chase's fingers were flying over the keyboard as he moved from one laptop to the next. "Yeah, I gathered that now."

"Who said there was a reception?" Andrew demanded.

Giovanni explained that Joseph Venturini's Compare telephoned to invite the family to the reception, and that Giovanni agreed to allow Sophia, Angel and begrudgingly, Olga, to attend.

"Who took that call?" Andrew said.

"It came to my home in New York. Carl Cusanelli relayed the message to me via my cell phone."

"Son of a ...." Andrew spewed and pounded his fist on the table. "Where was the reception to be held?"

"Your father's estate outside the city," Chase answered, never looking up from his computer.

"What time?"

"Eight o'clock," Chase answered.

Andrew ran his hand through his hair, his mind whirling with possibilities, all of which had horrible outcomes. It was 8:45pm, which meant at any moment from the time Angel left the Towers until now, they could have been ambushed anywhere along the way. Andrew spewed obscenities. He couldn't go to the police because he was still uncertain of the Captain's involvement and thereby unsure of what officers he could trust. He couldn't call the Venturini men for help because, his family was obviously somehow involved. They had gotten to Rex and only God knew who else. He couldn't trust any of them now. Pursing his lips, Andrew grabbed his cell phone and dialed Sammy, but the call went straight to voicemail. He left a brief message that said to call him, but didn't indicate why, and then he dialed Tony.

228

"I need help," he blurted right as Tony answered. Before Tony could utter a word, Andrew rambled a summarized version of what he believed was happening. "Angel could be anywhere by now."

Chase piped in. "I've got a visual!" And Andrew and Giovanni made a beeline toward his computer. "Do you recognize this place?" Chase asked Andrew.

Andrew nodded. "Tony, are you still there?" There was a pause that sounded like dead air and Andrew wondered for a moment if Tony had hung up on him. "I'm here," he said. "Where is she?"

"At my father's estate outside the city."

"All right, Ace," Tony gritted. "We're on our way."

"Not the house in the city," Andrew clarified.

"I know where it is," Tony barked.

Andrew disconnected the call and turned to Giovanni. "Can I take Alberto and Gunther with me?"

"Si," Giovanni responded.

"Chase, get Trig over here. I need him to chopper us in," Andrew ordered.

"Right on," Chase said, grabbing his cell phone.

"And tell him to bring weapons," Andrew added. He had to assume that whoever had lured Angel to his father's estate had access to everything there, including an arsenal of weapons.

Giovanni sank into his armed chair, with a look of exhaustion and despair. "I allowed them to walk out of here like lambs to the slaughter."

Checking the clip in his gun, Andrew shoved it back into his waistband and then watched Chase's fingers dance wildly across his keypad, retrieving data from the cameras, copying

faces of people in the room and sending the images
to Sal for ID recognition.

"That's Mrs. Rosen," Andrew said, pointing
to the computer screen. She was walking from the
kitchen into the family room with a serving tray of
hors d oeuvres. The women didn't appear to be in
any danger, at least not at the moment. "Is there
any way you can communicate with them?"
Andrew asked and Chase beamed.

"You think I'd send our Boss Lady
anywhere without being able to talk to her?"
Chase shook his head wildly. "I'm offended by the
insinuation." A few more clicks on the keyboard
and he turned to Andrew. "Which one do you want
to talk to?"

"Big Mike and the Snake," Andrew said.
"Where are they?"

"Uncertain," Chase said. "I have no video
coverage of them in the room and both of their
feeds are blank."

"Blank?" Andrew wrinkled his brow. "Let
me see." Chase pulled up the video and Andrew
grimaced. Their feeds were black. It could have
been a technological problem, but Andrew's gut
told him otherwise. For now, he needed to operate
under the assumption that both Big Mike and the
Snake had been incapacitated or otherwise
compromised and that Angel, Sophia and Olga
were on their own. Andrew scanned the room.
From Olga's camera he could see that Olga was
sitting on the far loveseat, facing the fireplace and
Sophia and Angel were sitting on the adjacent love
seat, closest to the dining room table and the
French doors that led to the kitchen.

"Let me talk to Angel," Andrew said and
Chase handed him the small, pen-like microphone.
Andrew took a deep breath. He didn't want to
alarm her because he needed her to remain calm
and not allow fear to show on her face.

Before he began speaking Chase piped in. "Did your dad have an internal security system in this house?"

"Yes," Andrew answered.

"Any chance you know the security codes?" Chase posed. "Because this would be a helluva lot easier if we could see the whole room and know how many people we're up against."

Andrew's eyes lit. He did know the codes. Setting down the microphone, Andrew helped Chase tap into the Venturini security system and within moments they had a clear picture of the entire living room. There was an armed guard standing by the staircase that led downstairs, one by the French doors that led to the kitchen and one by the secret opening in the bookshelf. "Three guards on the inside," Chase mumbled aloud. "Now, let's check the exterior." Clicking rapidly, Chase brought up a view of the garage and the perimeter of the house. An armed guard stood in front of the garages but the rest of the area looked clear. "It doesn't look like getting in is going to be a problem," Chase quipped and then clicked back to the camera feed that showed the living room.

Mrs. Rosen had placed the hors d'oeuvres in the center of the dining room table and now stood between the couch and the French doors. Seated at the dining room table was Emily and next to her sat Angel's bus boy, Ricky Dente. Across the room, on the other side of the white, brick fireplace, seated in a leather chair was Captain Senalli. He was doing all of the talking while everyone else stared at him.

"Son of a ..." Andrew mumbled under his breath. Lisben had been telling the truth. It wasn't that Andrew ever really doubted Lisben's story, but hearing it and seeing it were two different things. He couldn't believe the Captain would be an active participant in this level of corruption. Chase continued to copy the faces of everyone in the room and sent them off to Sal, while Andrew grabbed the pen microphone and took a deep breath.

"Sweetheart," he spoke softly into the microphone. "If you can hear me, I want you to wiggle your right pinky."

He stared at the screen as Angel, while keeping her eyes on Captain Senalli, slowly set her right hand atop her lap and wiggled her pinky.

"Okay, listen, but make no movements and remain calm. We are on our way." Andrew studied Angel's body language on the screen and could see her cheeks flush and her breathing grow more rapid. He knew what she was thinking. How could she protect her mother and Olga and get out alive? "You're in a position to buy time by keeping the Captain talking," Andrew told her.

Tino escorted Trig into the room, followed by Chito. "What's he doing here?" Andrew grunted, lowering the microphone and glaring at Chito. Andrew had come to accept Trig, only because he had proven himself by rescuing Angel when she was trapped in Iowa; but Chito was a different story. Chito was the leader of the Cobra gang, of which Andrew had spent a greater part of his job as a police officer trying to eliminate. He knew firsthand that Chito's main concern was Chito, so he wasn't apt to trust his proclamation of sudden loyalty to Angel.

Opening his jacket to reveal several guns beneath, Chito said, "I'm locked and loaded, and ready to bust some balls."

Andrew gritted his teeth. "One wrong move and I take you out," Andrew said. "Are we clear?"

"Geeze, man, lighten up. I thought you weren't a cop no more," Chito huffed and walked outside onto the patio to join Trig in the chopper.

Andrew's jaw tensed as he held the microphone to his lips one more time. "We're coming in the chopper. Sit tight, Sweetheart."

CHAPTER 29

Trig took off in the helicopter with Andrew in the co-pilot seat and Chito and Gunther in the back. Alberto was driving Andrew's Equinox and would meet them at the entrance to the Venturini estate. Andrew thought it necessary to have an extra vehicle on site, should they be unable to get back to the chopper. Tino stayed behind to clean up Rex's body and maintain security at the Towers. Andrew couldn't dismiss the possibility that all of this was a diversionary tactic to hit the real target which may or may not be the Capo di Tutti Capi. His gut told him that Giovanni was in no danger, but years of police work had taught him to never underestimate the enemy. Like Lisben always said, "You can't beat crazy until you start thinking like crazy."

Adjusting his ear bud, Andrew tested the wireless microphone Chase had attached to the button on his shirt. "I hear you loud and clear," Chase responded. "Remember, you'll be able to transmit to all of the ear buds. The only ones that can't hear you are Tony and his guys."

"We're going to set her down in the field to the north of the house," Andrew told Trig, who gave him an acknowledging thumbs-up.

As they approached the Venturini estate, Chito spewed obscenities and Gunther slid his .45 pistol back into his waistband and grabbed an assault rifle. Andrew looked down on a barrage of cop cars and flashing lights. Chicago's finest had barricaded the entrance to his father's house. He shouldn't have been surprised. After all, Captain Senalli had the entire force at his disposal.

"There's a lot of 'em, but I think we can take 'em all pretty easy," Gunther yelled while adjusting the rifle and taking aim. Several questions were plaguing Andrew. What exactly was the Captain's plan? How many of the cops down there were in on the plan, and how many were innocently following his random order to block off the street? They couldn't open fire on officers who were there only because they were following orders.

"Don't fire," Andrew hollered and then told Trig to delay landing for a few moments until they could come up with a plan. "Chase!" Andrew barked into his microphone. "We're covered with cops here. What's going on?"

"I'm hacking in now," Chase responded. "Scanners read that there's been a double homicide at your father's house," he said. "But I'm staring at the security feed and everyone is still in the living room and accounted for."

Andrew was racking his brain to understand what was happening. "Are you sure the feed you're looking at now is live?"

Chase's fingers danced across the keyboard. "Yep. It's crazy-ass live, no one's been tampering with it."

"Have they released the names of the deceased?" Andrew asked.

"They're not in the local feed yet, but let me see if Sal can tap in at the precinct," Chase answered. "Hold tight."

Andrew didn't want to wait for Chase so he instructed Trig to set the chopper down in the field on the north side of the house behind the tree line which surrounded his father's property. Andrew believed it would give them adequate coverage while sneaking closer to the house.

"The minute they see us set down, man, the cops are gonna be all over our ass," Chito blurted.

"I can handle the cops," Gunther said, holding up the rifle.

Andrew twisted his body around to face Chito and Gunther. "No kill shots unless absolutely necessary." They both stared at him as if he were crazy. Unspoken Mob rule 101 was that all shots were kill shots and a hitter never left loose ends. "Some of these guys are probably blindly following Captain Senalli's orders and probably had nothing to do with the attacks against us. Most of them probably don't even know who is inside the house."

"That was a lot of probablys," Gunther retorted.

"Yeah, man, like I don't like our chances if we're going to play it weak," Chito chided.

"Not weak," Andrew corrected. "Just careful."

"Ain't that the same thing, bro?" Chito quipped.

As they neared the ground Andrew directed his attention to Trig and instructed him to drop them and leave. "Once we're out, you get the hell out of here and wait until you hear from me or Chase. One of us will tell you where and who to pick up."

Setting her down, Trig held the chopper steady as Gunther, Andrew and Chito unloaded their weapons onto the grass. When the chopper lifted into the night sky, they grabbed their guns and made a dash toward the trees. Safely in the shadows, Andrew divvyed up the guns. Gunther carried a 357 magnum in a chest holster, a .45 pistol in his waistband and an assault rifle in his hands. Chito slung a handheld Uzi around his shoulder, had a 357 magnum tucked into his waistband and a .45 tightly in his grip. Andrew carried his .45, slung a rifle over his shoulder and wedged a 357 magnum into his waistband.

As they crept closer to the back of the house, they split up, Andrew heading straight for the garage, Chito heading to the left and Gunther to the right. Bending down, Andrew slowly squatted in the shadows and watched the guard pacing back and forth in front of the garage. He pulled a silencer from his interior jacket pocket and fastened it on to his .45.

A crunching sound from behind caused Andrew to whirl around with his gun, sending Tony face down to the ground. "It's me!" Tony whispered abrasively.

"You scared the crap out of me," Andrew scowled.

"I scared you? You just about took my head off," Tony berated.

"How'd you find me?" Andrew questioned as Tony crawled over and squatted next to him.

"I saw you land. Not too subtle, Ace." Andrew shook his head. What choice did he have? The cops were covering the entrance. "So, what's the plan?" Tony asked.

"Before you distracted me, I was about to take out the guard by the garage."

"You want me to do it for you?" Tony raised his .45 and took aim.

"The idea was for the shot to be silent," Andrew sneered, holding up his gun with the silencer attached and making an expression that said, *duh.* "I can do it."

"Then do it," Tony quipped.

"I'm not ready," Andrew uttered. He was trying to play out every scenario in his mind. If the shot wasn't heard, it would buy them some time to get inside unnoticed. If the shot was heard or if the body was immediately discovered, it would cause Senalli's men to flood the trees looking for the shooter. "This has to be timed perfectly."

Tony shook his head. "You're wound too tight, Ace. It's simple. Shoot the bad guys and rescue the girl. Don't overthink it."

"There's more than one damsel in distress inside. We've got to get Angel, Sophia, Olga and Mrs. Rosen out, preferably before everyone starts shooting." Andrew described the layout and told Tony where the guards were standing.

"Who's Mrs. Rosen?" Tony asked.

"She's sort of like a housekeeper. She was widowed and needed the work, and my dad felt sorry for her so he let her live here and take care of the estate."

"Where's your dad's escape tunnel?" Tony asked, as every Mafia Boss's home was built with at least one underground avenue of escape.

"It's on the left side and opens on the other side of the tree line; but I'm not sure it's a secure entrance." Andrew went on to explain that because of Rex's involvement with Emily, it was possible that she knew about the entrance and would have someone waiting there to ambush anyone who attempted to access it. "How many men are with you?" Andrew asked.

"Five, including me."

That, plus Andrew, Gunther and Chito made eight. When Alberto showed up, it would be nine; and if they could locate Big Mike and the Snake alive, they would have eleven. Eleven would be enough to put up a good fight. Tony took out his cell phone and text his guys, telling them to find the escape tunnel and work their way toward the house. The tunnel opened through the floorboards into the secret room that sat behind the bookshelf. They were told to get to that room and wait for further instructions.

Gunther, Chito, Tony and Andrew were on task to take out the guard in front of the garage. "There's a weapons room inside the garage," Andrew explained. "And I have a feeling we're going to need a lot more power."

"Unless they've already cleaned it out," Tony snipped. That was a possibility Andrew didn't like considering.

Holding his shirt close to his lips, Andrew whispered, "Chase, what's going on inside?" Before they put their plan into action, he wanted to make sure things hadn't escalated.

"The Captain is still talking," Chase answered.

"What about?" The Captain was usually a man of few words and Andrew couldn't imagine what topic could keep him droning on and on. All of a sudden, a thought popped into his head. "He's stalling," Andrew blurted.

"Who's stalling?" Tony asked.

"Captain Senalli. He's waiting for someone."

In the background, he could hear Chase's fingers dance across the keyboard. "Who do you think he's waiting for?"

"The Mayor," Andrew said without hesitating. It had to be the Mayor. Who else was involved and still alive? Ian Flanko was dead. Stephen Manucci was dead. Dr. Rainer was dead. Rex was dead. In fact, everyone that had any link to this entire thing was either inside his father's living room or already dead.

"That's one crazy-ass idea," Chase blurted. "Let me do some checking and I'll get back to you."

On the count of three, Tony and Andrew raced from the shelter of the shadows to the back of the garage, followed by Gunther and Chito. Andrew flanked around the side of the building and as the guard turned his back, he motioned for

239

Tony to join him, while Gunther and Chito went to the opposite side. They waited for the guard to turn again and then Andrew stepped out and put a bullet between his eyes. Tony dashed toward the body and he and Chito dragged him quickly through the side garage door.

"Clean up the blood," Andrew whispered to Gunther, who immediately began to push dirt and gravel atop the bloodiest spot in the driveway. The good news was that it was dark and from a distance no one would be able to see the blood on the ground, at least not until morning.

Three black SUV's were parked inside the five-car garage and Andrew slid by them, making his way toward a steel door located in the far corner. Punching in the code, the door slid open and Andrew retrieved several rounds of ammo, another handheld Uzi and two hand grenades. He tossed Tony the Uzi and some ammo.

"Looks like we're going to war," Tony quipped.

They were heading back outside when Chase's voice in his ear piece made Andrew stop in his tracks. "You're not gonna believe this," Chase uttered. "Channel 5 is at the entrance to your dad's estate broadcasting live and has just announced that the Mayor himself in on his way to the location of the alleged double homicide." Andrew could hear Chase fidgeting. "And get this, they've already announced that the victims in the double homicide were two Chicago Crime family Bosses."

"There aren't even two Bosses in there," Andrew huffed. "Angel's the only Boss."

"And you," Tony interjected, having been eavesdropping on Andrew's side of the conversation with Chase. Andrew locked eyes with Tony and the spectrum of his thoughts began to narrow. A flashback of conversations played in his head. Rex had called him Boss several times and referred to it as "old habits" when Andrew asked him to stop. How could it have been an old habit when Andrew had never been the family Boss? Had others been referring to him as the next family Boss? Also, Lisben had assumed that he had quit the force to take over the family, but Andrew had never officially tendered his resignation.

"They knew I'd come for her," Andrew uttered almost inaudibly, a devastating realization sinking in. "They're not waiting for the Mayor, they're waiting for me."

Andrew handed Tony his guns, except for the .45 that was holstered around his chest. "What are you doing, Ace?"

"It's simple. I'm going to shoot the bad guys and rescue the girl," he said, repeating Tony's earlier words.

"Oh, yeah? How do you plan to do that?" Tony posed. "The minute you walk in they're going to take your gun or maybe just shoot you right there."

"I stand corrected. You're going to shoot the bad guys and I'm going to rescue the girl," Andrew teased and Tony narrowed his brow. Andrew could tell he didn't like the idea. "What choice do we have?" He mumbled. "There are four women in there who are most likely not going to come out alive if we don't do something. We know they're already planning on killing Angel."

"And we can assume you are the other Boss they're planning on whacking, so why walk in there?" Tony stared blankly for a moment and then looked at Andrew as if he were studying him from the inside out. "You'd really die for her wouldn't you?"

"Wouldn't you?" Andrew shrugged.

Tony licked his lips. "No, but I'll kill for her. Let's do this."

The plan was for Andrew to walk into the downstairs door, leaving the door slightly ajar. While he made his way upstairs and to the living room, Tony and the rest of their men would immediately enter. Andrew instructed Gunther to give Tony his ear bud so that he could hear Chase. Gunther obediently dug it out of his ear and placed it in Tony's palm.

"This is more bodily fluid than I ever wanted to share with you," Tony quipped, pushing the bud into his right ear.

"Likewise," Gunther sneered. "I don't want it back."

Andrew pulled his shirt close to his lips and filled Chase in on the plan. He then dashed across the driveway, opened the door and stepped inside. The room was dark and he was somewhat surprised by the fact that the Captain hadn't assigned armed men to the lower level. It felt almost too easy. As soon as he neared the staircase he whispered, "Go" into his microphone and Chase gave Tony and the others the go-ahead to enter the house. It was imperative that they get into the house and hidden before Andrew was discovered, because once Andrew was seen, the Captain would assume that he hadn't come alone and begin searching for the others. It was their hope that Captain Senalli would send the guards from the living room to search the downstairs, at which time Tony, Gunther and Chito could easily pick them off.

Angel's eyes widened when she saw Andrew creep up the steps and place his hands in the air. "Who started the party without me?" He quipped sarcastically and the armed guard at the top of the stairs whirled around, flashing his gun in Andrew's face.

"Special Detective Venturini," Captain Senalli mused. "What a pleasant surprise." The

Captain rose from the leather chair and neared Andrew. "Or should I call you Don Venturini?"

Before Andrew could respond Sammy walked in from the kitchen. "Actually, you can call *me* Don Venturini," Sammy sneered.

CHAPTER 30

Angel's stomach knotted as she watched Andrew's expression upon seeing his brother. She could tell he was completely shocked by Sammy's involvement. Sammy grinned arrogantly at Andrew, while the armed guard searched him for a weapon, removed his .45 and then announced that he was clean. "Surprised to see me, brother?" Sammy mocked. "The big detective didn't see this one coming, did he?" He said to Captain Senalli and then smiled devilishly. "I have to say, Andrew, I expected more from you, but you played into our hands every step of the way; and now look at you. Daddy's favorite is gun-less, vest-less and gut-less."

"As usual, you've got things mixed up in your head," Andrew said calmly. "You're the gut-less one. You always have been. That's why dad was never going to let you take over the family."

Sammy's smile quickly faded. "Gut-less!" He seethed. "You think I don't have what it takes?" Sammy grabbed Andrew's .45 from the guard, stormed over to the dining room table and planted the barrel against Ricky Dente's forehead. Before anyone could utter a word, Sammy pulled the trigger and Ricky flipped backwards, blood splattering all over Emily, the table and the French doors. "How gut-less am I now?" He screamed.

"Merciful Heavens!" Olga gasped, while Sophia buried her face in her hands and Angel instinctively closed her eyes and leaned toward her mother. Mrs. Rosen sat stone-like, never even flinching at the sound of the shot.

Emily jumped to her feet cursing and stormed into the kitchen, returning momentarily with a wet cloth which she used to wipe Ricky's blood from her arm and cheek. "Was that really necessary?" She snipped.

"Now we don't have to pay him," Sammy grinned. "And Captain, let the record read that Andrew killed this man." Sammy sneered at Andrew. "After all, it was your gun."

"You two have been quite efficient at regulating the payroll for this project," the Captain interjected. "I ought to recommend you to the Mayor to help out with some of the city's budgeting issues."

Chase spoke into Angel's ear bud, "Tony, Gunther, and Chito are inside. Downstairs." Angel swallowed hard and tried not to let any emotion show on her face, which was not easy under the circumstances. "Listen carefully," Chase said. "There's a bathroom straight through the kitchen, left at the hallway and then the first right. There's a window in the bathroom. I need you to get to it and unlock it." Angel's heart sped up. How was she supposed to get to the bathroom? If she even requested using the bathroom it might set Sammy off again and Lord only knows who he would kill next. She licked her lips and gave her head a quick shake to indicate no.

"Boss lady, I know you've got to be scared shitless right now. I know I would be. This is one crazy-ass mother-fu...well, you know what I mean," he stopped himself before he fully cursed. "You're sitting in one secure-ass fortress with no second story windows except the one in the bathroom. From the staircase, Tony and the boys can't get a good enough angle to take out everyone without you, your mom, Olga and Mrs. Rosen getting caught in the crossfire."

Angel gave her head a quick twitch and Chase drew in a deep breath. "Alberto found the Snake and Big Mike and they're ready to move in, but we need the window unlocked so they can come in quietly and catch these crazy-ass mothers off guard." Angel's heart was racing and her mouth was beginning to go dry. She gave her head another quick twitch.

"I've seen you stare down a grenade launcher and walk out onto a pier in the middle of a war zone. You can do this," Chase said. "Boss Lady, your life depends on this. They've already got the news reporting that two Chicago Bosses were murdered there tonight. That's you and Andrew."

Swallowing the lump in her throat, Angel called out, "Sammy?" He spun in surprise and stared at her. Angel bit her lip. "I need to use the restroom." Sammy drew closer, his eyes penetrating and dark. Sliding onto the couch next to her, he took the barrel of his gun and ran it down the side of her left cheek.

"Instead of letting you relieve yourself, maybe I should just relieve the world of your presence?" He hissed.

"Knock it off!" Andrew hollered, drawing Sammy's attention away from Angel.

"Oh, you'll get yours brother, but first, I think I'll let you watch her die, so you can see that you failed to save her." Hate oozed from Sammy's eyes.

Captain Senalli exhaled loudly. "Just have Emily take her to the bathroom."

Sammy dragged the gun across Angel's chest. "Or I could take you," he seethed.

"I'll take her," Emily grunted and told Angel to get up.

As Angel rose from the couch, Chase cheered in her ear. "Right on, Boss Lady! That was shit-in-your-pants scary right there, but you rock!"

Emily nudged Angel along at gunpoint, past Ricky's body, through the French doors, across the long, narrow kitchen, left into the hallway and to the first door on the right. Angel noticed right away that Chase was right; there were no windows in the living room or in the kitchen. The bathroom was small, with a sink to the left, followed by the toilet and a window along the back wall. Looking at the size of the window, she couldn't imagine how it would be possible for Alberto, the Snake or Big Mike to fit through it, or how they were even going to get to the second story. Emily pushed her further into the bathroom and Angel held her hands up and slowly turned to face her. "Do you think I could do this alone?" Angel asked. "After all, you've already taken my gun and where am I going to go?"

Scowling at her, Emily rolled her eyes. "Fine, but the door stays unlocked and if you try anything, anything at all, I'll blow your head right off. You've got thirty seconds."

"Got it," Angel nodded. "I'll just be a second." She closed the door and quickly climbed atop the toilet seat so she could reach the window lock. Twisting the lock counterclockwise, she raised it ever so slightly, just to make sure it actually opened; and then pushed it back down, climbed from the toilet and hit the flushing lever. While the toilet flushed she quickly opened both drawers beneath the sink and the cabinet, in search of anything she might be able to use as a weapon; but there was nothing.

Emily pushed open the door as Angel began to wash her hands. "Can I ask you something?" Angel said.

"What?" Emily motioned with the gun for Angel to hurry up.

"How did you get the code to the elevator in the Towers?" Angel knew the information had to have come from Rex but she was trying to figure out if Rex was truly a traitor or if he had merely been used to gain information. Angel was having trouble accepting the idea that Rex was all bad, especially after learning from Sal that his record was squeaky-clean. After all, he had delivered Joseph Venturini safely to the morgue, and he had helped Andrew find her when she was missing in the hospital. It didn't make sense.

"None of your business," Emily spat.

"Will he be here later?" Angel asked and Emily lifted one eyebrow. "Rex? Is he coming?"

"I don't think that's possible," Emily snickered sarcastically and Angel knew by her reaction that Rex was most likely dead. "My Boss doesn't like to leave loose ends."

A shiver ran up the back of Angel's neck at the mention of the phrase "loose ends." Emily sounded exactly like Giovanni when she said it and it made the hair on the back of Angel's neck stand erect.

CHAPTER 31

"How much longer are we going to wait?" Sammy seethed, pacing back and forth between the dining room table and the bookshelf.

"He'll be here," the Captain hissed back and one didn't have to be a detective to realize something wasn't going according to their plan.

Chase's voice filled Angel's ears. "I'm transmitting to all ear pieces so listen up and remain calm." Angel saw Olga jump out of the corner of her eye. "This just keeps getting better and better," Chase quipped. "Sal's starting to upload data from the ID recognition search and I'm going to sum up what we know." Chase took in a deep breath. "Mrs. Rosen is not a victim in this game. In fact, she might be the crazy-ass mastermind behind the whole thing."

Olga narrowed her eyes and glared at Mrs. Rosen.

"Don't stare at her!" Chase blurted. "Don't look directly at anyone I'm going to talk about. It will be obvious there's some form of communication taking place, if all of you make eye contact with the same person at the same time."

Sophia lowered her eyes to the floor and Angel locked hers with Andrew.

"Mrs. Rosen's name is Martha Craden, well, that's her maiden name and also one of her aliases for a whole laundry list of criminal activity. Rosen is the other name she's used. She married Rinaldo Rosenalli and birthed a daughter named Amelia. That's right, you guessed it, Amelia is our very own crazy-assassin-ass nurse Emily, and her list of criminal infractions is longer than her mamas."

Angel saw Andrew's jaw tighten and heard Olga make a muffled humph sound.

"It gets better," Chase quipped. "Rinaldo Rosenalli was executed earlier this year, on the order of Joseph Venturini. Rinaldo's name was on the list we confiscated from the Tamolskaya Russian operatives who had infiltrated the families. We originally thought it to be a list of traitors within the families and discovered too late that it was a listing our loyal members."

Angel felt a sour pit sink deeper into her stomach. It all made sense now. Mrs. Rosen wanted revenge for her husband's death; revenge on the Venturini family and on Angel. That's why she had spoken with Angel about the list the very first time they had met. All of the dots were connecting and the realization that they may not make it out alive was beginning to sink in.

"We're still working on tying in Captain Senalli's connection," Chase said.

Angel and Andrew stared at one another from across the room. She could see the wheels spinning in his brain, as his experienced detective mind tried to piece the puzzle together.

"Andrew," Chase's voice rang through everyone's ear buds, "I need you to get away from the staircase."

CHAPTER 32

Andrew took three steps toward the fireplace and Sammy shoved his gun in his face. "Where do you think you're going?" He seethed.

"I'm going to sit down," Andrew answered calmly. "I've been on my feet all day and since we're obviously waiting for someone, I'd like to wait sitting down." He walked past the fireplace, scooted past Angel and Sophia and sat down on the couch next to Olga.

Sammy grunted. "You have no idea what we're waiting for, isn't that right, babe?" He turned to Emily with a grin, looped his arm around her waist and pulled her close, shoving his tongue in her mouth in what Angel considered to be a vulgar display of affection.

"Ugh, I think I'm gonna hurl," Chase quipped into their ear buds and Olga cracked a smile.

"Merciful Heavens!" She gasped quietly, but it was loud enough to set Sammy off. He whirled around, pointing the gun at Olga.

"You got something to say, old lady?" Sammy huffed and Olga's eyes bulged.

"Don't worry about it, baby," Emily soothed him. "They'll all be dead soon anyway."

A clanging sound from the other side of the French doors drew everyone's attention and Angel's heart raced, knowing it was probably Alberto, the Snake or Big Mike trying to get through the window. Captain Senalli sent the guard who had been standing next to the bookcase to check out the noise and he quickly disappeared through the

French doors and into the kitchen. For a few seconds, the room was dead quiet and then, there was an enormous explosion that shook the walls and shattered the French doors, throwing shards of glass across the room. Everyone instinctively ducked and Emily and Sammy dove toward the steps. Mrs. Rosen fell against the fireplace, and Captain Senalli called out, "Mom!" He then grabbed Mrs. Rosen and quickly helped her to her feet.

"Mom?" Angel thought. Could the Captain be Mrs. Rosen's son and Emily's brother? Angel studied all of their faces and suddenly saw a striking resemblance, especially between Emily and Captain Senalli.

"I heard that hot juicy piece of information," Chase blurted into their ear buds. "Looks like this might be a family affair, here. Hold tight, I'm checking with Sal."

The Captain yelled for the other two guards to investigate the explosion, which Angel thought to be a big mistake. She knew if her men had indeed made it into the house, the guards he sent would be dead in a matter of seconds.

Captain Senalli pulled a gun from a holster inside his jacket, stormed angrily toward Angel, gripped her by the throat and pulled her to her feet. "You're with me," he sneered, using Angel as a human shield and inching his way toward the kitchen.

"Senalli!" Andrew cried out. "I'll be your shield. Let her go."

Out of the corner of her eye, Angel saw Tony move quickly up the first two steps, rifle in hand. She forced herself to look the other way, not wanting to give away his position.

"Good," Chase said. "Andrew, keep him facing your way. Keep his funky-ass attention on you so Tony can take the shot. Angel, you need to lower your chin to your chest and for God's sake don't move."

Angel's heart was beating so rapidly she thought she was going to hyperventilate. She tried to control her breathing and remind herself of the fact that Tony was a great shot. If anyone could hit a tiny target at a great distance, it was Tony. Still, she didn't like the idea of being so close to the target. It felt as if everything around her shifted into slow motion. Turning her head toward Sophia, she saw her mother make the sign of the cross over her body, and then grip Olga's hand and begin to pray the Lord's prayer in Italian. Olga's eyes were wide and fearful. Andrew was standing next to Olga, yelling at the Captain, but the words were fuzzy in her ears, as if they were muffled beneath the sound of her own breathing. Just as Angel closed her eyes and dropped her chin to her chest, she heard the shot. Captain Senalli's grip went limp and he fell splattering blood all over the dining room and knocking Angel into the broken glass of the French doors.

"No!" Wailed Mrs. Rosen, as she dove across the room toward her son, throwing herself on top of him.

Sammy rose to his feet with his gun extended; taking aim at Angel, but Tony took him out with two shots at the knees, while Andrew raced toward Sammy and grabbed his gun before he could fire off another shot. Emily cowered beneath Andrew's aim, trying to console Sammy, who was writhing in pain. Gunther and Chito raced up the steps.

"Damn, I missed all the action," Chito blurted, while Gunther made a beeline to Olga and Sophia.

"You can frisk Emily and find out where she hid her gun," Andrew told Chito and then stepped away and spoke into the microphone on his shirt. "Chase, we need an ambulance for Sammy."

"Already on it," Chase answered.

Chito grinned a wicked smile. "With pleasure," he said and moved toward Emily, ordering her to stand up and hold her hands above her head. "This is my kind of action," he uttered. "Mamacita is lookin' hot." He ran his hand up and down her body, searching for a weapon, retrieving a gun she had stashed in the back of her jeans. "That was too easy. Maybe I should search some more."

Angel stepped away from the French doors, trying not to look down at Captain Senalli's body. She took two steps backwards, the glass crunching beneath her feet and then felt arms wrap around her waist. It was Tony.

"How you doin', Babe?" Tony spun her around to face him.

"Nice shot," she mumbled, still shaking from the experience.

"We've got two unmarked vehicles heading up the driveway," Chase blurted into their ear pieces.

"How many men?" Andrew asked.

"Can't confirm that yet," Chase quipped. "Working on it now."

Andrew paraded back over to where Sammy lie on the ground, gripping what was left of his knees and thrashing in agony. He aimed his .45 at Sammy's head. "Who are they?" He demanded.

"I don't know," Sammy wailed. "I swear, I don't know."

Tony released Angel and pulled his buzzing cell phone from his pants pocket. "My men are at the floorboard entrance of the tunnel," Tony told Andrew. "What do you want to do?"

Andrew spoke into his button. "Chase, direct Trig to the entrance of the escape tunnel.

It's to the north. Tell him to set down but keep the chopper running."

"Right on," Chase answered.

"Gunther and Chito, you take Olga, Sophia and Angel out the escape tunnel and get them safely into the chopper. Then get the hell out of here," Andrew ordered.

"Big Mike and Alberto are outside in the woods," Chase said. "They'll pick off as many they can as they exit their vehicles."

"Negative on that," Andrew blurted. "I want to see who is inside those vehicles and if we start firing we'll never get a glimpse of who's behind this."

Tony handed Sophia and Olga each a gun. "In case you need to protect yourself in the tunnel," he said.

"Where's the Snake?" Andrew questioned.

"Right here." His voice came from the kitchen and his boots crunched against the broken glass as he stepped through the French doors. "I had to get in through the window and set the grenade, and then get as far away from it as possible before detonation."

"Did you take out the guards?" Tony asked.

"All but one," the Snake answered. "I thought you might want to have a look," he said to Andrew. The guard was seated in one of the kitchen chairs and hunched over the table. He had been shot in the left leg and in the right shoulder.

"What's the problem, Ace? Just kill him," Tony blurted.

"I thought he might be more useful alive," the Snake retorted. "See, he's not from around here." A dark gleam in The Snake's eyes told Angel that something was very wrong.

CHAPTER 33

Andrew showed Gunther and Chito how to access the bookcase door and then unlocked the floorboards for Tony's men. After a brief introduction and review of the plan, they headed down into the tunnel. Tony's men went first, since they were familiar with the layout, followed by Chito and then Olga. Sophia refused to descend the ladder until Angel was with her and Angel was still talking to Andrew, Tony and the Snake in the kitchen.

"Ms. Buscetta, I urge you to leave now," Gunther said, but Sophia shook him off.

"I'll see what's keeping Angel," she said and strode back through the bookcase door and into the living room. She could hear Angel and the men's voices coming from the kitchen and so she headed that way, trying not to look at Sammy, who was bleeding all over the place, Emily, who was now handcuffed to the staircase railing or the bodies of Ricky Dente and Captain Senalli. All of a sudden, a cold reality hit. Mrs. Rosen was no longer crouched over her son. Sophia scanned the room, but it was too late, she felt the hard barrel against the back of her head.

"You and me are going to get out of here," Mrs. Rosen whispered. "You're going to help me."

Sophia didn't scream or panic. She didn't have to because she knew that Chase could see what was happening. Although, she wondered why he hadn't alerted her to the fact that Mrs. Rosen was sneaking up behind. "Listen," Sophia said calmly, raising her palms as high as her shoulders.

"You can just walk out of here. You don't need me. They're all busy in the kitchen and won't even notice until you're long gone."

"Mom," Emily whispered. "Don't leave me here."

"We've got trouble," Chase barked into their ear buds. "Hostage situation in the living room! Man, dealing with female assailants is like trying to herd a bunch of sneaky-ass cats. I can't look away for a second."

Andrew, Tony and Angel rushed from the kitchen, stopping just on the other side of the French doors. Before anyone could speak, Mrs. Rosen barked out orders. "Andrew, you're going to un-cuff Emily and she and I are going to walk out of here safely."

"Not with Sophia," Tony rebutted.

Mrs. Rosen narrowed her eyes and pursed her pointy lips. "If you want Sophia to live through this, you'll let me and Emily go."

Andrew stepped forward. "You know we can't do that, Martha, and even if we did, you'd spend the rest of your life, which would be a very short time, looking over your shoulder." Andrew took another step closer. "Why don't you let me help you and Emily? If you turn yourself in and tell me who is behind this whole thing, I can guarantee you police protection."   Mrs. Rosen scoffed. "You're not even a cop anymore, and as soon as word gets out that you killed the Police Captain, there will be a bounty on your head. The other officers will be after you."

Chase piped in, "I don't mean to hurry your wild-asses along or anything, but we've got men exiting the vehicles as we speak."

"How many?" Andrew asked.

"How many?" Mrs. Rosen questioned, unaware that Andrew was talking into a microphone. "Every officer will be lining up to kill you!"

Tony lifted his piece and took aim. "Forget this, Ace, we're out of time. I'm gonna drop her."

"No!" Emily screamed. "I'll talk. I'll tell you whatever you want. Don't shoot her."

Angel took a step toward Mrs. Rosen and Sophia. "Let her go," she said to Mrs. Rosen. "She has nothing to do with any of this. I was the reason your husband was executed. I was the one who misunderstood the list of names."

Hate filled Mrs. Rosen's eyes. "You! You think everything is about you. The only female Boss. The special one. Well, everything is not about you!" Mrs. Rosen seethed. "It's about HER!" She pulled Sophia's hair so hard that her neck whipped backwards and Sophia winced in pain.

"What do you mean it's about her?" Angel posed.

Gunther approached from the bookcase door with his gun extended. "I've got a clean shot from here," he said.

"I say you take it, Ace," Tony blurted.

"What do you mean this whole thing is about me?" Sophia re-stated Angel's question. She had never even met Mrs. Rosen and had nothing to do with her husband's death so how could everything be about her?

Tears formed in Emily's eyes. "Just tell them, mom." Emily kicked her feet and then let her shoulders sink down, as if in that moment she bore the weight of the world on her shoulders. "Daddy's dead, Charles is dead, they're just going to kill us too."

"Who's Charles?" Tony asked.

"Captain Senalli," Andrew answered, never taking his eyes from Mrs. Rosen. "His name was Charles Senalli."

"Charles Rinaldo Rosenalli, Jr." Mrs. Rosen's voice cracked with emotion as she spoke her son's name and big crocodile tears formed in her eyes and cascaded down her cheeks. Loosening her grip on Sophia, she lowered her gun to the floor. "My son," she whimpered and Sophia felt compassion tug at her heart. She knew what it was like to be widowed. She knew what it was like to have the mob destroy everything you loved. If she had been influenced by the wrong people at a critical time, Sophia could have become just like Mrs. Rosen, driven by hate and seeking revenge.

"Guys! They're pulling out several big-ass grenade launchers and it looks like they're gonna torch the place. You need to get out of there now!" Chase yelled through their ear buds.

Andrew hollered for the Snake, who hurried through the French doors, dragging the guard over his back and shoulders. "We'll take him for questioning," the Snake barked and headed toward the bookcase. Andrew unlocked Emily from the staircase and re-cuffed her hands together in front of her body, so she could maneuver down the ladder and into the tunnel. Gunther carried Sammy over his shoulder and Tony pushed Emily and Mrs. Rosen at gun point while Angel and Sophia grabbed hands and raced toward the bookcase. Andrew started for the bookcase, then stopped and ran back toward Captain Senalli's body. Flipping him over, he pulled out his cell phone, his wallet and his police ID badge, shoved them into his pocket and dashed across the room.

"Get out! Get out! Get out!" Chase yelled. The squealing sound of incoming artillery filled the air just as Andrew closed the bookcase. A sudden explosion turned the house into an inferno.

"Holy Shit!" Chase yelped into their ear buds. "I've lost visual contact, are you all there?

Did everyone make it out?" There was silence for several seconds and Chase cursed aloud.

"Affirmative," Andrew answered breathlessly. "We're all here."

CHAPTER 35

The tunnel was so dark that Angel felt as if the walls were closing in. She literally couldn't see the person in front of her or her own feet. They were all being led by the shuffling sound of Tony's men ahead of them. Everyone was quiet, with the exception of Olga who never stopped talking and Chito who was obviously afraid of the dark because he shrieked like a little girl every few steps.

"Chito, this is embarrassing, dude," Chase's voice came through their ear buds. "Man up."

"Yeah, Ace," Tony teased. "I thought you Cobras lived in tunnels below the city."

"We got lights down there, man," Chito defended.

Sammy, who was draped over Gunther's shoulder, periodically moaned in the darkness until he finally lost consciousness. Using his cell phone as a light, Andrew unhooked Emily's handcuffs and cuffed her to Mrs. Rosen, which then allowed Tony to grasp the cuffs in the middle and more easily drag them both along. It felt as if it took forever until the tunnel opening came into sight.

The chopper was on the other side of the tree line, exactly where Andrew had instructed Trig to land. Big Mike and Alberto were supposed to meet everyone at the tunnel opening, but they weren't there yet. "Merciful Heavens," Olga blurted breathlessly. "My knee highs are rolling down around my ankles. I've never walked so far so fast."

They had kept up a decent pace and Angel hadn't even thought about how difficult the jaunt would be for Olga. "We're almost there," Andrew assured her. "Straight through the trees and into the chopper and then you can relax."

"Well, let's do this then," Olga said, slapping her hands together and stepping through the tunnel opening. One of Tony's men hurried to get in front of her. After all, she was the sister of the Capo di Tutti Capi and it was thereby the unspoken responsibility of any and all family members to protect her. Another of Tony's men helped the Snake drag the armed guard out of the tunnel and into the woods, followed by Gunther carrying Sammy, Tony pulling Emily and Mrs. Rosen, Chito walking next to Angel and Sophia, probably because he was afraid to walk alone in the dark, and then Andrew and the two other Andriachini men who brought up the rear. Once they were all in the shadows of the woods, Tony instructed his men to retrieve their vehicle and bring it as close as possible to the chopper location. "We all aren't gonna fit in the chopper and I don't think we should make multiple trips," Tony deduced and Andrew agreed.

"Chase," Andrew spoke into his microphone. "Where's the Tank? Can you have Alberto or Big Mike bring the Tank and another vehicle to our location?"

"Working on it," Chase responded.

They could hear sirens off in the distance and the billowing smoke from Andrew's father's house filled the night sky. There was a growing sense of urgency among the group and Angel surmised that it was because they all realized that they needed to get out of there quickly. Not only were they sitting ducks without transportation, but undoubtedly media helicopters would be arriving soon and hovering over the Venturini estate to get an aerial view of the explosion. Other choppers in the night sky might provide coverage for Trig to get some of them out unnoticed. Then again, there was no guarantee and Angel knew that it wouldn't be hard for someone to shoot them right out of the sky with the same type of weapon they used to blow up Joseph Venturini's home.

The Snake let the guard he was carrying slide to the ground and then scooted him into a propped position against a tree. Angel then watched as he winced and stretched his back. Obviously carrying the guard all that distance had taken its toll on the Snake.

"Merciful Heavens, I can see the chopper from here," Olga snorted. "What are we waiting for?"

"Ssshhh," Andrew breathed, holding d up his palm. "Everybody get down," he whispered and Angel and Sophia lowered into a squatting position.

"What do you got, Ace?" Tony asked.

"Listen..." Andrew's voice faded and Angel strained her ears. She heard the whirring of helicopter blades in the distance, what sounded like the slamming of car doors and then, a very quiet, very distinct sound. It was the crunching of leaves beneath someone's feet. It was the sound of someone approaching.

Gunther laid Sammy down and pulled Olga, who was the only one still standing, onto the ground, simultaneously covering her mouth with his hand. It was obvious that he expected a verbal objection and was proactively heading it off. Chito readied his gun and peered into the darkness.

"Chase," Andrew whispered into his microphone. "We're sitting ducks and I think we've got company. Are we clear to approach the chopper?"

Chase's voice rang through their ear buds. "I've got no visual other than the sporadic images from the body cameras, but in the dark I can't see anything," he responded and Angel could tell by his tone that he was frustrated. "Sal is pulling up an infrared feed so I'll at least be able to tell you if someone is approaching, but it's going to take a few minutes."

Angel could sense that Andrew didn't think they had a few minutes and her pulse quickened. The guard leaning against the tree began to mumble, reaching with his left hand and fidgeting with his shirt collar. The Snake inched closer.

"What's he saying?" Tony asked.

The Snake shrugged. "He's speaking Italian, I think, but it has a different sound to it; maybe a different dialect or slang?" The man tugged and tugged at his collar until the Snake unbuttoned the top button and he reached inside and pulled out a gold chain with a cross dangling from the end.

"Grazie," he mumbled.

Tony left Emily and Mrs. Rosen on the ground and crawled over to the guard. Placing his ear toward the man's lips, he listened intently as the man prayed the Lord's Prayer in Italian. Angel could barely hear him, but she recognized several words. When he had finished praying, Tony asked him in Italian to name the man for whom he was working.

"La nostra missione non deve fallire, dobbiamo legare tutti," the man mumbled.

"Our mission must not fail. We must tie up all loose ends," Tony translated.

There was that terrible phrase again. Why was everyone talking about loose ends all of a sudden? It sent shivers up the back of Angel's neck.

"Non dobbiamo essere slegati con gli stati della corruzione, ma la nostra libertà e indipendenza."

"We must not be united with the states of corruption but demand our freedom and independence," Tony repeated in English.

"Independence from whom?" Angel asked and Tony translated her question into Italian.

"Voi, qui, gli Stati membri," the man uttered and then spit toward the ground.

"He said they want independence from you, here, from the States," Tony explained.

"From me?" Angel puzzled.

Sophia inched closer to the guard and spoke quietly. "Il mio nome è Sophia Buscetta, sapete chi sono io?"

"Sì. Siamo venuti per portare a casa," he mumbled and Angel beheld both shock and fear wash over her mother's face.

"What is it? What did he say?" Angel questioned, but Sophia didn't respond. She quickly looked to Tony and then to Andrew for a translation but both of them appeared as stunned as her mother. Spinning around on the ground, Angel faced Olga and her expression confirmed the worst. Whatever this man had said, it rendered all of them speechless.

"Don't look at me," Chito quipped. "It all sounded like mush to me."

Suddenly, two shots rang out and bullets ricocheted off the trees. Olga screamed while everyone else ducked and retrieved their weapons. More shots were fired but it was impossible to tell from which direction they came. They instinctively pressed their backs together and held their weapons out in front. "We've got to split up," Tony blurted. "We're too big a group, too easy a target."

"Agreed," Andrew huffed and ordered Gunther and Chito to get Olga, Sophia and Angel out of there. "Try to get to the chopper and take off. We'll cover you from here.

"No!" Angel objected. "We're not leaving you guys behind."

"With all due respect, Babe, you don't have a choice," Tony chided and then stood up, flipped Angel over his shoulder and took off in a dead sprint toward the edge of the trees and the awaiting chopper. Gunther looped Olga's arm and hurried behind them but Sophia didn't move.

"Sophia, you've got to go now!" Andrew scolded, but she appeared to be in a daze.

"C'mon chica, we've got to go," Chito begged.

"He's Sicilian," Sophia said quietly, ignoring Chito's pleas. "He is one of my own people."

"Sì. Se non ritorno Cosa Nostra sarà distrutto. Il padre verrà ucciso dalla Stidda," the man muttered low and emphatically.

Sophia gasped in horror and Andrew took her hand and squeezed it tenderly. "You must leave now," he warned. "You've got to get in the chopper and go."

"Holy Shiznick!" Chase's voice filled their ear buds. "There are people everyone. I can see them on the infrared feed by their body heat, but I can't tell you who's a friendly and who's not so you got to get your crazy-asses out of there! Trig get her airborne now!"

"No!" Angel yelled, even though she knew Chase probably couldn't hear her. After all that had happened, she wasn't even sure if her camera was still attached or working. "Not without my mom!"

Tony dashed back into the trees to find Sophia.

"Go!" Andrew yelled at Sophia. "Chito, take her!"

"What about you and him?" Sophia exclaimed.

"I'll bring him! Go now!" Andrew yelled.

Just as she stood to run toward the chopper, another shot rang out and this time it was followed by what sounded like a barrage of rapid gunfire and then silence. Sophia dove forward, flattening herself on the ground but Chito kept running. He ran in a dead sprint and dove into the helicopter. Emily wailed loudly and the Snake crawled toward her and Mrs. Rosen, noticing instantly that Mrs. Rosen had taken several bullets to the chest and was dead. He hollered to Andrew, who threw him the keys to the handcuffs and he quickly released Emily from her mother's wrist.

"Get them out of here!" Andrew yelled, as Tony and the Snake pulled Sophia from the ground and dragged her and Emily toward the chopper. By the time they reached the clearing Trig had already lifted the chopper with only Chito, Angel, Gunther and Olga inside. Tony swore aloud as they pulled the women back into the shadows of the woods.

Barreling through the grassy clearing in the Tank, Big Mike and Alberto were a sight for sore eyes. The Snake rushed Emily and Sophia to the Tank while Tony hurried back to get Sammy and help Andrew, who had lifted the guard over his shoulder and was making his way through the trees. Tony bent over Sammy to lift him from the ground and realized instantly that he was dead.

Rushing back to Andrew, Tony blocked his path. "Put him down, Ace," he said.

"What are you, crazy?" Andrew barked. "He could be the only person left that can lead us to whoever is behind this whole thing." Andrew maneuvered around Tony. "Grab Sammy and let's go."

"He's not gonna lead you anywhere," Tony barked and then cleared his throat. "And neither is Sammy."

Andrew slid the guard off of his shoulder and watched as he fell in a heap to the ground; his head almost completely blown off. Glancing over at Sammy's body, Andrew swallowed hard and then he bent down and pulled the golden cross necklace from the guard's body.

CHAPTER 36

Back at the Towers, they all gathered in the secret meeting room and tried to make sense out of everything that had transpired. They were muddy and blood-soaked, but more than that, they were confused. Pacing in front of the windows, Angel chewed on her fingernail and tried to make sense out of what had happened. Who had the resources to pull this off? How was Sophia connected? No one spoke for a long time. Instead, they took turns using the restroom, washing their hands and scrubbing dirt or blood from their faces and arms. With the help of Tino, Olga and Sophia served coffee, hot tea, Cannoli and Cinnamon Strudel and turned the bar into a mini-buffet. "It's going to be a late night," Olga told Angel, "and nothing keeps the mind alert like a little caffeine and sugar."

Chase was fidgeting behind three laptops, preoccupied with uploading images to Sal for possible ID recognition and running them through his database as well.

Sophia telephoned and left a message for Salvatore. It was possible that he hadn't returned home to Sicily yet, as no one was certain of the exact route he had taken. A man of his position had contacts throughout Italy and Sicily so he may have stopped any number of places along the way. Angel knew that Sophia was anxious to talk with him about whatever the guard had said to her before he died. They were all hopeful that Salvatore could shed light on what was happening.

When everyone had a chance to get something to eat and drink, Giovanni took a seat at the head of the table, with Angel to his left, then Chase, Andrew, the Snake and Gunther. To Giovanni's right sat Sophia, Olga, Tony and Big Mike. Trig and Chito stood guard at the elevator outside of the meeting room, while Tino stood guard at the front doors to the Towers and Alberto stood guard one floor up, outside of the holding room where Emily sat with her wrists and ankles duct taped.

"Here it is," Chase said, twirling a pencil in his fingers. "The Mayor's about to speak." He transferred the feed to the big screen and they all watched as Mayor Tompkins stepped up to the podium filled with microphones from every major network.

"It is with both sadness and hope that I address you this evening. The corruption in our city has run deep into our own Chicago police force. Captain Charles Senalli was murdered this evening in a mob related attack by the Venturini family, particularly the new head of the family, Special Investigator, Andrew Venturini. His father was murdered earlier this week, as were his brothers and we have substantial reason to believe that Andrew Venturini murdered his family so that he could take over as the next Don. Captain Senalli was killed while attempting to apprehend him." Chase muted the feed and shook his head.

"This is crazy-ass effed up, man," Chase snarled.

Andrew lowered his head, his jaw tightening and his face tinting an angry shade of red. Angel wanted to console him but there was nothing she could say. He had lost his family, his career and was now being accused of crimes he didn't commit. The whole city would be against him.

"Senalli was my hit," Tony blurted. "I was the trigger man."

"My condolences to you Andrew," Giovanni said and then cleared his throat. "These are life altering events and we will deal with them. Now is not the time to get caught up in personal loss. This battle is not over. There are more loose ends to be tied."

There was that phrase again. It sent a shudder through Angel every time she heard it. Giovanni said it, Emily had said it and all of a sudden, the light bulb went on in Angel's mind. Salvatore had said it too. He said it in reference to Olga, but it was said nonetheless. "Is there mafia significance to the term 'loose ends'?" Angel asked.

"Estremità libere," Giovanni sighed. "They are very dangerous."

"I understand that, but is there some other significance?" Angel couldn't escape the feeling that that particular phrase was old and held a deeper meaning.

"No, Babe," Tony said. "Everyone knows you don't leave any loose ends because they'll come back to bite you in the ass."

Giovanni lowered his brows and shook his head and then motioned toward Chase. "Perhaps we should begin with a review of what we know to be certain."

Chase nodded, put his pencil between his teeth and let his fingers fly wildly across the keyboards of all three laptops. When he finally stopped, Mrs. Rosen's picture shown on the big screen with a picture of Rinaldo Rosenalli, Emily and Captain Senalli. "Meet the Rosenalli family," Chase quipped, bouncing excitedly from his seat and walking toward the big screen with a red laser pointer in hand. "This is Martha Craden," he said as he put the pointer in the middle of her forehead. "She obviously became Martha Rosenalli after marrying Rinaldo." Chase moved the pointer to Rinaldo's forehead. "They got busy and had Emily

271

and the Captain." Chase stood back and circled all of them with the laser pointer. "One big family of crazy-ass whack jobs, right there; but don't get too attached, they're almost all dead," he joked.

"Perhaps we could move this along?" Giovanni grunted, obviously not impressed with Chase's laser pointing antics.

"What you might not know is that Martha wasn't a virgin when she wed 'ol Rinaldo here. She had been hob-knobbing with Mayor Tompkins before he was the Mayor, of course," Chase explained and then took a breath before continuing.

"Before and after," Andrew interjected and was met with expressions of surprise around the table. He proceeded to explain what Mayor Tompkins had told him in the hospital about his affair with Martha. "The Mayor said Martha threatened to go public with their affair if he didn't meet with her in the old alley cellar the night of the CoBroGas attack."

Skepticism shown on Giovanni's face. "Do you believe his story?"

"Not entirely," Andrew responded. "I believe he and Martha had a relationship in college and that they reconnected after they were both married to other people; but beyond that his story has holes."

Chase rushed toward the table, plunked back into his seat and began clicking across his keyboard. "This just keeps getting better and better," he muttered to himself.

"Something you want to share with the class, Ace?" Tony chided.

Chase glanced over the top of his laptop. "Like I said, Martha wasn't a virgin and what I was about to tell you was that she had another child prior to marrying Rinaldo." His fingers danced across the keyboard. "I didn't bother to look the

272

father's name because I didn't think it would be relevant, but if the father was Mayor Tompkins, well, that's a whole 'nother set of crazy-ass circumstances right there."

"Emily may be able to shed some light on all of this," Andrew said.

Big Mike instantly stood up. "I'll go get her." Giovanni gave a nod of approval and Big Mike left the room.

Angel glanced at her mother who sat, statue-like, staring down at the top of the table. "While Chase searches, I'd like to ask a question," Angel announced. "The guard that the Snake nabbed said something while we were in the woods…something that left all of you speechless. Anyone want to share that juicy piece of information?" She tried not to sound sarcastic, but it had been driving her crazy.

No one answered. They all looked to Sophia, as if they were waiting for her to grant permission to disclose the translation. She blinked slowly and then let out an exasperated sigh. "He sounded Sicilian and so I asked if he knew who I was…"

"Why would you assume he knew of you?" Giovanni interjected.

"Because Mrs. Rosen, I mean, Martha, had said that this whole thing was about me." Sophia's voice cracked with emotion and Angel could tell that, for some reason, her mother was feeling somehow responsible for the CoBroGas attack and Joseph's death.

"This isn't your fault, mom," Angel added but Giovanni cut her off.

"What did the Sicilian say to you?" His nostrils flared. It was no secret that the Italians and the Sicilians were long-time rivals.

Swallowing hard, Sophia interpreted their brief conversation. "I asked him if he knew me and

he said yes, that he had come to take me home."
Tears formed in her eyes. "He said that if I did not
return, the Cosa Nostra would be destroyed and
my father would be murdered by the Stidda."

"Stidda!" Giovanni exploded; his face
turning bright red. He pounded his fist on the
table and ranted something seemingly hostile in
Italian, but Angel couldn't understand a word of it.
Judging by Olga's bulging eyeballs and the
shocked expressions on Tony and Andrew, she
knew that whatever he had said was not good.

"Merciful Heavens!" Olga gasped. "You've
got to control your temper before you give yourself
a heart attack," she scolded Giovanni.

Giovanni turned toward Chase. "I want to
know if Stidda is in this city!" He seethed and
Chase's fingers flew across the keys.

"Who is Stidda?" Angel posed.

"Stidda means star in Italian," Sophia said
quietly.

"La Stidda is a mafia-want-to-be
organization. Their members are known as
stiddari and they are enemies of the Cosa Nostra,"
Giovanni rambled.

"Where did they come from?" Angel asked.
"Are they here in the States?"

"No, at least none of which I am aware.
They originated in Sicily as an off-shoot of
disgruntled Cosa Nostra members," Giovanni
explained and Sophia interjected.

"They formed in the late eighties and were
somewhat low profile," she said. "They're made up
of many smaller factions that operate
independently. Here in the States they would be
more like street gangs."

"To take on the Cosa Nostra would mean
they have come together as one powerful
organization," Giovanni added.

Chase clicked on his keypad and a picture of a man's hand appeared on the big screen. "According to the internet, Stidda members have a star-shaped tattoo between their thumb and index finger that looks like this," Chase said. "Man, that's gotta be a painful-ass place for a tattoo."

Giovanni glanced around the table. "Have any of you encountered anyone with this marking?" Everyone shook their heads to indicate they had not.

"Stars," Andrew muttered quietly and then tightened his jaw and cursed under his breath. "The stars," he repeated, this time loud enough that everyone could hear him. "Just before Manucci died, he said 'the stars.'"

"I'll be damned, you're right," Chase uttered. "He was trying to tell us that Stidda was here."

"Then Emily killed him because she knew that he was working against Stidda," Tony added. "Which proves that Emily is Stidda."

"That's what we'll find out as soon as she gets here," Angel remarked.

Big Mike raced through the door with Chito and Trig behind him. "She's dead," he muttered out-of-breath. Alberto and I entered the room to get Emily and she was dead.

"How did she die?" Angel blurted.

"I don't know. There's no exterior wound," Big Mike uttered.

"Check her mouth for a cyanide capsule," Chase said in monotone. "That's how she killed Manucci so it's stands to reason that's how she'd kill herself." Big Mike and Alberto carried Emily's body to the secret meeting room and laid her in one of the hospital beds that still lined the far left wall. Prying open her mouth, Chase used his pencil to dig into her back molar and retrieve a tiny casing. "Bingo," he blurted. "I'd bet my balls if we sent this to a lab it would show traces of cyanide."

"Clean up this mess." Giovanni waved his hand and mumbled in disgust.

Chase's cell phone beeped and he hit the speaker button as he walked back to the conference table to sit down. "You're on speaker. Talk to me, Sal-baby," he said.

"I've run Manucci's phone through our database, as well as Rex's and Emily's. There are no phone calls between Rex and Manucci or between Emily and Manucci and only one call between Emily and Rex," Sal explained and this information fit with Angel's gut feeling about Rex being used for information and not really being a player in the game. Sal continued. "The last call Manucci made from his phone was to a Chicago number, but I've run it and it shows up as a temporary cell, which means there's no name associated with the account."

"Can you trace the phone?" Andrew asked.

"Only if it's in use for at least ninety seconds," Sal explained.

"I can set up an automatic trace from here. Whoever it is probably won't be on long enough for us to pinpoint a location, but it can't hurt to try," Chase said.

"I also thought this information might be helpful," Sal added. "Manucci has a clean record in the States but is wanted for questioning in Italy for several bombings allegedly against a Sicilian group that calls themselves Stidda. We have Intel that suggests there was a contract on Manucci which may be one reason he ended up here in the States."

Everyone's ears perked at the mention of Stidda. It was the confirmation they were seeking, the assurance they were at least on the right path.

"So, if Manucci wasn't Stidda, does that mean that he was working on behalf of the Cosa Nostra?" Angel asked.

"If we go strictly on his past record, I'd say yes," Sal answered.

"Is there any connection between Emily and Stidda?" Andrew asked.

"Not any that I can find," Sal responded. "But I'll keep looking."

Placing his pencil between his teeth, Chase bounced excitedly in his seat while his fingers continued working their magic on the keys. He was intense and Angel hated to interrupt his train of thought; but she also thought it only fair to mention what he had just done. "Um..." she grimaced. "Chase, you just put that pencil in Emily's mouth."

His eyes bulged and then Chase spit the pencil across the table. It rolled in front of Olga, who leapt to her feet and blurted, "Merciful Heavens! That's disgusting!"

"Sorry," Chase winced. "My bad. Does anyone have a mint?"

Tony chuckled and slid a tin of Altoids across the table. Shoving a couple mints into his mouth, he slid the tin back to Tony and immediately redirected his attention to his laptop. "Sal, I have a wild-ass idea and I'm gonna need your help tying it all together."

"What do you need?" Sal asked.

"Somebody had to fund the CoBroGas attack," Chase said. "I need to know where the money came from."

"That's brilliant!" Andrew added. "We can follow the money trail back to the source."

"Maybe," Sal said. "If you're thinking that the money came from a group like Stidda, it'll be damn near impossible to prove, but there is one thing we might be able to trace...." His voice faded, as if the thought had just entered his mind and he was mulling it over. "CoBroGas is currently being developed and tested for military use but variations are also being tested for use in crowd control situations and other hostile environments. The difference is in the potency of the mixture. It's possible for me to find out if someone specifically requested a particular dose of it for testing in Chicago."

"Someone like Captain Senalli?" Andrew scoffed.

"It would take someone with more clout than a Police Captain to transfer in an agent like CoBroGas," Sal responded. "I'll see what I can dig up."

It was nearing midnight when Giovanni resigned himself to go to bed and Olga and Sophia followed shortly thereafter. "We will reconvene first thing in the morning," he said. Angel promised her mother that she wouldn't stay up much longer, but she also knew that she would not be able to sleep until they could get to the bottom of this. Angel sent everyone home or to bed except Tony, Andrew, Chase and the Snake.

"Why isn't Big Mike sticking around?" The Snake asked after everyone else had gone.

"The same reason Alberto isn't here," Angel remarked. "I need to know who I can fully trust."

"What do you have against Big Mike, Babe?" Tony questioned, pouring himself another cup of coffee and lifting a Cannoli from the platter on the bar.

"He and Alberto were the ones that allegedly found Emily dead. What if one of them killed her so she wouldn't talk?" Angel posed and then continued before anyone could offer an objection. "Also, Big Mike was missing in action at the Venturini estate when all of..." The Snake cut her off.

"Ms. Maratinzano, with all due respect, so was I. As I explained earlier, after we were ambushed, we were dragged into the trees near the entrance to the grounds," the Snake said.

"Ambushed by whom?" Andrew asked and Angel could tell by his expression that this was the first Andrew had heard of the story.

"The moment we pulled up to the Venturini Estate and stepped out of the vehicle, Big Mike and I were Tasered."

Angel nodded. "They were. Two men with long range Tasers hit both the Snake and Big Mike the moment they got out. Then they led me, mom and Olga inside."

"Who led you inside? The same two men that Tasered the Snake and Big Mike or different men?" Andrew asked using his investigative expertise.

"Does it matter, Ace?" Tony quipped and Andrew shot him an unappreciative glare.

"Actually, I don't know." Angel narrowed her brow as she tried to remember. "There were the two men with the Taser guns, but I didn't really see them, not their faces anyway."

"How could you not see their faces? How far away were they?" Chase asked, taking a sudden interest.

Angel shrugged. "It all happened very quickly. The Snake and Big Mike stepped out of the Tank and opened the back doors for me, mom and Olga. We slid out and then, all of a sudden, Big Mike and the Snake just dropped." Angel paced as she spoke. "I reached down to draw my gun, but before I could get it out of my thigh holster, the door to the house opened and two men took us inside at gun point."

"So that had to be two different men," Andrew surmised.

"If you didn't even see them, but they Tasered our guys, then they had to be using something like an XREP," Chase said excitedly.

"Those are illegal," Andrew said.

"Yeah, well, something gives me the crazy-ass feeling that these people aren't law-abiding citizens to begin with," Chase snipped, running his fingers over his keyboard.

"What's an XREP?" Angel asked.

"An Extended Range Electro-Muscular Projectile. It's a projectile that's fired out of a shotgun and allows the user to incapacitate a victim up to 98 feet away," Chase explained. "Total kick-ass technology!"

Chase dove into the archived surveillance data of the exterior of Joseph Venturini's house and began wading through the feed. To save time, he diverted feed to the other two laptops, which allowed Tony and Andrew to help search. "What are we looking for?" Tony asked.

"We want to find a visual of Big Mike and the Snake getting Tasered to see if we can identify who Tasered them, and the men who took the ladies inside," Chase explained. "I've got a hunch..." his sentence was cut short by the buzzing of his cell phone. "Sal-baby, tell me the good news," Chase answered, putting the call on speaker.

"That depends on what you call good news," Sal retorted. "The Polizia di Strato in Rome has a man in custody that is connected to several criminal acts which link him to the Cosa Nostra. According to a confession he made to law enforcement, Stidda has commissioned hits on Salvatore Buscetta and his daughter, Sophia Buscetta."

"Why?" Angel blurted.

"The statement reads: 'Stidda views the Cosa Nostra as genetically weakened by the

Buscetta name and their involvement with the brotherhood in the States. They plan to take care of the problem on American soil, blame the Americans and then take over the Cosa Nostra."

"Does he give names of the American contacts?" Andrew asked.

"No," Sal responded. "The statement implies that Stidda will financially fund the house cleaning project but does not give specific details about whom, how or when. It does, however, mention a nasty cyber cell which we know has ties to Emily."

"Anonimi?" Chase burst out. "Is Anonimi working with Stidda?"

"Anonimi works with no one. They do what they do either for money or personal vengeance. If they have teamed up with Stidda on this mission, you are up against a very dangerous organization. Their members are everywhere and their resources are limitless," Sal warned.

Chase disconnected the call and silence fell over the room. Angel imagined that they were all mentally assessing the many possible scenarios. "Well," Angel pronounced, breaking the quiet. "Since Mrs. Rosen made the comment that this whole thing was about my mother, I think we can assume that she, Emily, Captain Senalli and Sammy were all working with the Stidda Anonimi group."

"We can't make that assumption yet," Andrew said. "We have no evidence to support it."

"This isn't a trial, Ace, we don't need evidence," Tony chided.

Chase redirected everyone back to the surveillance feed of Joseph Venturini's estate. "I've got it," he said and transferred the images from his laptop onto the big screen. They watched as it played out just as Angel and the Snake had described. Big Mike and the Snake exited the

Tank at the same time, both opening a back door and allowing all three women to slide out. The moment the doors were shut, each man was Tasered, lost consciousness and fell to the ground. "Here's the part we need to see," Chase said excitedly, and then began isolating the feed to show the faces of the men who escorted Angel, Sophia and Olga inside. Pausing the feed, he zoomed in on their faces, copied them individually and sent them to Sal for data ID recognition. They all watched intently as the two men, presumably the ones responsible for the Tasering, neared Big Mike and the Snake, lifted them into the back of the Tank and then got into the vehicle and drove away from the house.

"That explains how we woke up in the woods," the Snake stated.

Chase copied their faces and sent them off to Sal. He then stopped typing and looked up from his computer. "Why didn't they kill you?" He posed. "I mean, call me crazy, but Stidda members don't seem to be the guys that are gonna all of a sudden go all moral on your ass."

"That's bothering me too," Andrew agreed. "Why didn't they just shoot you? Why take the time to Taser and relocate you?"

"Yeah, something's not right about this," Tony added. "You guys should be dead."

"Thanks a lot," the Snake sarcastically sneered.

Angel refilled her coffee and began to pace around the room. Assuming Emily was working with the Stidda Anonimi group, and that everyone at the Venturini estate was linked to Stidda, it did seem odd that they hadn't killed Big Mike and the Snake; unless one of them was secretly a Stidda member? Angel immediately dismissed her doubts. She was beginning to think like Giovanni, over-wrought with paranoia. "So, what happened after you and Big Mike woke up?" Angel asked.

"Somehow Alberto found us and un-taped our wrists and ankles and..."

"Alberto found you?" Andrew interrupted, his tone indicating disbelief.

"I know it sounds unbelievable, but when I came to Alberto was cutting the tape off of my wrists." The Snake threw his hands in the air.

"Let me get this straight, Ace," Tony scoffed sarcastically. "First, they don't kill you, and then Alberto just happens to magically find you unguarded?" Tony drew his gun and took aim at the Snake. "Let's say we try that story one more time."

The Snake didn't flinch as he stared down the barrel of Tony's .45. "I'm not lying. Ask Alberto and Big Mike."

"You know the rules. If you lie, you die, man," Tony said. "It's real simple."

The Snake didn't acknowledge Tony, but instead turned his head toward Angel. "Ms. Maratinzano, I've never lied to you or to your grandfather and I never will."

Looking into the Snake's face, Angel saw no fear. Her gut told her that he was telling the truth, but she knew she had to investigate his story nonetheless. Spinning on her heels, she ordered Chase to retrieve Big Mike and Alberto immediately.

CHAPTER 37

Big Mike corroborated the Snake's story, word for word and Angel breathed a sigh of relief. When asked how he just so happened to stumble upon Big Mike and the Snake in the woods, Alberto said he was directed to their location by a cop.

"A cop?" Andrew repeated with disbelief. "What cop?"

Alberto shrugged. "A young guy, real big with a red crew cut and freckles. He told me where they were and said I should get 'em out of there."

Angel watched the color drain from Andrew's face. Alberto described Monahan; naïve, annoying Monahan, whom Lisben warned him not to trust. What role could he possibly have in all of this? Andrew ran his hand through his hair and paced in front of the windows.

It was almost 2:00am when Chase yelped, "Hot diggity, wild-ass dogs!" He said it so loudly that it startled everyone in the room. "We're dealing with two factions," he blurted. "My crazy-ass hunch was right!"

"What hunch?" Angel asked.

"The Stidda and the Cosa Nostra are enemies that live right on top of each other. I mean, it's not spread out like over here. Sicily isn't that big, so I got to thinking that if the Cosa Nostra caught wind of Stidda's plan to take out Salvatore and Sophia, they would most assuredly take action to protect them," Chase ranted while pulling up images and placing them on the big screen. He showed an enlarged image of the two men that led Sophia, Angel and Olga into the Venturini home at gunpoint. "Look at their hands," he said excitedly, zooming in closer to reveal a star shaped tattoo between the thumb and index finger of each man. They were Stidda. "Now, look at the men who loaded Big Mike and the Snake into the back of the Tank and dumped them in the woods," he said, changing the image. As he zoomed in it became clear that there were no star tattoos on either man. "I'd bet my balls that both Stidda and the Cosa Nostra were at the Venturini estate tonight!" He bounced up and down excitedly. "That would explain all of the people we picked up on the infrared scanners."

"It would also explain some of the gunfire and the fact that they didn't hit any of us," Andrew added.

"Exactly!" Chase blurted. "You guys were caught in the crossfire of Stidda trying to whack Sophia and the Cosa Nostra trying to protect her."

"This isn't exactly concrete evidence," Andrew said.

"You're not a cop anymore, Ace," Tony berated. "You can stop with the evidence crap."

Angel was certain that Tony didn't intend for his words to hurt Andrew, but she could tell by his expression that they did. Andrew had loved being a cop. It was who he was. It was his life and now it was gone.

Angel freshened her coffee, kicked off her heels and sat down at the table. It had been a long night and everyone looked as exhausted as she felt. "We should all get some sleep and reconvene in the morning," she said, yawning as she spoke.

"I can't sleep," Chase uttered, bouncing his knee rapidly up and down. "I'm crazy-ass wired right now. I feel like we're so close to this whole thing unraveling."

"Agreed," Tony said. "I say we make some more coffee and press on."

Andrew's cell phone buzzed and he stepped away from the table to take the call. It was Lisben and he wanted Andrew to meet him right away. "Where are you?" Andrew asked, placing the phone on speaker so they could all hear what he was saying.

"I'm outside Monahan's home. They're here and they're gonna kill him," Lisben wailed.

"Who's there?" Andrew asked. "Who's going to kill him?"

"Stidda," Lisben whispered with angst in his tone. "I don't know who to trust on the force now. You've got to come. Hurry!"

Andrew disconnected the call and made a beeline for the door. "Andrew!" Angel called after him. "You're not going alone."

"My family's dead, the rest of the Venturini members think I killed them so that I could become Boss, and the entire Chicago police force thinks I murdered Captain Senalli; so until I can find the person behind all of this, I have no choice but to go alone," Andrew said.

"You have all of us," Angel retorted. "It may be unorthodox, but we're sort of like your family."

Big Mike and the Snake stood up and headed toward the door. "We're with you," Big Mike said.

"Sweetheart..." Andrew began but was interrupted by the door swinging open and Sophia rushing inside. She was wearing black silk pajamas and had a frantic look in her eyes.

"Mom, what are you doing up? What's wrong?" Angel rushed toward her, taking her mother's hands in hers and leading her toward a chair. Olga rushed in behind her, out of breath and dressed in her yellow fleece robe.

"Merciful Heavens!" Olga gasped. "I didn't think we were going to make it."

"Make it?" Angel questioned.

"There's a helicopter hovering over the building," Sophia said.

"We were making tea when we heard the whirring blades and rushed right down," Olga said, plunking into the chair next to Sophia and fanning herself with her hand.

Tony, Andrew, the Snake, Alberto and Big Mike immediately drew their guns. Chase called Tino, who was guarding the front entrance to the Towers, alerting him to the intrusion and then called Gunther to have him awaken Giovanni and move him to the secret meeting room. Next, he telephoned Trig and Chito in case they would need back-up from the street.

After disconnecting the call, Chase brought up the feed from the surveillance cameras on the Penthouse level. "Let's see who's paying us a visit at this hour," Chase said, clicking wildly across his keyboard.

The camera from the patio showed a chopper hovering directly above. "That is one sweet-ass chopper, man," Chase mumbled. "Do you know what that is? That's an A129 Mangusta. They call it the Mongoose. It's one bad-ass Italian attack chopper. Its blades are almost completely silent which allows it to engage in some sneaky-ass maneuvering." A genuine look of awe filled his face. "What I wouldn't give to fly one of those babies."

"Well, they can't set her down with our chopper parked there," Tony said, stating the obvious.

"Are you kidding?" Chase scoffed. "That thing could blow our chopper right off the patio and set down wherever it wanted."

Just then, three men dropped from the Mongoose onto the patio and broke through the glass door, parading into the dining room and fanning out. They each carried what looked like a shortened shot gun. One man paused to scan the living room and the kitchen and then headed into Angel's room, while the other two men rushed down the hallway toward Sophia and Olga's bedrooms.

Chase transferred the feed to the big screen. "Look at that," he said excitedly. "See what they're carrying?" He pointed at the screen. "That's a Lupara. It's basically a sawed-off shot gun predominantly used by the Cosa Nostra in Sicily."

This caught Sophia's attention and she neared the screen to get a better look. "They're my people?" She uttered. "They've come to take me back to Sicily, just like the guard in the woods said." Sophia's expression changed from fearful to determined and she raced toward the door but Big Mike and the Snake blocked it. "I've got to get up there," Sophia raged. "They may know something about my father."

"You still haven't heard from him? Angel asked and Sophia shook her head to indicate she hadn't.

"We can't let you go up there," Tony said.

"Merciful Heavens!" Olga exclaimed. "She's gone completely mad."

"I'm not crazy, Lucia," Sophia barked at Olga. "But if they have my father..."

"You want me to Taser her?" Olga asked, pushing her chair back and standing up. "I'll Taser you for your own good, Missy," Olga threatened Sophia.

"Everybody take a chill-pill," Chase scolded. "I've got an idea." Before Chase could share his idea, his cell phone buzzed and he placed Sal on speaker.

"Andrew asked if there were any American contacts listed during the confession made to the Italian police," Sal began. "I've just received the name of the man in custody. His name is Sergio

Puccio. He's Cosa Nostra, one of Salvatore's men.
I did a preliminary search and he has a brother in
Chicago, named Saulto Puccio."

Andrew ran his fingers through his hair
and shook his head, pacing by the windows. Angel
could tell that this information triggered a
disturbing thought so she approached him,
blocking his path. Looping her fingers with his she
opened her mouth to say something but he shot a
quick glance toward Tony and then pulled his
hand away. Angel didn't know what to make of it.

"I've got Saulto's location," Chase blurted.
"He's on the west side." Chase's fingers danced
rapidly over his keyboard. "Hold the phone," he
blurted. "My trace on the last number Manucci
called just went live." Andrew rushed toward
Chase's computer screen and hovered over his
shoulder. "C'mon....c'mon....stay
connected....keep talking," Chase cheered the
mystery caller on.

"Can you get the number of the person he's
talking to?" Andrew questioned.

"Thirty more seconds," Chase answered.
"Almost there." It was obvious that the
anticipation was killing everyone in the room.
"Bingo baby!" Chase exclaimed. "We got 'em!" All
of a sudden Chase's face went ashen. "He's here,"
he uttered in disbelief. "He's in the building."

Tony drew his .45 and aimed it in the
direction of Big Mike, the Snake and Alberto.
"Which one is it?" Tony sneered. "It'd be my
pleasure to take him out."

"He's upstairs," Chase uttered and switched
the big screen back to the Penthouse surveillance
feed. In the middle of the living room stood
another man, with the original three who had
descended from the Mongoose.

"Omigod," Andrew gasped.

"That's the dude who told me where to find the Snake and Big Mike!" Alberto blurted, pointing excitedly at the screen.

"That's the cop who took me to the morgue," Olga gasped. "Give me one minute alone and I'll Taser his ass into tomorrow!"

"That's Monahan," Andrew said.

CHAPTER 38

Chito and Trig arrived at the Towers and, with Angel's permission, were escorted into the secret meeting room. "What's up, man? We just got home and then you called us right back here? Do you know what time it is?" Chito complained.

Gunther escorted Giovanni in. "What is the meaning of this?" Giovanni growled, staring at the image of the Penthouse intruders. "Go upstairs and kill them," he ordered.

"Grandfather, we have reason to believe that they may be Cosa Nostra, who have come to protect Salvatore and my mother from Stidda or Anonimi or both," Angel explained.

"Who is this Anonimi?" Giovanni barked.

"A cyber cell that Emily was a part of and who we believe was used by Stidda to gain access to the CoBroGas," Chase rapidly explained.

"Bah! Salvatore would have told me if he were sending men to the States," he huffed. "He would not have sent his men to the Towers without alerting us. These are not the Cosa Nostra. Kill them."

"What if he didn't know that they were coming?" Sophia interjected. "What if he didn't know about Stidda's threats against us? What if those men have my father or know where we can find him?"

"There's only one way to find out," Tony said, holding his gun up. "Let's go up there and ask them."

Giovanni narrowed his brow and stared at the image on the screen. Monahan and the other men hadn't moved. They stood perfectly still, as if they were waiting for something. Did they know that Angel and her men were watching? Were they waiting for them to provoke a confrontation? Were they waiting for someone else to arrive or for someone to give them further instructions? There was only one way to find out.

"Big Mike, Snake, Alberto, Tony, you're with me," Andrew said. "Gunther and Chase, stay here in case anything goes wrong."

"What about us, man?" Chito said. "You brought us back here, now we want to be a part of the action."

"Speak for yourself," Trig blurted. "This brother gets enough action."

"Who are you jiving?" Chito cracked up. "Your black ass don't get no action," he teased.

"I get more than you," Trig rebutted.

Giovanni gave them an unappreciative glare and they both cowered into chairs next to Chase. "On second thought, we'll just sit down and shut up," Chito mumbled.

"That's the first sign of intelligence I've seen from you," Chase grunted.

With a bug clipped to the inside of his shirt, Andrew led the way up the staircase to the Penthouse door. Tony and Alberto walked behind him with Big Mike and the Snake bringing up the rear. "Monahan!" Andrew yelled through the door. "I'm coming in."

Monahan instructed the three men surrounding him to lower their weapons.

Pushing open the door, Andrew stepped inside. "There is no time to explain," Monahan said, as Tony, Big Mike and the Snake filed inside, each flanking in a different direction and taking aim at the men while Alberto stood guard at the door.

"I disagree," Andrew chided, noticing immediately that one of the men was Mayor Tompkin's security guard whom Monahan had conversed with in Italian in the hospital hallway. "I think you have a lot of explaining to do."

"Sophia Buscetta is in imminent danger and we must get her to safety. After which I will answer your questions."

"You expect me to turn over Sophia without any information?" Andrew scoffed.

"We are members of the Cosa Nostra, sent here by Salvatore to protect his daughter," Monahan said. "I'm sure you already know that. We learned too late of Stidda's plans to attack with nerve gas. We were unable to stop the attack but we were able to intervene at the hospital."

Angel and Sophia neared the big screen next to Giovanni and watched intently. Giovanni's expression was one of skeptical hostility, while Sophia appeared to be more curious and concerned. Angel found herself trapped somewhere in the middle, trying to decide if Monahan was trustworthy or just another loose end that needed to be tied up.

"How exactly did you intervene?" Andrew seethed.

"We have extensive knowledge and experience with nerve gas agents. When we found out what was used against Sophia and Salvatore and Sophia's family, we moved as many as we could to the morgue."

"YOU placed us in refrigeration?" Tony asked.

"Our people did, yes. It was the only way to slow the effects of the gas and it was a contained area where we believed we would be able to provide adequate short-term protection."

"Your men placed Angel in refrigeration as well?" Andrew seethed.

"Yes. We had no other option. She was wondering around the hospital, indiscreet, and had she encountered Stidda they would have killed her on the spot. We sedated her and placed her where we felt she would be safe," Monahan explained.

"He knows where my father is," Sophia muttered, studying Monahan. "He's telling the truth."

"Bah," Giovanni waved his hand in the air. "You are too trusting. This is all a lie, a rouse to lure you from safety."

"Egli non è un bugiardo. Lo vedo nei suoi occhi," Sophia demanded.

"Bugiardo!" Giovanni's jowls tightened and Sophia exploded into an Italian tirade, one that left even Giovanni wide-eyed and speechless. Angel wasn't certain what Sophia had said, but she could tell by Giovanni's response that her mother had basically told him to kiss off. Sophia turned on her heels and stormed toward the doors.

"Like it or not, I'm going up there," she sneered and Giovanni let out a long, tired sigh.

"Michelangela," he turned to face her, stern warning lit in his eyes. "Control your mother."

Angel pulled Sophia into the hallway by the elevator.

"We also killed the Stidda members that had infiltrated your families, the Venturini family in particular," Monahan continued and then pressed his fingers to his right ear as if he were receiving a transmission through an ear bud. "There's a chopper headed in this direction. We need to remove Sophia from the building now!" Monahan demanded.

"That ain't gonna happen, Ace," Tony blurted, keeping his aim steady.

They could hear the whirring sound of chopper blades in the distance. "How did Captain Senalli get involved?" Andrew demanded.

"Through his mother, Martha Rosenalli who wanted revenge on your father for the murder of her husband." Monahan spoke quickly and then took two steps toward Andrew. "Please, let us get Sophia to safety and you have my word that I will come back and give you all of the details."

Just then, Sophia appeared in the doorway with Angel. "Do you have my father?" She asked Monahan.

"Dios mio!" Giovanni barked. "Get up there and protect them!" He raged and Chase, Trig and Chito leapt to their feet and raced out of the door.

"What the hell are you doing up here?" Andrew barked. "Alberto, get them back downstairs."

"Yes, Ms. Buscetta," Monahan lowered his head in a gesture of respect. "Salvatore is in a secure location. He's waiting for a confirmation that you have been retrieved," Monahan explained.

"We're gonna need proof of that, Ace," Tony sneered.

The sound of the approaching chopper grew louder just as Trig, Chase and Chito rushed through the Penthouse door. "We're running out of time," Monahan hollered. "Andrew, if Stidda comes here, she will not survive. No one will."

Trig flipped his dreadlocks over his shoulder and shot Chase a sideways glance. "It's time for this brother to go black ops on their ass, man," he said and took off running toward the chopper that was parked on the patio.

"What are you doing?" Chase yelled, following after him.

"If I take her up, man, there's a chance they'll think Sophia's on board and I can lure their sorry asses away," Trig explained while hooking his belt and starting the chopper.

"You might be up against a military attack chopper," Chase yelled over the sound of the blades, but Trig didn't respond. He gave Chase a thumb's up and then lifted the chopper into the air. Rushing back inside, Chase ordered Monahan to have his pilot immediately move the Mongoose away from the Towers. "Tell the Mongoose to take protective action over our chopper so that Stidda will think Sophia is on board."

Monahan relayed the message and then turned to Andrew. "If they think Sophia Buscetta is in that chopper, they'll blow it clean out of the sky." The Mongoose lifted away and tailed Trig while Monahan pulled from his pocket what looked like a small oral transmitter and spoke loudly and clearly into it. "Sophia Buscetta is aboard an unmarked chopper. We are escorting her to safety. I repeat, target is in custody. Mongoose out."

"That was frickin' brilliant!" Chase slapped Monahan on his back. "You've got that set on an open-frequency, don't you? So, the Stidda are sure to intercept it and follow our choppers."

Monahan nodded. "That's the hope, but I doubt it will work."

Andrew instructed Chase and Chito to take Angel and Sophia back downstairs, just in case the Stidda didn't fall for their trick and returned in full force.

"Now what?" Tony asked.

"Now we wait and make sure they don't return," Monahan answered.

While Tony, Big Mike, the Snake and the three Cosa Nostra men were keeping a watchful eye on the night sky, Andrew and Monahan stepped into the living room, sat down on the couch and began to piece the puzzle together. Monahan explained that he wasn't really a cop. He hadn't gone to the Police Academy nor received official training. "When we caught wind of the fact that Stidda had plans to attack the Buscetta family on American soil, I was placed on the force as an undercover Cosa Nostra operative."

"How did you learn of Stidda's plans?" Andrew asked.

"From my father, Saulto Puccio, who heard it from his brother, who is sitting in an Italian prison for crimes he did not commit."

"Why did you need to infiltrate the force? Why didn't your men just come into the city, locate Stidda and then leave?" Andrew posed.

"We had reason to believe that the nerve gas was funded locally," Monahan explained. "I went undercover to find out who had funded it. We hoped that the money trail would lead us to the Stidda here in Chicago and we could take them out before they found the Buscettas." Monahan dropped his chin to his chest. "It didn't exactly pan out that way."

"No, it didn't," Andrew gritted and then pursed his lips together. "Why didn't you tell me all this when you were first assigned to the force?"

"I didn't know if you could be trusted," Monahan shrugged. "At that time I had reason to believe that the Captain was working with Stidda and that made me suspicious of anyone close to him." Monahan leaned against the back of the couch. "I had to let it all play out."

Andrew's jaw tightened and he cleared emotion from his throat. Letting it all play out had cost the lives of Andrew's family and his career. "I'd like to tell you I understand how it all happened, but I don't." He exhaled. "It would help me if you would connect the dots. I mean, why didn't Stidda wait until Salvatore returned to Sicily before contracting the hit?"

"Because this whole thing started as something more personal than Salvatore and the

Cosa Nostra." Monahan shook his head, "It's true what they say, hell hath no fury like a woman scorned."

"I'm not following," Andrew quipped.

"This whole thing began with Mrs. Rosen." Monahan went on to explain. Mrs. Rosen's husband, Rinaldo Rosenalli, was originally from Sicily, where most of his family still remained. The Rosenalli family held a substantial amount of wealth and power in Sicily but had always remained neutral, claiming loyalty to neither the Stidda nor the Cosa Nostra, despite both sides trying to recruit them. "They remained neutral, that is, until your father had Rinaldo killed," Monahan explained. "At that time, being totally obsessed with avenging Rinaldo's death, the Rosenallis joined Stidda."

"Why would Stidda be interested in avenging one man's death half way around the globe?" Andrew questioned.

"Because Rinaldo was murdered by the brotherhood in the States and some people don't like Salvatore's close relationship with the stateside mafia." Monahan shook his head. "Some people, like Stidda, as well as some of the other smaller Mafioso outfits, view the Buscetta's partnership with the Maratinzano family as a conflict of interests, a weakness, if you will," he explained. "There are even Cosa Nostra members who are unhappy with the Buscetta's new stateside romance, as they call it." Andrew nodded, as Monahan's words confirmed what the guard had told them in the woods.

"So, Stidda decided to attack while Salvatore's defenses were down..."

"Yes. With Rinaldo's widow already secure in your father's home and Rinaldo's son being the Captain of the Chicago Police, Stidda saw a window of opportunity to kill two birds with one stone."

"Avenge Rinaldo's death by killing my father and take out Salvatore and Sophia in one fail swoop," Andrew uttered. The dots were finally starting to connect. "All they needed was a military-grade nerve gas."

"Exactly," Monahan said. "At least in theory."

"Why spend the money financing the CoBroGas? Why not just hit their targets and get out of dodge?" Andrew wondered.

"That's where they got greedy." Monahan said. "Originally, it was supposed to be a normal contracted hit, but when they heard about Angel Maratinzano's dinner party at Tetterbaum's Pub, wherein all of the big players would be present, Captain Senalli came up with a better idea."

Andrew leaned back on the couch, exhaled loudly and placed his palms on his forehead. "Kill everyone at once."

"Yep," Monahan said. "All they needed was someone with enough political power to approve a CoBroGas shipment to Chicago and enough clout to have the paperwork buried."

Andrew quickly sat up and stared at Monahan. "Mayor Tompkins?"

Monahan slowly nodded. "I don't have the evidence to prove that, but I have a hunch it was him. He and Senalli were tight."

"But Tompkins wouldn't have the clout to bury his request for the gas..." Andrew pondered, his voice fading.

"No, but being a member of Anonimi, Emily could easily destroy the paper trail or divert it to someone else entirely."

"So you placed one of your Cosa Nostra guys on the Mayor's security detail," Andrew said in an a-ha tone. It was starting to make sense.

Andrew stood up and paced across the living room, stopping at the edge of the dining room table, turning to lean against it and crossing his arms over his chest.

"If everything went as planned then Mrs. Rosen and the Rosenalli family would get revenge for Rinaldo's death, Captain Senalli would get hailed as the first Captain to clean up the crime scene in Chicago by ridding it of just about every mafia family in the city, and Stidda would overthrow the Cosa Nostra," Monahan summed up. "It was a win-win-win; but what I can't figure out is what Mayor Tompkins stood to gain by funding the operation?"

"I think I can help there," Andrew said and told Monahan about his private conversation with Mayor Tompkins in the hospital. "If what he told me was true then Martha Craden, a.k.a. Mrs. Rosen, blackmailed him into funding the CoBroGas by threatening to go public with their affair. So, it wasn't what he stood to win, but what he stood to lose."

"Poor bastard," Monahan sighed.

"Hell hath no fury," Andrew added with a raised eyebrow. "So, when Mayor Tompkins was shot in the alley, what was he really doing there?"

"We assume that he went there to meet the three Stidda members that you and Angel took out," he surmised. "Possibly to give them money or exchange information?" He shrugged. "We were never able to find out."

"Holy...!" Tony yelped from the patio. "Andrew, get out here! You gotta see this!"

Andrew and Monahan rushed onto the patio and saw Trig's chopper whirring by, followed by the Mongoose and the Stidda. "Trig damned near turned the chopper upside down with an evasive maneuver!" Big Mike whooped.

"I've never seen anything like it." Tony's eyes widened.

"That's Trig, man, one of the best pilots around. That's some good 'ol USA military training at work right there," Chase bragged. Having been able to see only part of the scene on surveillance, he had sneaked up to the Penthouse to take in the live action.

"What are you doing up here?" Andrew scolded.

"It's hard to see what's happening in the night sky from the surveillance feed. It's too dark," Chase retorted.

"They'll pursue him until they kill him," Monahan warned.

"Your guys are in a frickin' Mongoose, man," Chase scowled. "That ride was specifically built for military attack operations. Turn her around and blast the Stidda out of the sky."

Monahan licked his lips. "That action would officially declare war between Stidda and the Cosa Nostra and could result in hundreds of deaths worldwide."

"Trig is out there risking his neck to save Sophia's life and you're just going to let him get blown out of the sky?" Chase raged. "You do that and you have my personal guarantee that the Cosa frickin' Nostra is gonna have a war with the brotherhood of the U.S. frickin' A!"

Andrew had never seen Chase's face so red nor heard him sound so angry. Tony, Big Mike and the Snake huddled around Chase with their guns extended. "What'll it be, Ace?" Tony growled.

Monahan looked to Andrew, as if he expected him to help talk some sense into everyone else, but Andrew shrugged, meandered over and stood next to Chase. "Take the Stidda down," he said, "and then we'll come up with a solution to avoid a war."

"One life does not carry more value than hundreds," Monahan objected.

"If it's one of ours it does," Tony retorted.

"Damn straight!" Chase blurted in agreement.

Monahan shook his head. "Salvatore would not make this call."

"Salvatore isn't here," Angel said, having crept through the Penthouse door with her 9mm extended and Chito right behind, clutching a handheld Uzi. "And since I am the only bloodline Buscetta in the room, I'd say this is my call to make." Angel walked closer to Monahan, her 9mm aimed at his forehead. "Take the Stidda down."

CHAPTER 39

The explosion lit up the Chicago skyline and Angel imagined it must have awakened the whole city. Within an hour, Sal from the FBI released a statement to the press, local and abroad, declaring that the FBI had concrete evidence that the Stidda crime organization out of Sicily had attacked and killed Sophia Buscetta, daughter to the head of the Cosa Nostra. In addition, Sal informed the press that Captain Senalli had been working with Stidda and in conjunction with Anonimi was responsible for the CoBroGas attack on Tetterbaum's Pub and ultimately for the death of Joseph Venturini and his sons, Joe Jr. and Sammy. As a bonus, Sal threw in that it was Chicago Special Investigator Andrew Venturini, who was responsible for uncovering Captain Senalli's criminal activity and notifying the FBI.

"The Stidda will know that we took down their chopper," Monahan said.

"Yes, but they'll think Sophia was killed in the process," Angel rebutted. "In her death lies her freedom."

"And a war between Stidda and the Cosa Nostra," Monahan objected, as they all gathered around the dining room table and watched the various media releases on Chase's laptop.

"We'll figure something out, Ace," Tony quipped. "Relax."

"I cannot relax when a war with Stidda endangers my family," he seethed.

Andrew glared at him, his jaw tightening; and Monahan, obviously realizing the irony of what he had said in front of Andrew who had just lost his entire family, backed down.

Sophia and Olga worked diligently in the kitchen preparing a breakfast fit for kings. They filled the table with scrambled eggs, bacon and sausage, homemade biscuits with sausage gravy, and cheese strudel.

"Come and get it," Olga hollered, and everyone grabbed a plate and found a seat either around the table or in the living room. Sophia, Angel and Chito served coffee and then sat down to eat with everyone else. When they had all dined, Giovanni got down to business.

Because of his bravery and willingness to risk his life for Sophia, coupled with the fact that he had previously delivered Angel to safety, Trig was given the opportunity to take the Omerta oath and became a Made member of the Maratinzano family. Kissing him on each cheek, Sophia also declared him an honorary Cosa Nostra member.

Trig blushed and looked to Chito. "See, I told you this brother gets more action than you."

"Get over yourself, bro," Chito huffed

"It's the dreads, man. The chicks dig the dreads," Trig teased, raising his eyebrows into his forehead and grinning ear to ear. Angel wondered if Chito was feeling jealous of the fact that Trig was Made. She considered offering Chito the opportunity but wasn't convinced that he would risk his life for the family. He would have to prove his loyalty first.

Sophia was finally able to connect with Salvatore via a security encoded signal set up by Chase and Monahan. She learned that Salvatore would have to remain in hiding until the Cosa Nostra could rid Sicily of the Stidda threat, which Angel felt certain left Sophia wondering when she would be able to see him again. Her mother appeared concerned but also relieved. Salvatore was alive and in lieu of everything that had transpired, that was a blessing that could not go unappreciated. Angel could also sense a certain excitement in her mother. With the world believing Sophia Buscetta to be dead, she was truly free for the first time in her life. That had to feel good.

Angel telephoned her bartender, Johnny, and invited him to the Towers, at which time she offered him Tetterbaum's Pub for a very low price. Johnny eagerly accepted. "Johnny loves the pub," he told her, speaking in his typical third-person manner. "Johnny will take good care of her." Olga was elated that Angel had finally taken her advice and sold Tetterbaum's, and although Angel would miss it, she had come to realize that the only way to protect the public and her family from random attacks at the pub, was to officially get rid of it. The Maratinzano family would remain financially invested in a behind-the-scenes manner; but that knowledge would never be made public. It took a year and several attempts on her life to realize that being a Mafia Boss was a full-time job and one which has to be taken seriously. If the past year had taught her anything, it was that carelessness and distraction could result in losing loved ones. Like it or not, and there were times when she didn't like it at all, she had the responsibility of protecting her family.

Salvatore's men left the Towers en route to Sicily, with the exception of Monahan, who was going to remain in Chicago with his father, Saulto Puccio. Because of his service in protecting Giovanni and his family at the hospital and at the Venturini estate, Giovanni offered Monahan the Messaggero position which he and Salvatore had previously offered to Sophia. Monahan accepted with enthusiasm. "Well, all right then!" He said, clapping his hands together.

Walking Monahan to the door, Andrew asked about Manucci and Monahan dropped his chin to his chest. "Manucci was a good man. Loyal. One of Salvatore's best. He will be missed."

"My condolences," Andrew uttered.

"What about Chef Conaletti?" Angel asked, joining them in the doorway. "We could never find him at the hospital."

"You couldn't find him because he never made it to the hospital. We took care of him," Monahan responded. "Nothing you need to worry about."

"One more thing," Andrew interjected. "What about Lisben's role in all of this?"

"Captain Senalli saw Lisben in the morgue and knew Lisben saw him hit Ian Flanko, so he put out an internal ABP on him. Before we could get there, Stidda found him at his home, slobbering drunk," Monahan explained. "They made him an offer he couldn't refuse and dropped him at you house, to wait for you to return home. We were in route to get him when Angel and her men showed up and brought him here, to the Towers. At that point, he became an inside security risk and we notified Salvatore of the potential danger."

"That's why Salvatore ordered Tony to kill him?" Andrew said.

"Yes. We believe Lisben's job was to report your whereabouts to Stidda, create a diversion when needed and become an inside informant. He was also influential in persuading the force to turn against you, spreading the rumor that you had murdered your family and Captain Senalli," Monahan explained.

Chase piped in from across the dining room. "So, when Lisben called to tell Andrew that

Stidda was at Monahan's home and that they were going to kill him..."

"That was obviously a lie to lure Andrew and all of your men away so that they could more easily get to Sophia," Monahan interrupted.

Tony approached Andrew and gave him a pat on the back. "It would be my pleasure to tie up that loose end for you, Ace," he said.

"Thank you, but with Giovanni's blessing, that will be my first order of Venturini business," Andrew said.

"Merciful Heavens!" Olga exclaimed. "The birthing of a new Boss right here in our living room."

Angel studied Andrew's face. She couldn't help but feel shocked that he appeared so sure of taking over the Venturini family. His reputation had been cleared, he would be hailed as a hero on the force for exposing Captain Senalli's criminal activity, and he could even become the next Captain. Police work was always his first love, so Angel couldn't help wondering if Andrew's desire had changed or was he sacrificing his dream because of the overwhelming responsibility he now felt toward what remained of the Venturini family?

Giovanni rose from the armed chair and stepped toward Andrew. "You have my blessing. We will arrange for a meeting and make it official."

As everyone migrated from the Penthouse to their homes or assigned apartments below, Angel stepped out onto the patio and drank in the fresh morning air. Well, it was city air, polluted with the extra stench of an exploded military grade, Italian helicopter, but it felt good in her lungs nonetheless. Maybe it was just the fact that she was finally able to take a deep breath and relax for the first time in days. There were still details to work out, like what life would be like for Sophia, when Salvatore could come out of hiding and how life would change with Andrew being the Venturini Boss. They'd also have to discuss what was to be done about the Mayor. Should a man who was blackmailed into participation be killed for his service to the enemy? Should he be held accountable for a loose end that came back around to ensnare him? Angel would say no, but she feared that she would be the only Boss with that opinion. What about Stidda and Anonimi? Surely there would be backlash from all that had transpired, not to mention the fact that the soda delivery man who planted the CoBroGas tanks and administered the gas was still at large. There would definitely have to be a manhunt and Angel hoped that they would be able to take him alive and gain enough information to curtail future attacks. The other thing on her mind was finding the right moment to give Andrew the ring she had found in his father's pocket.

Giovanni stepped onto the patio and walked toward her. "This old man is going to bed," he told her, taking her by the shoulders and planting a kiss on her forehead.

"Goodnight, Nonno."

"Goodnight and good day," he said with a grin. "And today is a very good day." He gave her a wink and turned to go inside.

"Grandfather?" Her words stopped him. "I was just thinking...wondering..." Angel let out an exasperated sigh. "Will we ever stop the violence?" She shook her head. "This whole thing was caused because I made a mistake. I misunderstood the Tamolskaya list which resulted in Rinaldo's murder." Tears pricked the back of her eyes. "If I had been smarter none of this would have happened. Joseph and Joe Jr. would still be alive." Guilt rushed over her and she buried her face in Giovanni's shoulder and wept.

He took in a deep breath and exhaled, stroking her hair gently. "We cannot avoid conflict. It will always find us. But we can learn from every experience so that we are hopefully wiser the next time around." He lifted her face from his shoulder and wiped a tear from her cheek. "A leader isn't born with knowledge, he..." Giovanni paused and smiled, "... or she acquires it." He gave her a wink. "You have done well, Michelangela. You cannot hold yourself responsible for the fact that Don Venturini contracted a hit on Rinaldo. There may have been other factors involved in Joseph placing Rinaldo at the top of his death list. Perhaps there were other actions of disloyalty of which you are not privy." He draped his arm around Angel's shoulder. "When confronted with adversity, you protected the family and at the end of the day, that is a job well done."

Giving her shoulder a squeeze, Giovanni turned to walk inside and then stopped briefly. "A good leader always ties up loose ends." He gave her a wink and disappeared through the door.

Loose ends. How in the world was she supposed to tie them up? The day was approaching when she would have to focus on building the family, on getting a Compare and an Underboss, and even a husband. She would have to tie up the loose ends of her heart and settle down. Tony? Andrew? Just the thought of losing them made her stomach twist into tight knots. How many loose ends were out there? Was there really a way to tie them all up?

"Babe?" Tony's voice jolted her from her thoughts and she whirled around to face him. Taking her face between his palms, he leaned down and kissed her tenderly on the lips. "I never got to tell you how great you look in that dress."

Angel glanced downward. She had forgotten that she was still wearing it. What a wreck she must have been, standing there in bare feet. She imagined that she was probably the only woman on the planet who had crawled through the woods on her hands and knees while wearing Versace. "Thanks," she whispered.

An awkward moment of silence fell between them and for the first time, Angel couldn't tell what Tony was thinking. The look in his eyes was distant and contemplative, almost sad. She intertwined her fingers with his. "Tony...I...." Angel paused, feeling as if she should explain what happened with Andrew in the elevator, yet uncertain of what to say and even more uncertain of what to feel.

Bringing her hand up to his lips and placing a gentle kiss atop it, Tony nodded. "I gotta go, Babe," he said. "We'll talk soon." And then he was gone.

Angel turned back toward the view of the city and closed her eyes. Tony's knowing about her escapade with Andrew created a knot in her stomach that she didn't know how to untie. She regretted the fact that her actions had hurt him, yet she didn't regret what had happened between her and Andrew. Maybe Giovanni was right. Maybe it was time to let them both go; to tie those loose ends into a proverbial platonic bow.

Creeping up behind her, Angel was startled when Andrew wrapped his arms around her waist. "Everyone's gone home and Olga and your mom have gone to their rooms to nap," he said. "I believe you and I are due for a conversation. Where should we start?"

"Let's start at the beginning," she said, leaning back against his chest. "In the pub, before the CoBroGas attack, you were about to tell me something. You said, 'Sweetheart' and then all hell broke loose." Angel turned to face him. "What were you going to say?"

A smile filled his face and lit up his chocolaty brown eyes. "I was going to say, 'Sweetheart, you look amazing in that dress.'" She spun around, leaning against him and interlocking her fingers with his. "I was beginning to think Versace was bad luck."

Andrew bent down and planted a tender kiss on the nape of her neck. "Then, just to be safe, we should get you out of it."

ABOUT THE AUTHOR

S.R.Claridge, nominated for the 2010 Molly Award, 2013 Pushcart Prize and awarded the 2011 Rocky Mountain Fiction Writers Pen Award, writes full-time and lives in Colorado. She loves autumn, moonlight and Grey Goose martinis with bleu cheese or jalapeno stuffed olives. She believes Friday nights are for indulging in Mexican food and margaritas and Sunday mornings warrant an extra-spicy Bloody Mary. Growing up in St. Louis, Missouri and earning her BA in Psychology from the University of Missouri, Columbia, S.R.Claridge is a mixture of mid-western family values and western wild nights. She loves Jesus, believes in the power of prayer, in the freedom of forgiveness and that life is a gift that should be enjoyed to the fullest. With a background in theatre, S.R.Claridge creates characters with dramatic flair and is known for her intense plot twists and engaging humor. S.R.Claridge would rather walk dangerously where there's a view than sit in idle safety and let life pass her by. Her spirited outlook comes shining through in her novels, as she takes readers to the edge of their seats with bone-chilling suspense.

AUTHOR ACCLAIM

"The Just Call Me Angel series is suspense at its best."
- RipeReviews

"A unique series from a one-of-a-kind author."
- APEX Reviews

"Riveting!"
- TrueBlueEbookReview

"One thrilling moment after another!"
- CanadaReviews

"A best-seller candidate indeed."
- BookWatchMagazine

BOOKS BY S.R.CLARIDGE

Tetterbaum's Truth *(book 1 in the Just Call Me Angel series)*
Traitors Among Us *(book 2 in the Just Call Me Angel series)*
Russian Uprising *(book 3 in the Just Call Me Angel series)*
Death Trap *(book 4 in the Just Call Me Angel series)*
Loose Ends (*book 5 in the Just Call Me Angel series*)
Divine Intervention *(book 6 in the Just Call Me Angel series)*
Petals of Blood *(short story; Pushcart Prize Nomination 2013)*
House of Lies (*Political cult suspense*)
No Easy Way *(debut novel; nominated for The Molly Award from the HODRW 2010)*
The Candy Shop *(Suspense Thriller)*

S.R.Claridge has also ghostwritten over ten novels.